GEEK GIRL

MODEL MISFIT

Photograph © Georgina Bolton King

Holly Smale is the author of *Geek Girl* and *Model Misfit*. Clumsy, a bit geeky and somewhat shy, she spent the majority of her teenage years hiding in the changing-room toilets. She was unexpectedly spotted by a top London modelling agency at the age of fifteen and spent the following two years falling over on catwalks, going bright red and breaking things she couldn't afford to replace. By the time Holly had graduated from Bristol University with a BA in English Literature and an MA in Shakespeare she had given up modelling and set herself on the path to becoming a writer. Between then and now she also spent two years living in Japan. Holly is currently writing the third book in the *Geek Girl* series.

For my sister, Tara.
In calm or stormy weather.

GEEK GiRL

MODEL
MISFIT

HOLLY
SMALE

HarperCollins *Children's Books*

First published in paperback in Great Britain
by HarperCollins *Children's Books* in 2013
HarperCollins *Children's Books* is a division of HarperCollins*Publishers* Ltd,
1 London Bridge Street, London SE1 9GF

The HarperCollins website address is: www.harpercollins.co.uk

1

Typeset in Frutiger Light 11/17.5 pt by Palimpsest Book Production Limited,
Falkirk, Stirlingshire

Printed and bound by CPI Group (UK) Ltd, Croydon, CR0 4YY

fit adjective

1 Appropriate or suiting
2 Proper
3 Qualified and competent
4 Prepared
5 In good physical condition

NOUN

1 Fashionable clothing
2 An onset or period of emotion

COLLOQUIAL SLANG

1 To be really, really good looking

ORIGIN from the Old English *fitt*: 'conflict or struggle'.

1

My name is Harriet Manners, and I am a model.
I know I'm a model because:

1. It's Monday morning, and I'm wearing a gold tutu, a gold jacket, gold ballet pumps and gold earrings. My face is painted gold, and a long piece of gold wire has been wrapped around my head. This is not how I normally dress on Mondays.

2. I have a bodyguard. The earrings cost so much I'm not allowed to go to the toilet without a large man checking my earlobes afterwards to make sure I haven't accidentally flushed them.

3. I haven't been allowed to smile for two hours.

4. Every time I take a bite of doughnut to keep my strength up everybody breathes in sharply

as if I've just bent down and given the floor a quick lick.

5. There's a large camera pointing at my face, and the man behind it keeps saying, "Oi, model," and clicking his fingers at me.

There are other clues – I'm pouting slightly, and making tiny movements every couple of seconds like a robot – but they're not necessarily conclusive. That's exactly how my father dances when a car advert comes on TV.

Anyway, the final reason I know I'm a model is:

6. I have become a creature of grace, elegance and style.

In fact, you could say I've really grown up since you last saw me.

Developed. *Blossomed.*

Not literally. I'm exactly the same size and shape as I was six months ago, and six months before that. As far as womanly curves go, much like the netball captain at school, puberty is making no bones about picking me last.

No, I'm talking metaphorically. I simply woke up

one day, and *BAM*: fashion and I were at one with each other. Working together, helping each other. Just like the crocodile and the little Egyptian plover bird that climbs into its mouth to pick bits of meat out of its teeth. Except obviously in a much more glamorous and less unhygienic way.

And I'm going to be totally honest with you: it's changed me. The geek is gone, and in her place is somebody glamorous. Popular. Cool.

A brand-new Harriet Manners.

2

Anyway. The really great thing about being totally *synergised* with the fashion world is that it makes shoots very smooth and focused.

"Right," Aiden the photographer says, "what are we thinking, model?"

(You see what I mean? What are *we* thinking: fashion and I are basically sharing a brain.)

"We're thinking mysterious," I tell him. "We're thinking enigmatic. We're thinking unfathomable."

"And why are we thinking that?"

"Because it says so on the side of the perfume box."

"Exactly. I'm thinking Garbo and Grable, Hepburn and Hayworth, Bacall and Bardot, but it might be best if you think reality TV show contestant and do the opposite."

"Got it," I say, shifting slightly in my position on the floor and moving my foot so that the sole is pointing towards me. Then I lean towards it gracefully. *Mysterious.* I grab the corner of my jacket and lift it slightly, like a

butterfly wing, angling my face downwards. *Enigmatic*. Finally, I arch my back and poke out an arm so I'm staring at the crease of my inner elbow. *Unfathomable*.

"Got it." Aiden looks up from the camera. "Model, Yuka Ito was right. These are some very strange shapes you're pulling, but it works. Very edgy. Very high fashion."

What did I tell you? Me and fashion: I walk in and out of its mouth and it doesn't even *try* to eat me any more.

"Now point your elbow in the other direction for me." The photographer crouches down, adjusts the camera shutter and then looks back up again. "Towards the camera."

Sugar cookies.

"You know," I say without moving, "enigmatic, mysterious, unfathomable. They're tautological. Yuka could save a lot of room on the box by just picking one."

"Just move your arm."

"Umm, has she considered 'baffling'? It's from an old word used to describe a wind that buffeted sailors from all directions. It's sort of appropriate for a perfume, don't you think?"

Aiden pinches the bridge of his nose with his

fingers. "Right. How about you show me the bottom of the shoe? We should try to get the contrasting sole in the shot."

I clear my throat, mind starting to race. "Erm... but what about Saudi Arabia, China and Thailand? It's considered culturally impolite to show the bottom of your feet there..." I look around the room in a blind panic. "We don't want to risk alienating them, do we?" I sweep my arm out in a wide, persuasive gesture.

And something on my sleeve catches Aiden's eye.

Oh no. No no no.

"What's that?" he says, standing up and walking over to where I'm now scrabbling to get off the floor but my feet are caught in the enormous tutu. The photographer grabs my arm and peels a tiny gold sticker from the inside of my jacket elbow. "What's *this*?"

"Hmm?" I say, swallowing and straining to make my eyes as round as I physically can.

Aiden peers at the sticker. "F = M x A?" he reads slowly. Then he pulls three more from inside the lining of the jacket. "V = I x R? Ek = ½ x M x V2? W = M x G?"

Before I can move he grabs the shoe from my foot, turns it over and pulls a sticker from the heel. Then he pulls one from my inside elbow and four from the inside folds of the tutu netting.

He blinks at the stickers a couple of times while I stare at the floor and try to look as small as humanly possible. "Harriet," he says in a slow and incredulous voice. "Harriet Manners, are you studying maths in the middle of my fashion shoot?"

I shake my head and look at the air behind the photographer's left ear. You know the crocodile and the bird? I think one of us is about to get eaten.

"No," I answer in my littlest voice. Because a) It's physics, and b) I've been doing it all the way through.

3

OK, so I *may* have stretched the truth a tiny bit.

Or – you know: a lot.

I haven't changed. In fact, I'm even more of a geek than I used to be because:

a) the grey matter in my brain is still developing extra connections on a daily basis
b) I know even more facts than I did before
c) I'm just coming to the end of exams, which means my short-term cognitive abilities are on overdrive.

I'm also not graceful, elegant or stylish, but I guess you've already worked that out for yourself.

"Unbelievable," Aiden mutters, clicking through the images as I slip behind a curtain at the back of the room to get changed into my school uniform.

"I'm so sorry, Mr Thomas," I call out. "I honestly didn't mean to disrespect you and the crocodi— erm,

fashion industry. Did you get OK photos?"

"That's not the point. Do you know how many other models wanted this job?"

Yes. Last time I was at Infinity Models, two of them locked me in a cupboard so I missed a really big casting. I had to wait until the cleaner came round to let me out again.

"I'm sorry, it's just it's my final GCSE today," I try to explain as I tug off the massive tutu and smack an elbow painfully against the wall. "At 2pm, the British education system is going to decide whether I have any chance of ever becoming an award-winning physicist. My entire future is going to be shaped by today."

I pull on my school jumper, which promptly gets caught in the gold wire still wrapped around my head. There's silence while I hop in and out of the 'changing room' with my jumper over my face and my arms waving in the air like manic bunny ears.

"Hmm," Aiden agrees still clicking through images. "You're clearly a genius destined for a Nobel Prize."

"GCSE physics is not about *literal* spatial awareness," I puff, clutching blindly at my head and simultaneously smashing my knee against the wall. "It's *conceptual* spatial awareness. Two very different things."

Which is lucky, because the wire on my head now

appears to be caught on everything in a two-metre radius. I have a detailed Get To School On Time Plan in my satchel, and nowhere at all does it say: Detach Myself From A Curtain Ring.

"It's OK, Harriet," I say, spinning helplessly in little circles. "You still have an hour and eleven minutes to get to school by train. Or an hour and sixteen minutes by taxi. You've got ages."

"Erm... you know the clock on the back wall is slow. Right?"

I abruptly stop circling.

Oh my God. OH MY GOD. I *knew* there was a reason they made us study karma in religious education.

"*No*," I squeak, ripping myself free from the wire at the cost of quite a few hairs, a scratch on my cheek, a curtain ring and half a school uniform. "*How* slow?"

"An hour," Aiden says.

And – just like that – both my Get To School On Time Plan and entire life trajectory fly straight out the window.

4

This is so incredibly *typical*.

The *one* time my dad isn't at the back of a photo shoot, trying to 'liven things up a bit' by stealing bits of mannequin and pretending he has three arms and four legs, is the one time I really need him here.

But Dad's at a job interview and I now have less than fifty minutes to get to a destination over an hour away.

As the taxi driver points out cheerfully after I clamber into the back and beg him to hurry: "I can only go as fast as the traffic, Goldilocks. I'm part of it, ain't I?"

Which I would probably look at as a kind of poignant universal truth if I wasn't preoccupied by trying to make myself as light as possible, in the hope that the decreased weight would allow the car to accelerate faster.

And also with correcting his grammar.

There's nothing else I can do. Thanks to the laws of physics – and irony – the factors dictating how fast I get to my exam apparently do not include a) crying,

11

b) hyperventilating or c) repeating 'sugar cookies' until the taxi driver shuts the internal window and flicks the switch that stops him being able to hear me.

So I may as well use the remaining time constructively to update you on what's been happening in the past six months.

Here's a brief synopsis:

1. I've become even less popular. Geek + Model = a whole new set of graffiti on your belongings.

2. I'm trying to cry less about it. We each expel an average of 121 litres of tears in a lifetime, and I can't afford to dry up before I even hit sixth form.

3. My dad is still out of work, and Annabel is still working as a lawyer. This is worth noting, because my stepmother is now seven months pregnant, and Dad is definitely not.

4. Apparently the average person eats a ton of food a year: the weight of a fully grown elephant. Annabel is doing her best to single-handedly challenge this statistic. She is *huge*.

5. My best friend, Nat, has turned sixteen, and I have not. This means that Nat can now legally play pinball in Georgia, USA after 11pm and fly a plane solo in the UK, and I cannot.

6. I have modelled twice for Baylee, gone on a few go-sees (when not spending time productively locked in a cleaning cupboard) and that's it.

7. I've finally reached the painful conclusion that my hair is not strawberry blonde.

8. It's ginger.

And that's it. Everything else has stayed exactly the same.

My stalker, Toby, still orbits me like some kind of slightly snotty moon and my nemesis, Alexa, still inexplicably hates me.

My agent, Wilbur, still makes up words whenever he feels like it, and the fashion designer, Yuka Ito, is still totally terrifying.

My dog, Hugo, is still fond of sampling anything sticky he spots on the pavement and I still keep my textbooks lined up in alphabetical, chromatic and subject order.

Because that's how real life is: people and situations and dogs don't change that often, even when you have written *very* careful plans and tried to force them to.

And if I could leave my list there, I would. Because it's a nice list, isn't it? A lovely, positive list that looks forward to an entire summer with Nat, a brand-new graffiti-less satchel next term, and – quite soon – the legal ability to fly planes on my own whenever I feel like it.

But I can't leave it there, because one more thing happened. And – for a little while, anyway – it made all the other points seem less important:

9.   Lion Boy dumped me.

5

Reasons Not to Think About Nick

1. He told me not to.

Don't worry. It's not as bad as it sounds.

I mean, in some ways it's *exactly* as bad as it sounds. Four months after our first kiss, Nick told me we shouldn't see each other any more and then he abruptly disappeared from my life. I haven't seen or heard from him since. Not a text. Not a phone call or a voicemail. Not an email. Not a tweet or a Facebook message. Not even a fax (even though I'm not sure who faxes these days, but the option is still sort of there, isn't it?).

But it's totally OK. You don't spend nearly sixteen years reading novels about love and scanning poetry about love and listening to songs about love and watching films about love without coming away with a pretty good idea of how love stories go.

15

Everybody knows the dramatic ups and downs are what make the difference between a *real* love story – the kind that people make into films – and a boring one that nobody bothers writing or singing about.

Would *Pride and Prejudice* be popular if Darcy and Lizzy hooked up at the first ball?

Would *Wuthering Heights* be a classic if Cathy chose Heathcliff?

Would *Romeo and Juliet* be studied in school if they dated for a few years and then got married and moved to the suburbs of Mantua?

Exactly.

So even if your love story involves somebody dumping you and moving back to Australia, as Shakespeare said you just have to refuse to "admit impediments", and then they'll come back to you. Everybody knows that.

And, yes, it's been more than two months so it's taking Nick a little bit longer than it probably should, but he must be on his way.

All I have to do is wait.

In the meantime, I'm trying not to think about him. I don't think about his coffee-coloured skin, or his big black lion curls, or his green smell, or his eyes that slant up at the corners. I don't think about the tilt of his nose, or the wideness of his smile, or the way he used to rub his thumb across my knuckle when we were holding hands and tap the end of my nose after I sneezed (which was very unhygienic, but for some gross and deeply disturbing reason I liked it).

I don't think about how he makes me feel like a lightning bug: as if part of me is full of fire, and the other part of me can fly.

I don't think about how I'd be with him all the time, if I possibly could.

And I absolutely never think about the fact that I'm not really enjoying this bit of my love story, and that I'd have *much* preferred the boring kind where Nick stayed and everything carried on exactly as it was before.

Even if it broke all the rules of romance straight down the middle.

The driver clears his throat.

"In love, Goldilocks?" He winks at me in the rear-view mirror, waving his hand in my direction. "That explains a lot."

I look in surprise at the anatomically correct heart I've been sketching on the window, and then blush and wipe it away. *Subtle, Harriet.*

"Nope," I say as nonchalantly as I can. "I'm just... prepping for next year's biology module."

"Course you are." The driver grins. "Anyway, thought you was in an 'urry? Some kind of exam?" He nods. "You got four minutes left."

I blink a few times. The car has stopped and we're sitting directly outside my school. I hadn't even noticed we'd stopped moving.

"But…" I say as I scrabble in my satchel for my purse, "how is that even physically possible?"

The driver shrugs. "I'm magic, ain't I," he states matter-of-factly. "Like that fat dude in 'Arry Potter."

I glance up. He certainly looks… other-worldly. Ephemeral. Slightly over-blessed with body hair.

"And I went well over the speed limit," he adds brightly. "That's eighty quid, love. Magic is pricy these days. Now get a hop on, you got three minutes left."

6

I swear on my *Oxford English Dictionary*, I have never moved so fast in my entire life.

By the time I've slid through the closing door of the gym hall, my breathing is so strained I sound like our vacuum cleaner when Annabel's cleaning the sofa. Sweat is dripping down my neck and the only thing I have to mop it up with is the edge of my school jumper now hanging in three ripped pieces around my neck, like a piece of modern art. Or something Wilbur would wear.

I'm barely two steps into the room when Toby's fluffy head spins around. I can only assume he spotted me out of the back of it with what he calls his 'Harrietenna'.

"*Toby,*" Miss Johnson says in a warning voice, and Toby immediately stops waving and starts blowing me kisses and blinking instead.

I nod hello at him, hurry past and put my little plastic bag of stationery carefully on the right-hand

19

side of my desk. Then I sit down and close my eyes.

Only a minute left to gather my thoughts, summon The Knowledge of the Stickers and Zen my environment. Just a few precious moments to allow the stress hormones to dissipate, to regulate my breathing, stop working out what time it is in Australia and to get my mind back on physics.

Midnight. It's midnight in Sydney right now.

Somebody snorts.

Focus, Harriet. There are two types of electron: negative and positive. Like charges repel. Opposite charges attract.

Somebody snorts again, and there's a faint giggle from a few seats away.

When insulating materials are rubbed together, electrons are knocked off one atom and on to the other.

There's another laugh, and suddenly I'm vaguely aware of eyes burrowing into my forehead.

Not just Toby's, I know what they feel like.

Cautiously, I open mine and glance around the room. There are a hundred and fifty-two other students in the hall, and every single one of them is staring at me.

I have absolutely no idea why. It's not as if nobody

here has seen sweat before. Or a ripped jumper. Or a single sock and scratched face. That's how a large chunk of my year end lunch break.

I look at Toby and see he's inexplicably patting his cheeks. When I search the room for Nat and see her – a long way away – she's trying to mouth something at me.

"Go," she's saying, subtly pointing at me. "*Go.*"

I love Nat. She's my favourite person in the entire world (followed by my dad and Annabel). But I'm not going anywhere. I've only just got here.

"Go," she mouths again, and then she rolls her eyes and smacks her head with her hand.

Now *that* gesture I'm familiar with.

"Everybody *face this way*," Miss Johnson shouts furiously, and three hundred and two eyes suddenly snap away from my face. "*Toby Pilgrim, that includes you*," Miss Johnson yells, and the final two revert to the front. "You have thirty seconds before your exam begins."

The only person not focusing on our imminent exam is Alexa, who is sitting diagonally directly behind me. She's got a standard smug expression on her face and she's rolling something between her fingers. Before I can work out what's going on, she subtly leans down and rolls a little paper ball forward so it's positioned directly under my desk.

"Twenty seconds."

I stare at the ball in confusion, then in a flash I know: Alexa's trying to sabotage my exam. She's trying to plant revision notes on me. Yet another round of her ultimate plan – Ruin Harriet's Life.

Oh my God. If I pick it up and get caught, I'm going to be thrown out of this exam. If I don't pick up it up and it gets found under my desk afterwards, I'll get disqualified for cheating. *What do I do?*

"Ten seconds."

Pick it up or don't pick it up? Don't pick it up or pick it up?

"Five seconds."

I bend down swiftly and grab it. If I can destroy the evidence before the exam starts, I'm not cheating. I'm just… disposing of rubbish responsibly.

But, like Pandora, I need to know what's in the box. I need to know what's intended to destroy me. So I tuck the note under the desk and quietly open it:

GEEK, YOU'RE FACE IS BRIGHT GOLD.

Oh, I think.

Oh.

"Please turn your papers over," Miss Johnson announces as I shrink into my seat with my hands over my face. "You may now start."

1

I spend the rest of my final exam looking like something actresses hold once a year and cry over. According to a test I did on the internet, I have 143 IQ points. Clearly I have no idea what to do with *any* of them.

Toby isn't quite so sure.

"Harriet," he says happily as I walk out of the hall and head outside to wait for Nat. "I am honoured to stalk you. I honestly cannot think of anyone I'd rather follow obsessively around."

Somehow, Toby's gotten even more thin and stretched-out looking: as if he's a bit of melted cheese somebody's just pulled off a pizza. His hair is fluffier, he has dark shadows around his eyes, and he's bobbing along with his hands neatly by his sides, his little nose twitching slightly. He looks even more like a meerkat than he did last time you saw him.

Let's put it this way, I wouldn't be even vaguely surprised if a plane flew past and he bolted for cover.

24

"What are you talking about, Tobes?"

"Gold is traditionally the colour of success, achievement and triumph," Toby explains in a voice brimming over with admiration. "You're the perfect colour for the last exam. I don't know why nobody has thought of it before."

I stare at him, and then burst into an explosion of laughter. Only Toby could possibly think I painted myself gold today on purpose.

Except... *In love, Goldilocks? That explains a lot.*

I abruptly stop laughing. Oh my God: the taxi driver did too. I clearly just look like the kind of girl who goes insane and colours herself in on a regular basis.

That's not the impression I'm trying to give to the world at *all*.

As Toby starts chattering excitedly about exam questions and oscillations of light waves, I glaze over and listen to the sound of his chirpy words going up and down and round and round.

Every time I try to remember what it was like not having him around, I can't do it. Toby's like a fact: once you know him, you can't *unknow* him. Over the last few months, he's started spending a little more time where Nat and I don't have to pretend we can't see him. And we've...

Well, we've kind of let him.

He's not so bad in small doses. As long as he doesn't irritate Nat too much. She has limited interest in irrelevant facts, and I fill that quota already.

We finally get outside, blink a few times in the bright sunshine, then start wandering, half blind, towards a small patch of shade. Nat's surname is near the beginning of the alphabet, so she always gets stuck at the back of an exam room: picking at her nail varnish and making impatient huffing sounds, like a pretty, swishy-haired dragon.

By the time we spot Alexa it's too late.

She's just outside the school gates with a big group of her friends: all clad in their cunningly edited school uniforms like a fashionable army. Rolled skirts and tucked tops and pink streaks and bra-straps showing. Sprawled menacingly across the grass, as if they own the school.

And how can I put this?

In a very non-literal way, they sort of do.

8

No, by the way.

If you think a polite but firm conversation with my bully six months ago totally fixed everything between us, you've obviously never met Alexa. Or me.

Or any other teenage girl.

I want to pretend Alexa and her friends aren't waiting for me, but a quick glance at her face tells me otherwise. She's practically salivating. That's the not-so-great thing about the last day of school: no repercussions.

"Hey," she says sharply, taking a step towards me. "Manners."

I instinctively look for another exit. But, short of using Toby to hurdle the fence, there's no other way out of the school. So I duck my head and try my hardest to become completely invisible.

Thanks to not being a member of the Fantastic Four, this doesn't work.

"HEY," Alexa says again, blocking my path. She

glances briefly at Toby. He scratches at the inside of his ear and then sniffs his finger. "Did you have *fun* in that exam, geek? Bet you did. I bet it was the best fun you've had in *ages.*"

I flush slightly. She's absolutely right: it was awesome. When I got to the essay question about the life cycle of a star, I actually got a bit dizzy with excitement. "Maybe," I say with the most non-committal shrug I can muster.

"Bet you knew all the answers, didn't you, you total spod."

I shake my head. "Only about ninety-three per cent of them."

Everyone snickers – I don't know why: that's still a solid A* – and Alexa scowls at me. I try to walk away, but she blocks me again. "So you've heard about the massive house party I'm having tonight?"

The answer to this question is obviously: *yes.* There are Eskimos in Siberia who woke up this morning, fully aware of the house party Alexa is having tonight.

"No."

"*I've* heard about it," Toby interrupts eagerly. "You're having tiny jellies, aren't you? Alexa, they sound *brilliant.* I've always found normal-sized jellies unhygienic. All those different spoons. It's much more sanitary to have lots of little ones each, isn't it?"

Alexa ignores him. "A guy who used to be on TV is coming. So it's technically a *celebrity* party."

Toby nods sagely. "No green jelly then. Just awesome red and purple, right? My mum makes mine in the shape of a rocket with liquorice where the engines would be."

Years from now, historians will look back at records of these days and wonder how Toby managed to get through them alive.

"That's nice for you, Alexa," I say, finally managing to dodge round her and start walking in the opposite direction.

"So, Manners" – and she clears her throat – "Want to come?"

I stop mid-stride. Apparently when people have their heads cut off there are five or six seconds when they can hear and see and blink, but they can't move because they've already been severed in half.

That's sort of how I feel now.

Slowly, I turn back round. *"Pardon me?"*

Out of the corner of my eye, I see Nat come out of the school doors, pause and then start legging it towards us.

"Do you want to come to my party?" Alexa says,

her face totally blank. "We've got a TV star, so you'd be the perfect celebrity addition. A model."

"*Really?*"

"Yeah," she says slowly, and the smirk appears again. "And if we fancy a dance, we can tie you to the ceiling by your feet and spin you round really fast. You can be our very own human disco ball."

Then she points at my face and bursts into hysterical laughter, and a few nano-seconds later everyone starts snickering behind her.

It takes thirty minutes for a human body to produce enough heat to boil half a gallon of water. I think from the temperature of my cheeks right now I can probably cut that down to eleven or twelve, maximum.

Why didn't I just keep walking? What's *wrong* with me? Other than a gold face and an entire lack of survival instinct, obviously.

"Bite us, Hockey-legs," Nat snaps, suddenly appearing next to me. "As *if* we'd want to go to your wannabe party."

"As if I'd *want* you to want to. I'm still scrubbing the loserness off my doorstep from your last visit." Alexa sneers. "Anyway, why the hell would I want *her*," and she points at me like I'm a bit of toenail stuck in a carpet, "in my house, spreading her geekiness around? There's no level of cool that can cure *that*. I'd have an *epidemic* on my hands."

She spins round and adds, "Nobody wants that, right?" Then starts ceremoniously high-fiving her friends.

As if I'm not still standing there with my cheeks burning.

As if I don't matter.

As if I never will.

As if nothing has changed at all.

9

I count slowly to ten, and then I take a deep breath, reach into my pocket and pull out a small bit of crumpled-up paper.

I tap my still-triumphing nemesis on the back and hand it to her.

"What the hell is this?"

YOUR
GEEK, ~~YOU'RE~~ FACE IS BRIGHT GOLD.

"*You-apostrophe-r-e* is a contraction of *you are*, Alexa," I say. "If you needed help with grammar, you should've asked."

There's a stunned silence followed by a couple of desperately suppressed snorts, and I suddenly wonder whether *everyone* likes Alexa as much as they pretend they do. Or whether some of them are only here for the 'celebrity' parties and tiny jellies.

Alexa's smirk has finally gone. "I *know* the

32

difference," she hisses furiously. "It was a *typo*."

She scrunches the distinctly handwritten note back up and throws it hard at my face. It hits my left ear with a small *pop*.

"What do I care, anyway?" she adds. "School's over. Nobody in real life cares about that kind of rubbish."

"I do," I say quietly.

"So do I," Nat says loudly, putting her arm around my waist and giving me a quick peck on the cheek.

"Me too," Toby agrees. "Never underestimate the power of a well-placed apostrophe."

We turn to leave and Alexa suddenly loses it, as if all her anger has just exploded in one bright firework of hatred. "*Don't walk away from me*, geeks!" she screams, slamming her hand against a parking bollard. "We're not done here! You just *wait* until next year! I'm going to… I'm going to – you – you – you're…"

"Hey!" Toby says, "I think she's finally getting it, Harriet!"

"We'll look forward to hearing the rest of that sentence in sixth form, Alexa," Nat calls back. "That should give you enough time to work out something really terrifying."

We grin at each other and keep walking. Alexa's

shouting gets fainter and fainter until all I can hear is a harmless buzzing sound, like a tiny mosquito.

I look upwards.

The sky is bright blue, the trees have parted, and now there's nothing but summer stretching endlessly in front of us.

10

We don't even wait until we turn the corner to start dancing.

That's the beauty of the summer holidays. It's as if life is just a big Etch-A-Sketch, and once a year you get to shake it vigorously up and down and start again. By the time we go back to school, the whole year will be wiped clean.

Sort of.

Enough to ensure nobody remembers Toby breakdancing across the road with his satchel on his head, anyway.

"Did you see Alexa's *face*?" Nat shouts, doing a little scissor kick and punching the air. "That was *magic.*"

I give a happy little hop, even though it does mean I may now have to apply to a different sixth form if I don't want to spend the rest of my teens lodged down a toilet of Alexa's choosing. (The Etch-A-Sketch isn't *that* thorough.) "Do you think I did something horrendous to Alexa when we were little that I've forgotten about, Nat?"

"Who cares if you did?" Nat yells as she does a series of excited little spins, high-fiving me on every turn. "Alexa's gone! Exams are *over*. Do you know what that means?! No more physics! No more chemistry! No more history! No more *MATHS*!"

My A Levels will be in physics, chemistry, history and maths and I fully intend to start studying for them before the week is over, but I high-five my best friend anyway.

Nat giddily grabs a calculator out of her bag and throws it on the floor. "I am *never going to use you again*," she yells at it. "Do you understand? Me and you: we're through!"

Toby bends down and picks it up. "Aren't you going to study fashion design, Natalie?"

"Yup." She tosses her shiny black hair and beams at him. "It's going to be clothes, clothes, clothes for the rest of my life."

"Then you're going to need this," Toby says, handing it back to her. "To calculate fabric measurements, body shapes, profit margins, manufacturing costs and loan repayments, not to mention pattern cutting and size differentiation."

"*What*?" Nat's face collapses. "Oh for the love of..." She looks at me. "I didn't have to know that for *months. Seriously*. Does he *have* to be here? Can't we send him back to wherever he came from?"

"Hemel Hempstead," Toby says helpfully. "I can get the 303 bus."

"We've got an entire summer ahead of us," I remind Nat jubilantly, ignoring him. I feel a bit like Neil Armstrong immediately before he boarded the *Apollo* in 1969: as if we've just been handed all the space in the universe, and we can do whatever we want with it. "In fact, I've got it all mapped out." I start rummaging in my satchel and then pull out a piece of paper with a flourish. "Ta-da!"

Nat takes it off me and frowns. "Nat and Harriet's Summer of Fun Flow Chart?"

"Exactly!"

I do a little dance and then gesture at the coloured bubbles: yellow for me, purple for Nat, and – thanks to the nature of the colour wheel – an unfortunate poo brown for everything in between. "I've got every detail planned out for maximum fun and entertainment value," I explain, pointing proudly. "Starting with Westminster Abbey, which is where Chaucer, Hardy, Tennyson and Kipling are buried, and then Highgate

Cemetery to visit George Eliot, Karl Marx and Douglas Adams. We're working our way through dead writers chronologically."

I've focused our Summer of Fun Flow Chart on London because all there is locally is a roller-skate rink and a Mill museum, and as much as I love both wheels on my feet and bread we totally exhausted both of those options before we left primary school.

"The Charles Dickens Museum?" Nat reads slowly. "Glass-blowing in Leathermarket? The Ceremony of the Keys at the Tower of London?"

She's impressed. I can tell from how quiet she is and the fact that she's not making eye contact.

"Amazing, right? They've just discovered traces of ancient blue paint on the Parthenon statues at the British Museum, scientifically proving that ancient Greece looked like Disneyland. We can go and see the new exhibition!"

Nat nods a couple of times and scratches at her neck. "Uh-huh."

I suddenly realise how selfish I sound. "Nat," I say quickly, "there's loads of stuff for you on here too. There's an exhibition on ball gowns at the V&A, and the London College of Fashion are doing a graduate show that I'm sure Wilbur can get us tickets to."

Toby nods knowingly. "Did you know the Victoria and Albert Museum employs a hawk every summer to discourage pigeons from the gardens?"

"And *tonight*... I thought we could celebrate together with *these*!" I pull DVDs of *The Devil Wears Prada* and David Attenborough's African documentary from my satchel. "And *these*!" I pull out some sparkly purple nail varnish and toe-dividers and a pack of *Game of Thrones* playing cards. "And – wait for it – *these*!" I pull out a pack of no-calorie caramel popcorn and an enormous chocolate muffin.

Then I look at Toby. "I didn't forget you," I add fondly. I hand him a *Lord of the Rings* Lego set.

"Harriet Manners," he says solemnly. "I shall begin constructing a YouTube stop-frame video sensation *immediately*."

"What do you think, Nat?" I squeak, bouncing up and down on my toes. "Are you ready to start the Most Incredible Summer Of All Time™?! I'm calling it MISOAT for short, by the way."

"Umm," Nat says, and glances at me then back into the middle distance. All signs of laughter or twirling have completely disappeared. "Toby, can you leave us alone for a second?"

"Girl stuff?" he says wisely. "Natalie, I know all about menstruation. We studied it in biology."

"*Toby.*"

"Ah. Not menstruation then." Toby cocks his head to the side. "Perhaps bras?"

Nat scowls so hard her forehead looks like something out of *Star Trek*.

"Kittens?"

Just as Nat reaches out a hand to physically throttle him Toby ducks behind a tree.

I guess old stalker habits die hard.

"What's going on?" I ask nervously. "Have you already seen *The Devil Wears Prada*?"

Nat's lips twitch. "Of course I have. It's not that... I'm so sorry, Harriet. I only found out two days ago. I didn't want to upset you during exams."

My stomach tightens into a hard ball. I can already feel our trips to the Natural History Museum and the Imperial War Museum shutting down, like tiny little lights being turned off. "What's going on?"

"I'm..." and she takes a deep breath. "I'm going to France."

A couple more bulbs break. "What? For how long?"

"A whole month," Nat says miserably. "I'm leaving tomorrow."

And – just like that – my entire summer goes completely dark.

=

*F*rance? What has *France* got that my Summer of Fun Flow Chart doesn't have?

A French Home-stay Programme, apparently.

Nat's mum is making her go, as punishment for catching Nat in Boots when she should have been doing her French GCSE. Nat quickly explains this as her mum pulls up at the kerb alongside us and makes the universal gesture for Get In This Car Right Now, Young Lady.

Then she waves miserably goodbye at us from the back windscreen.

"Harriet," Toby says, when he comes out from behind the tree two minutes later. "Do you know what this *means*?"

"No," I say curtly, because obviously I do.

Don't say it, Toby, I will him silently. *Please. Just don't say it.*

But as always Toby's ability to read minds, verbal

inflections or really-quite-obvious facial expressions remains non-existent.

"It *means*," he says – staring at me with eyes like lava lamps, all liquid and glowing – "you're going to be spending the whole of summer with *me*."

OK, I'm going to bed for the next month.

I'll just spend the next six weeks under my duvet, learning how to embroider hieroglyphics by torchlight. I'll get Annabel and Dad to whizz up all my food so I can drink it through a straw from under my duvet, like an old lady's budgerigar. By the time I start A Levels I'll be the same shape as a mattress, covered in fungus and shrivelled into an even smaller and even more muscle-less mass than normal.

As Robert Burns once wrote, "The best laid schemes o' mice an' men gang aft a-gley" and the same can obviously be said for teenage girls. My plans are aft-agleying all *over* the shop.

"Harriet?" Annabel shouts downstairs as I slam the front door as hard as I can behind me. "If you're trying to break all the windows in the house simultaneously, that is an incredibly efficient way to do it."

"Hey!" I hear my dad say indignantly. "How come

Harriet gets *complimented* for slamming doors when I get in trouble? I demand a retrial."

"There hasn't been a trial, Richard," Annabel laughs, "so we can't technically 're' anything."

"Oh, fine, you win again. It's a good thing you're about to pop out a mini-me or I wouldn't be letting you triumph so easily."

"Thank you, darling. Your gallantry is, as ever, much appreciated."

I hear a loud cheerful kiss, echoing down the stairs.

"You know," Dad muses afterwards, "I *am* pretty gallant. I'm a bit like a modern-day Lancelot. Except with no horse. Why don't I have a horse, Annabel? How are we expected to be real men these days without horses?"

Yup. If you think that the prospect of creating a new human life has in any way forced my father to grow up even *slightly* over the last six months you'd be wrong.

There's a jellyfish called the *Turritopsis nutricula*, which Marine Biologists say is the only animal in the world that renders itself immortal by reverting back to adolescence every time it starts to age too much. All I'm going to say is: they obviously haven't met my dad yet.

Let's just see how long *he* sticks around.

Throwing my satchel into the corner of the hallway, I start a slow, stompy climb up the stairs. Six months ago they were pretty, white-painted wood; they are now covered in horrible beige, hard-wearing carpet with fiddly stair gates at either end. There used to be a space under the banister where the cat would climb the stairs and headbutt me from eye-level, as a kind of greeting. It's been blocked up.

There are also fake plug-coverings in all of the plug sockets and padding around the edges of the tables and more gates in doorways, just in case we need to be herded safely from room to room like cattle.

I reach the newly safe and sanitised landing and stare at my parents. "What are you *doing*?"

"Hello, Harriet." Annabel is wearing an enormous, elasticated, pin-stripe suit, and is calmly wiping one of my fossils with a cloth. "Sweetheart, why is your face gold? And what on earth happened to your jumper?" She looks down. "I know I'm full of pregnancy hormones, but I'm certain you were wearing two socks this morning."

"Oh *amazeballs*!" Dad cries from the study. "You coloured yourself gold! To win an exam! That is creative *genius*!"

I think my head is about to explode. "I'm serious, what are you *doing*? You can't *clean fossils,* Annabel. You are literally wiping away 230 million years of history!"

"I think this is a coating of dead skin cells and dust mites, actually. When was the last time you dusted these, Harriet?"

I grab the fossil from her. "This is an Asistoharpes! This is 395 *million years old*! Why don't you just stick it in the washing machine while you're at it?"

My stepmother raises her eyebrows in silence.

"I think if it's survived that long it can handle a bit of wet cloth, don't you?"

I ignore her and turn to Dad, who is standing on the office chair, trying to get down my collection of books about the Tudors. Every time he reaches for one he swivels slightly and has to hang on to the shelf for balance. "What are *you* doing?"

"There's a whole load of stuff here that's yours, Harriet," he explains, reaching for a biography of Anne Boleyn and swivelling again. "So we've built some more shelves in your bedroom. This is going to be the baby's room."

I grab a few of my books off the bed from where they've just been thrown, willy-nilly. "This room is called the *study*, Dad. If this was a room for a baby, it would be called something else!"

"It is, Harriet," Dad says, laughing. "We just renamed it."

I can feel every single cell in my body fizzing and bursting like those crackly sweets that pop on your tongue. First Alexa, then Nat, now this. Today isn't even making an *effort* to go to plan any more.

"There isn't *room* in my bedroom for all my stuff!"

"Then throw some of it away," Annabel suggests with a tiny smile. She's cleaning another fossil. "Or we can put it in the attic. Or maybe in the garden. I imagine these rocks would probably be very happy there."

My throat is getting tighter and tighter. "What do you mean *throw it away*? You can't just throw preserved evidence of natural evolution in the bin!"

Annabel puts her hand gently on her enormous straining belly. "Harriet, what's going on, sweetheart? Did your last exam go badly? What's the matter with you?"

"Me? What's the matter with both of *you*? Baby, baby, baby! It's all baby, baby, baby!"

"Are you about to start singing Justin Bieber?" Dad asks. Annabel snorts with laughter and then puts her hand guiltily over her mouth.

My head pops.

"*Oh my GOD*!" I yell. "I hate you, I hate this house and *THIS IS GOING TO BE THE WORST SUMMER EVER*!"

And with one grand gesture, I burst into tears, sweep every single fossil I can into my arms and storm into my bedroom.

Leaving every window in the house rattling behind me.

12

Reasons Not to Think About Nick

1. He told me not to.
2. I've got much more important things to think about.

OK. So maybe I didn't tell you *everything*.

I told you the stuff you might tell a teacher, or a neighbour or the old lady who works at the corner shop and won't stop asking questions. But I didn't tell you the real stuff. Not the stuff that counts.

I slide down the back of the door and stare blankly at the jumble of fossils now sitting in my lap. Here are some interesting facts I've discovered recently about the animal kingdom:

- The cuckoo is built with a small dip in its back so that it can toss out the other eggs as soon as it's born.

- Mother pandas only care for one of their cubs, and allow the other to die.
- Shark embryos fight and eat each other in the womb and only the winner is born.

Don't even get me started on what the spotted hyena does to its relations. Trust me, you really don't want to know.

What I'm trying to say is, I'm incredibly excited about having a new brother or sister. Of course I am. Babies are cute – in a baldy, screaming kind of way – and a really big part of me can't wait to meet my new sibling and buy it cute little dinosaur T-shirts and a miniature satchel and (eventually) matching crossword puzzles so that we can do them together over breakfast.

But another part of me is anxious.

Literature, history and nature repeatedly remind us that it's not always TV deals and record contracts and matching outfits when it comes to siblings. If *King Lear* and the Tudor dynasty taught us nothing else, it's that you might want to watch your back. Especially if you're a *half*-sibling like me. Because if push comes literally to shove, somebody normally ends up getting kicked out of the nest.

Over the last six months, the baby has started taking over everything:

- First breakfast streamlined into one topic: did you know that the baby's heart starts beating after twenty-two days? Did you know that by seventeen weeks it has fingerprints?
- Then random questions: do you think it'll hate mushrooms, like Annabel, or cinnamon, like Dad?
- Then it started demanding olive milkshake and ketchup on ice cream and once – to my absolute horror – a bit of the white chalk from my maths blackboard.
- People started visiting and walking straight past me to 'The Belly'.
- Annabel started looking tired all the time. Dad started looking anxious and being extraordinarily loud to make up for it.
- And the photograph of my mum on the mantelpiece mysteriously moved to the guest bedroom, as if that would help everyone forget what happened to the last person in this house who tried to have a baby.

Or the fact that the baby was me.

And – bit by bit, gate by gate – the house started changing, and my room started feeling smaller, and my parents stopped talking or thinking about anything else.

Then – without warning – Nick dumped me.

So I threw myself into the thing I'd kind of been neglecting for once: schoolwork. I studied at breakfast, lunch and dinner. I studied in the bath, and on the toilet, and on the bus, and in the shower by sketching maths equations into the steam on the glass. I even studied during modelling shoots, as you already know.

Basically, I stuffed my head with facts and formulas and dates and equations and lists and diagrams so there wouldn't be room for anything else.

But now exams are finished, and school is over.

Nat is leaving for France.

Lion Boy is still gone.

I'm less important to my parents than someone who isn't even born yet.

And all I can do is sit in my room, staring at my overcrowded new bookshelves and wondering what to do next.

Because that's the truth about people with

obsessively organised plans: we're not trying to control everything in our lives. We're trying to block out the things we can't.

But now there's nothing left.

Nothing but the baby.

13

Anyway.

By the time I wake up the next morning – owner of the world's most sparkly pillow – I feel a bit more hopeful. On the bright side, there is no *way* my life could get any worse.

Last night, everyone else in my year was getting ready to party. Sneaking out of the house in one outfit so they could change into a smaller one. Discussing in excited whispers who was going to kiss who, and who was going to wish they hadn't. Giggling and laughing and getting ready to celebrate the end of compulsory education in a way they would never, ever forget.

Meanwhile, I was sitting on my bedroom floor on my own, painted gold, crying, with a shredded school jumper pulled over my head. I think that's pretty much rock bottom, even by my own socially redundant standards.

Things always look better in the morning, though, and by the time I wake up I'm actually quite entertained

to discover that I've left a trail of damp gold glitter behind me, like an enormous sparkly fairy.

Hugo's lying patiently at my feet. I give him a quick cuddle to let him know I'm mentally stable again, then hop out of bed to grab my phone and switch it on. It gets so little activity these days, sometimes I actually forget I have one.

Which is why it's a bit of a shock when it rings immediately.

"Hello?"

"Ferret-face, is that you?"

I never know what to say to questions like that.

"Hi, Wilbur. It's Harriet."

"Oh, thank holy dolphin-cakes," my agent sighs in relief. "I was starting to think you'd spontaneously combusted. I just read about a man that happened to, Kitten-cheeks. One minute he was washing up and the next minute, POOF. Just a few bubbles and a broken plate."

I blink a few times. Sometimes talking to Wilbur is like falling out of a big tree: you have to just try and catch a few branches to hang on to on the way down. "Is everything OK?"

"Not enormously, Baby-baby Panda. I've left nineteen messages on your answer machine, but you're a naughty little lamp-post and haven't answered a single bunny-jumping one of them."

Sugar cookies. I'd totally forgotten about the mess I made of the shoot yesterday. "Is this about Yuka?"

She's going to hang-draw-and-quarter me like they did in the sixteenth century. Except she's going to do it with words instead of a sword and it's probably going to hurt more.

"It most certainly is, Poodle-bottom. Time is, as they say, of the essential oils. Where have you been?"

I swallow with difficulty. "I-I-I-I'm so sorry, Wilbur."

"It might be too late now, my little Monkey-moo," Wilbur sighs. "There are forms to fill in, things to sign, governments to inform."

They're going to tell the *government*? That seems a little bit excessive, even for Baylee. "Please, Wilbur. I won't do it again."

"Once is enough, Cupcake-teeth. It normally is."

I close my eyes and sit heavily on my bed.

I don't believe this. I actually don't believe it.

It's not even eight o'clock in the morning yet; I haven't even opened the curtains. There's sleep in my eyes and the imprint of Winnie the Pooh's nose on my cheek. And it looks like I've just been fired.

14

It was only a matter of time.

I'm like the donkey in the Aesop's fable who dressed in a lion skin and got away with it until the fox heard him bray. I've been waiting for six months for the fashion industry to realise I'm their donkey and chuck me back out again.

I quickly put Wilbur on speakerphone, throw the mobile across my room and climb miserably back into bed. Then I pull a pillow over my head.

You know what? I think I *am* just going to stay here. I'm almost certain that nobody will notice. I'll be like Richard III, and in hundreds of years archaeologists will find my skeleton buried under some kind of car park, where future people keep their spaceships.

Or jet packs.

Or magnetically levitating transporters.

Or flying bubbles.

I'm just trying to work out if in 500 years they'll

have finally found a way to replace the wheels in my trainers with rockets when some of Wilbur's nonsensical words start filtering in through the pillow. "Candle-wick." "Rabbit-foot." "Potato-nose." "Tokyo."

Tokyo?

I lift the sparkly pillow so I can hear a bit better.

"...so there's going to be a lot of work to do before you go... and oh my *gigglefoot* that reminds me you need to pick up some spot cream because we do not want any dermatological disasters like last time you went abroad, do we, my little Baby-baby Unicorn? Eat some more vegetables before you get there and..."

The tiger beetle is proportionately the fastest thing on earth. If it was the size of a human, it could reach 480 mph. I'm on the other side of the room so quickly I reckon I would leave it panting and retching behind me.

"Hello?" I pick the phone up, drop it and then grab it again and start randomly whacking buttons. "Hello? Hello? Wilbur? Hello? Are you there? Hello?"

"Where else would I be, Owl-beak? This is my phone, isn't it?"

"What did you just say?"

"Love bless you, Plum-pudding. I forget your family

has a problem with earwax. I *said*, try and eat some more vegetables before you land in Tokyo, or Yuka's going to kick off again and we all know what that means."

My entire body suddenly feels like it's been electrocuted. *Before I land in Tokyo?* "I'm *not* fired?"

Wilbur shrieks with laughter. "*Au contraire*, my *petit poisson*. Yuka has a brand-new job for you in Japan, and if we get moving I should be able to get flights sorted in time."

I stare at the wall in silence.

I've been obsessed with Japan since I was six years old. It's the Land of the Rising Sun: of sumo and sushi; karaoke and kimonos; mountains and manga. Homeland of Ryuichi Sakamoto and Studio Ghibli; of Hayao Miyazaki and Haruki Murakami. Mecca for geeks and freaks and weirdos. I have dreamt about visiting Japan ever since...

Well. Ever since I realised it existed to visit.

Oh my God: this could fix *everything*. It will be my New and Infinitely More Glorious Summer Plan 2 (NAIMGS2). I can make a brand-new flow chart. It's *perfect*.

And, yes, it might only be a temporary solution, but everybody knows that if you put enough temporary solutions together you've got something that lasts a very long time indeed.

"YES!" I shout, picking Hugo up and giving him the biggest, most twinkly kiss of his life, right between his eyebrows. "When do I leave? What's the plan?"

"You leave on Saturday, my little Panda-pot. And *BOOM!*" he adds after another stunned silence. "Your fairy godmother strikes again."

15

Right. Time to initiate the New Plan.

The first and most important step to convincing your parents that you are a responsible nearly-adult, capable of foreign jaunts, is obviously not being painted gold. So I hop in the shower and scrub myself until I no longer look like the death mask of Tutankhamen.

Then I peruse my wardrobe for something that says *I am an authoritative and totally trustworthy girl on the cusp of womanhood*. Something that says *I can be sent very far away without any repercussions*.

In a moment of poetic inspiration, I put on the most expensive thing I own and grab the matching accessories. I spend a few minutes fiddling on my laptop, then stride confidently into the kitchen to face my parents.

"Zac?" Annabel's saying, pouring ketchup into an open tin of pears and mixing it up with the end of an empty biro. "For a boy or a girl?"

"Either. It's very gender neutral." Dad pauses and then adds, "Plus it's the name of a Macaw from San Jose who can slam twenty-two dunks in one minute."

"Vetoed."

"What about Zeus?"

"*Zeus?* As in the lightning-lobbing Greek father of Gods and Men?"

"As in the world's tallest dog. Great Dane. Nice eyes."

Annabel laughs. "I don't care how nice his eyes are, Richard. Vetoed."

"Archibald, the world's smallest bull?"

Annabel looks calmly at Dad. "I think it's time to give Harriet back her *Guinness Book of Records*."

Dad shakes his head. "I'm surprised at you, Annabel. Do you have no respect for the majesty of the animal kingdom?"

"I have plenty of respect for it, Richard. I just don't particularly want it coming out of my uterus."

"Liz?"

"You'd better be referring to the Queen."

"Of course I am," Dad says indignantly. "Two of them, in fact. Both fierce examples of female power, independence and majesty." He pauses. "And, you know... Hurley."

I quickly cough from the doorway before there's only one parent left alive to appeal to. Then I walk regally into the centre of the room.

"Father. Annabel." I look at Hugo who scampered down here at the first whiff of cheesy-bacon. "Dog. I would like to open this session by apologising *profusely* for my behaviour yesterday. It was an untimely display of vivaciousness due to the unexpected ruination of my Summer of Fun Flow Chart. I should have found a way to express my entirely valid opinions more reasonably."

I pause to see if this heartfelt apology has sunk in. They're both staring at me with wide eyes. Ha. I feel a bit like Atticus Finch in *To Kill a Mockingbird*. I'm totally going to nail this.

"Secondly," I say, putting my laptop down on the table and pressing a button so that it shines at the wall. "I have something very important to show you."

There are a few seconds of impressed, awed silence.

Then my parents burst into laughter so loud that Hugo steps back and starts barking at the ceiling.

"*Brilliant*," Dad gasps. "What's she wearing this time?"

"I think it's her bridesmaid dress from Margaret's

wedding," Annabel whispers, wiping her eyes. "You can still see where she sat on a candle during the after-dinner speeches."

"Oh, thank God. I thought my daughter had turned into an enormous toilet-roll holder."

I wait patiently for them both to stop giggling. I'm totally going to remember this moment when it comes time to put them in a retirement home.

"This outfit," I say, nobly deciding to rise above both of them, "may be a bridesmaid dress, but if you use your *imagination* it represents something much bigger."

I press a button on my laptop, and an image of a cygnet shines on to the wall. "I was once an ugly duckling—"

Dad puts his hand up. "With feathers all stubby and brown?"

I stick my tongue out at him and press the button again. The picture changes from cygnet to swan. "But in the last six months, I have grown up a lot. I have transformed." I click quickly through a few photos of tadpoles and frogs, caterpillars and butterflies I copied from Google. "But what happens at the end of a transformation… is that where the story ends?"

I point at the slide that says:

TRANSFORMATION → WHAT NEXT?

"Yes."

I scowl. "It's a rhetorical question, Dad. The implied answer is clearly no."

"Keep going, Harriet," Annabel says through a mouthful of ketchup pear. "I'm curious to see where this will end up."

"Does a caterpillar sit on the same leaf when it's a butterfly? No! It goes for a little fly and sees something of the world. Does the tadpole stay in the same pond once it's a frog? No! It stretches its legs, goes for a jump, explores other waters." I gesticulate energetically with my matching fake flower bouquet. "Did Cinderella go back to cleaning hearths once she married the prince?"

"Probably," Dad says. "They didn't have women's rights back then. She had to do the cooking too, and probably a bit of laundry."

"For the love of sugar cookies, Dad, *stop answering rhetorical questions*."

I take a deep breath and compose myself again.

"Transformation means moving *forwards*. If a butterfly stays on the same leaf and a frog stays in the same pond, then they may as well have stayed a caterpillar or a tadpole. There was no point in metamorphosing."

"Wrap it up now, Harriet," Annabel says gently.

I had an entire slide about a dragonfly, but maybe I'll leave that for the encore. I click to the final slide, and a picture of Mount Fuji shines on to the wall with my face hastily copied and pasted on top of it.

"So, in summary: I assert my right to go to Tokyo for a modelling job. Thank you for listening." And I plonk myself triumphantly down on a chair.

Excellent. That should do it.

Maybe I won't be a physicist after all. I'll be a lawyer, and my poetic and powerful Powerpoint presentations will be made into poignant fridge magnets for years to come.

Dad's expression reminds me of Hugo when we get takeaway pizza. "*Japan?* The agency wants Harriet to go to *Japan?* Annabel, that's where those little trees that look like big trees but smaller come from. Can I go with her, Annabel? Please?"

"Richard," Annabel says, "if you had a full-sized koala lodged in your abdomen, would you want me to stay with you?"

Dad looks horrified. "Definitely."

"Then let's assume I feel the same way, shall we?"

She turns back to me with a softer voice. "We can't take you to Japan, sweetheart. I wouldn't be able to get through the doors of the aeroplane, for starters, and I need your dad here because I could go into labour at any moment. You understand, don't you?"

I nod. Of course I understand that.

Annabel's eyes widen. "So what you're *actually* asking is to go to Tokyo, entirely on your own? At fifteen years old?"

"Yuka will be th—" I start, and Annabel looks at me sharply.

She has a point: Cruella De Vil would make a more reassuring guardian.

I clear my throat and clutch my fake flower bouquet as tight as I can. "Like Cinderella, I believe it is my turn to stop cleaning hearths."

"Harriet," Dad points out. "You don't even make your own bed."

"I'm talking *symbolically*." Dad clearly doesn't understand the subtleties of the English language. "*Please?*"

Annabel smiles. "Come here," she says affectionately, and when I perch on the sofa next to her she nudges me with her shoulder and spikes another pear with her biro. "Listen, we know things are hard for you at the moment, Harriet. Don't think we haven't noticed."

I shrug.

"But I'm sorry, you can't go to the other side of the world on your own. You might be older than your age in some ways, but in quite a few of them you're also much, much younger."

What?

"Just because I don't have any boobs yet doesn't mean you can stop me going abroad! That's discrimination!"

Annabel laughs. "That's not even slightly what I'm talking about, Harriet."

Then I turn to Dad with my widest, most beseeching eyes. "Tell her I can go, please!"

"I'm sorry, sweetheart, but for the first time ever I'm with Annabel on this one." Dad twinkles at me but I block it with my firmest scowl.

"So what am I expected to do all summer? Just sit here and rot in a corner?"

"I don't know, Harriet," Annabel sighs. "Draw. Read. Paint. Go for walks. Build nuclear warheads. Take your dad to the zoo. Whatever you want as long as you remain within a 500-mile radius of this house."

"So what you're telling me," I shout furiously, "is

I can't go to Japan because of *that*?" and I point at Annabel's belly.

Annabel suddenly looks incredibly tired. "No, Harriet." She puts the pear tin down. "I am saying that you can't go to Japan because of *that*."

And she points directly at me.

16

Obviously the most important thing at a time like this is to remember to maintain the moral high ground. To react with dignity and self-control: noble in defeat, gallant in loss.

Which is why it's a massive disappointment when I throw the fake flower bouquet across the kitchen and yell, "Stop trying to ruin my life! This is so unfair! I wish I'd never been BOOORRRN!"

And charge over to the front door, pull it open and stomp out with as much vigour as I can muster. Leaving it hanging wide open behind me.

Before I actually run away, I'd just like to point out how incredibly unreasonable my parents are being.

I'm nearly sixteen. By this age, Isaac Asimov was at university, Eddie Murphy was doing stand-up comedy shows in New York, Louis Braille had invented raised writing, chess champion Bobby Fischer was an international grandmaster and Harry Potter was well

on his way to saving the entire world of magic.

It's not that I don't appreciate having people in my life who want to be with me, every step of the way. But still.

I bet Isaac Asimov didn't get this kind of disrespect from *his* parents.

My plan is to stomp all the way to Nat's house and then stay there a) forever or b) until my parents are so prostrate with grief at my absence that they'll let me do whatever I want as long as I come home again.

Unfortunately the huge silk skirt of my bridesmaid dress gets caught on a bush at the bottom of the road, and by the time I've managed to rip myself free I don't really have any stomping energy left. I just feel like a bit of an idiot.

Nat's door swings open before I've even knocked, and – not for the first time – my brain spins slightly. When Nat's mum isn't covered in colourful miracle paste and wearing a dressing gown, she looks so much like Nat it's like having a worm-hole into the future.

"Harriet, darling!" she says, beaming at me. "What a pretty dress!" She leans forward to give me a kiss. "And I adore the tiara."

"Hello, Ms Grey," I say politely. "I've run away and I'm living here now."

"Are you, sweetie? How terribly exciting."

"Is Nat in, please?"

"She's upstairs, packing for her trip." Nat's mum pauses and sniffs. "And by the smell of it she's taking my Chanel perfume with her."

"IT'S NOT THE CHANEL ACTUALLY, MUM," Nat yells downstairs. "IT'S THE PRADA. SHOWS HOW MUCH YOU KNOW."

Nat's mum leans up the stairs. "You're being punished, Natalie. You're not taking *any* perfume, mine or otherwise. And no high heels, make-up or jewellery either. I *will* be checking."

Nat appears at the top of the stairs in about half a second, like a magic genie. "*Mum*. I can't leave the house without make-up. I'm not a *savage*."

"Maybe the next time you decide to skip an exam because you feel like testing out lipsticks, you'll think twice."

"Or maybe I'll just check first that my mum isn't testing out eyeshadow in the aisle behind me."

Nat's mum laughs. "*Touché*, Natalie. Unfortunately only one of us is Mum and it's not you."

Nat looks furious. "Fine. *Whatever*. Have it your way, *as always.*"

She looks at me and makes her Can You Believe This? face.

Then she looks at me again with her What The Hell Are You Wearing? face.

"Harriet, why do you look like something that just got kicked off the Disney Channel?"

I hold out my skirts. "Parental manipulation."

"Did it work?"

"Nope. Not even a little bit."

"I honestly don't know why we bother making an effort in the first place." Nat glares at her mum again, then beckons to me. "Anyway, come on up, Harriet. I think I might need your help."

Nat needs *somebody's* help, that's for sure.

I can barely open the door to her room, and – when I finally do – I realise it's because every single piece of clothing she owns is on the floor. It looks like our garden after a mole has been through it, except that instead of mounds of soil there are about fifteen hills of shoes and dresses and jumpers and handbags and scarves and vest tops and leggings, erupting from the carpet.

Nat's already crouched in the middle of her bed, holding a box of tampons.

"Hop up here," she says as I squeeze my way in, pointing at a spot on the bed with her foot.

I carefully clamber over a pile of skirts. "What on earth are you doing?"

Nat holds up a tampon with a grim face. "This." She pulls the cotton wool out of the applicator and rams a pink lipstick in. "I reckon I should be able to get five in a box, and quite a few eyeliners and

lipglosses as long as they're short ones." Then she holds up a small conditioner bottle. "This is foundation." She pulls out a tiny tub of moisturiser. "This is cream blush." Finally, she pulls out a ridiculously thick copy of *Harper's Bazaar*. "I need you to cut a hole in the middle of all the pages so I've got somewhere to put my eyeshadows and mascara."

I stare at her in awe and then take the magazine off her.

"You could put a pair of strappy high heels inside a tissue box, with tissues on top? And maybe little sachets of perfume inside sanitary towels?"

Nat grins at me and holds up her hand. "Harriet Manners, what would I do without you?"

I high-five her. "Be slightly shorter and less fragrant, I'd imagine." Then I pick up the scissors and start neatly cutting through a few pages of a beautiful model with blonde waves down to her waist.

After several hours of industrious productivity, during which I tell Nat all about the awesome trip to Japan that I won't be going on, I say, "Seriously, Nat, what am I going to do without you? At least you'll be in France. I'm going to be stuck here on my own."

"And Toby. Don't forget Toby." Nat wrinkles her

nose at me so I hit her with the magazine. I said *small doses*. "I've got it worse. I'm staying on a *farm*. An actual working *farm with animals* in it and stuff. What's the prison on that island called?"

"Alcatraz?"

"Yeah. I'd rather have been sent there. At least I could have jumped out and swum to the shops in San Francisco. I'm going down in style though." She holds up a lipstick. "I'm going to look like one of the women who works behind a beauty counter in John Lewis by the time I'm finished."

"Are you going to milk cows and make butter and collect eggs?"

"I most certainly am not." Nat shudders. "You realise eggs come out of chicken's butts, right?"

"They don't, Nat," I laugh, cutting through another piece of paper. "They're actually called cloacas, and all birds and amphibians and reptiles have them. For joint reproductive and digestive purposes."

"Ew. That's actually more gross." Nat sits on the bed next to me, looking miserable. "Oh, God, Harriet. This summer is a total disaster. I bet there's going to be some disgusting boy on the farm with a little wispy moustache and a habit of accidentally walking into my bedroom while I'm getting changed."

76

I giggle. "And every time you take a shower he'll lurk outside so when you come out in a towel he's *right there*."

"Yeah," Nat says, starting to laugh. "And he'll ask for the salt at the dinner table with, like, *meaning*."

"And every ten minutes he'll offer to give you a massage with olive oil he stole from the kitchen."

"I bet he wears shiny green lycra cycling shorts around the house and his T-shirts are too short." We're both giggling uncontrollably now, and rolling around on the bed making vomiting sounds.

"I'm going to have to run away," Nat says decisively. "I'm going to steal a pig and ride it into Paris."

My phone beeps and I grab it out of my pocket. "Pigs can trot at up to eleven miles per hour at top speed," I say, clicking on a message from an unknown number. "It's definitely faster than walking."

"Or a tractor. I can't drive but I reckon if you're in a tractor everything else gets out of the way for you. Do you think a tractor has gears, like a car…"

Nat continues chattering but I can't really hear her any more.

The human brain consists of eighty per cent water, and for the first time in my life that's exactly what mine feels like: as if it's swishing and swirling around inside my head. My ears fill with the roaring sound you get when you sit at the bottom of a swimming pool.

Because I've just received this:

Hope you smashed your final exam. Would love to talk. Thinking of you. Nick x

18

<u>Reasons Not to Think About Nick</u>

1. He told me not to.
2. I have much more life-changing things to think about.
3. It's all I do.

January 22nd (156 days ago)

"A seagull," Nick said, leaning his head against the rope of my tyre-swing.

We were both wrapped up in big coats and scarves; I was wearing the big furry hat I got from Russia with the flaps in the sides. I leant back and looked at him, pointing at the faint scar just above his eyebrow. "A *seagull* gave you that?"

"Yeah. So I wrestled it to the ground with my bare hands. Then another seagull joined in so I fought that too. By the end there were, like, fifteen seagulls, all totally defeated. They called me Seagull Dundee after that."

I narrowed my eyes. "How old were you?"

"Four. I was a very strong little boy."

I laughed. "Now tell me the truth."

Nick's mouth curved up at the corner. "I cannot *believe* you don't trust that I wrestled fifteen seagulls with my bare hands before I was out of kindergarten. What kind of rubbish girlfriend are you?"

"The kind with quite detailed knowledge of seagulls, unfortunately for you. No knowledge of boys but it balances out."

He shouted with laughter. "I *knew* I should have gone for the girl on the Dolce & Gabbana shoot." Then he pushed my swing a few times while I stuck my tongue out at him. "OK. What actually happened is I ran away from my parents when we were collecting rocks at the beach. I was pretty tiny so I didn't get very far, but a massive seagull freaked me out and I fell over and smacked my head on a rock. When I woke up a few minutes later, it was standing on my chest."

"Were you scared?"

"No. Heroes don't get scared." Nick thought about it. "One of us definitely pooped, though. I'm pretty sure it was the seagull."

I laughed again. "I hate seagulls. Did you know that they're so smart that they hang around bridges so they can steal the heat coming off the roads, and that they tap on the ground with their feet and pretend to be rain so earthworms come out?"

"That doesn't surprise me at all. They're so sneaky."

"How big was this one?"

"The size of a tiger. Comparatively, anyway."

I tried to imagine Nick small and frightened, but I couldn't quite do it. "So what gave you the scar? The rock or the seagull?"

"The rock. Although the seagull got really close to my face too. Really, really close. Like, this close." Nick suddenly stopped the swing and put his face near mine.

I held my breath. I could see the different shades of black and brown in his eyes, and the tangle of black lashes underneath them. I could see my hat reflected in his pupils. I could see the little mole on his cheek and smell the greenness which – I had finally managed to establish – was the result of a fondness for lime shower gel combined with a tendency to constantly sit on wet grass in his jeans.

"That's pretty close," I just about managed to say as he put his hand gently on my cheek and brushed away a bit of hat fluff.

"Yup," Nick said with a smile that went up in one

corner and seemed to stretch out forever. His hand stayed where the fluff had been. "But not quite close enough to hurt me."

And he leant in and kissed me.

19

Scientists say that music can literally change the speed of a heartbeat. They failed to add:

So can a text message.

It's as if Nick is suddenly in the room with me.

I drop the phone.

"Harriet? What's going on?"

Humans are supposed to have 70,000 thoughts a day; I'm about to hit my limit in four and a half seconds.

"It's Nick," I summarise.

"*Seriously?*" Nat grabs the phone off me and reads the message. Then she chucks it back to me, jumps off the bed and starts folding a jumper messily.

I'm breathing too fast and my heart is starting to skitter around like Bambi on a frozen lake. My entire body is suddenly full of a triumphant, almost painful buzzing sensation. What did I *tell* you? It wasn't a matter of *if* he was going to change his mind. It was just a matter of *when*.

83

Although I'm going to be honest: he really took his time. We're not Jane Eyre and Mr Rochester, for goodness' sake. I could have set up an entire school since we last spoke.

I jump off the bed, spin around the room and start hugging my phone to my chest. "Should I ring him now, Nat?" I say breathlessly, breaking off just long enough to kiss my phone and start hugging it again. "Or should I text? What do you think he wants me to do? Do you think he's coming straight here from Australia?" My eyes widen and I fly to the window. "Oh my God, Nat. What if he's already here?"

I push the window open and then remember that I'm at Nat's house. He's very unlikely to come here first. I need to go home and get ready *right now*. I need to wash my hair. I need to clear away my chemistry kit.

I start putting my shoes on.

"How long should I wait until I reply to look cool?" I continue breathlessly. "Five minutes? Ten minutes? An hour?"

I'm so excited I can't get my shoelaces to tie up properly. "Or should I just ring now? I don't want him to get the wrong impression."

I look at the text again. The answer to these

questions must be in here somewhere. Maybe it's in code. Maybe it's a haiku. Allegory? For goodness' sake, I've studied English literature for five whole years. I can analyse the imagery in *Macbeth* and the symbolism in *Hamlet*. I should be able to work *this* out.

"You know what?" I decide. "I think I'll just ring him straight away. I can't wait any longer."

My phone abruptly disappears.

"Like hell you will," Nat snaps, and before I know it she's standing on her bed, violently waving my mobile in the air like some kind of rectangular hand grenade. "You'll have to kill me first."

I stare at my best friend. It's only now that I notice her cheeks are bright pink, and her hands are shaking. Her angry rash is starting to climb up her chest. And it's only now that I notice she's folded and unfolded the same jumper five times. "What on earth are you talking about?"

"You're not contacting Nick," she says loudly. "I'll eat this phone if I have to. And the charger."

I'm not sure that's even physically possible. "*What*? Why?"

"Because you need to wake up, Harriet."

I blink and then look down at myself. "I'm pretty sure I'm awake, Nat."

"This isn't an epic romance. It's just a boy who used you. A boy who made you forget about everything that was important to you before he came along. You've read so many books you can't even tell the difference between fiction and reality any more."

I flinch. Just because I sometimes use the words 'thou' and 'mayst' for fun does not mean I think I'm in an Austen novel. Not all the time, anyway.

"I can," I say indignantly. "I am well aware of the difference between what's real and what isn't." I'd be prettier in a book, for starters. "Give me my phone right now."

I jump for her, like some kind of killer whale trying to get a particularly nice seal.

"Harriet," Nat says urgently, moving a little further away. "Nick hasn't contacted you for *two months*. He *dumped* you weeks before the most important exams of your life and ran away. That's not what somebody who cares about you does. You have to believe me. I understand boys better than you do."

I flinch again and something in me pinches slightly. "You might know boys in general," I say defiantly. "But you don't know Nick. He cares about me. I know he does."

I jump for her again and miss.

"He doesn't," Nat says, moving until she's pressed against the wall and holding me back with a foot. "He's an idiot and I'm not letting him suck you back in with his pointy cheekbones and his pointy hipbones and his stupid pointy hair. *No.*"

Fury suddenly surges through me. My best friend is acting like some kind of crazy, masterminding puppeteer. She's calling my Lion Boy an idiot. She's just reminded me about his lovely hipbones.

And – most of all – I'm furious that a very tiny part of me suspects she might be right.

"*Natalie!*" I yell. "Nat! Give me my phone NOW!"

"Don't make me do this," Nat shouts, and her cheeks get even pinker. "For once in your life just listen to me, Harriet."

"*Give me my phone!*" I shout again, and – with a lurch of my stomach – I suddenly know what Nat's going to do.

If she gets rid of that text, I will have no way of contacting him. I deleted Nick's number so I wouldn't be tempted to text him after he left. He doesn't 'do' social media. And I can't remember his email address.

He'll give up on me.

And if that happens, I'm not sure our ten-year friendship will survive. More importantly, I'm not sure

Nat will. There's a really good chance I'll just kill my best friend on the spot.

There's a red dot in the centre of each of Nat's cheeks. "I'm doing this for you," she announces, tapping the screen. "I honestly am."

"*No!*" I yell, and bundle myself at her legs in an attempt to desperately wrestle my phone out of her hands. Nat scrabbles away while I hold on to her feet, and the next thing I know she's only wearing one sock and there's yet another rip in my bridesmaid's dress.

By the time I've finally managed to claw my phone back, we're huffing and puffing and scratched and bright red all over and it's too late.

The message has gone.

My last chance with Nick has gone with it.

You really don't want to know what I say next.

Let's just put it this way: in no way do I leave my feelings about the situation open to interpretation. I am very clear about every single one of them.

I end the conversation by telling Nat I hope she doesn't get eaten by French chickens in a way that very much intimates the opposite, and then storm out of the house.

"Harriet?" Nat yells out of the window as I stomp down the road, silk dress rippling after me. "I'm *sorry.* I lost my temper! I shouldn't have done that!"

"No," I yell back, without turning round, "you shouldn't!"

Then I keep stomping. What kind of friend *does* that?

Who the sugar cookies does Nat think she *is*?

20

For the next couple of days, I simply refuse to leave my room.

There's no point. The alternative is to watch my parents take all my impeccably arranged books out of the study and pile them in a not-even-vaguely alphabetical order outside my door.

By the time it gets to Friday afternoon, I'm so sick of hearing Dad say "*another* book of random quotations? Seriously?" I decide to go for a long, cathartic walk. My ex-best friend will be in France by now, getting chased about by Mr Green Lycra Cycling Shorts.

Good. Serves her right.

I hope he doesn't even use proper virgin olive oil, and opts for low-grade cooking oil instead.

Unfortunately my stress-reducing exercise efforts are ruined within two minutes by a small, fluffy-headed figure creeping from tree to tree in front of me. I have

to keep looking in the opposite direction so I don't hurt his feelings.

"Toby," I finally say as I turn back on to my road. He flattens himself behind a lamp-post considerably thinner than he is. "I can see you."

"Are you sure?"

"Pretty sure, yes."

"Oh dear," he says sadly. "My homemade camouflage stalker kit may need some more work." He points at his grey T-shirt and grey trousers. They have faint black lines drawn on them in criss-crosses.

I stare at him, and then totally give up. "What on earth are you camouflaged *as*?"

"Pavement." Toby lies down on the floor and holds himself very rigid and still. "See? It's only for urban settings, obviously. It wouldn't work in the countryside."

I laugh and carefully step over him.

"Harriet," he says, jumping up and running after me. "Are you and Natalie OK? I couldn't help overhearing a small amount of very loud fighting the other day when I was sitting in the rhododendron outside her house waiting for you to come out."

Clearly Toby hasn't moved on quite as much as I thought he had. "I've had an unexpected best-friend position open up," I say tensely. "Would you like it?"

"*Would I?*" Toby shouts, jumping up and down. "I mean, *I would*. Just to make that clear."

"Great," I say sharply. "We're now Best Friends. We can go and get some badges made up or something."

Toby bounces along next to me in contented silence, and then sighs. "I'm afraid I don't think I can take the job, Harriet," he says sadly. "You and Natalie are soulmates, except you don't kiss. It would be wrong to try to ever separate you."

I make an ambiguous snorting noise. Soulmates are usually happy for each other when supermodel ex-boyfriends text them. "Either way, now I'm not going to Tokyo, it's just you and me this summer."

"Actually, maybe not," Toby says solemnly.

I'm already thinking about my abandoned Summer of Fun Flow Chart. Maybe I can re-use it after all. I just need to find the right colour pen so I can cross out *Nat* and replace it with *Toby* and my holiday will be none the wiser. "Hmmm?"

"I think you already have a visitor."

My stomach suddenly flips and every hair on my body stands on end. *Nick?*

I look up. There's a bright pink Beetle parked outside my house.

The hairs flatten back down again. Oh no. No no. No no no no – I turn around and start walking in the opposite direction.

"Harriet?" a voice calls. "Come and give your favourite old person a nice big cuddle."

And there – standing in the doorway covered in bells and sequins, like some kind of summery Christmas tree – is my grandmother.

I just want to make something perfectly clear.

There are many, many other old people I prefer to this one. My grandad, for instance. Nat's grandad. Nat's grandma. My old piano teacher, Mr Henry. The ancient lady who works in the local newsagent and gives me free sweets without being asked.

It's not that I don't love my grandmother. I just don't really know her very well.

Or at all, actually.

"Sweetie!" she says as I approach with tiny steps, the way you might a rampaging hippopotamus. "Your hair is even redder than it used to be!" She sweeps me into her arms and all the bells on her wrists tinkle like she's an enormous cat. "From a distance it looks like your head is on fire!"

I think I'm about to get an embroidered daisy

imprinted permanently on my forehead. "It's strawberry blonde," I tell her left breast as politely as I can. She smells of wood and beetroot.

"Look how mucky you are!" she laughs, pulling back and spitting on her long wizard-like sleeve. Before I can escape she starts scrubbing it hard on my nose. "Oops. No. They're freckles, just like Richard's. Adorable! How long has it been since I saw you last? Five months? Six?"

"Three and a half years," I say, staring over her shoulder at my parents who have finally emerged. Needless to say, Annabel's eating. This time it appears to be toast with Neapolitan ice cream spread in a layer on top.

"Whoopsy," my grandmother says, beaming at us. "I took over a coconut stall in India for an afternoon and next thing I knew I was running a *roaring* backpacker trade. Good for copious amounts of diarrhoea, coconut water."

Toby races forwards with his hand out. "I am Toby Pilgrim, Harriet's stalker. Nice to meet you, Mrs Grandmother Manners."

"Bunty," she says cheerfully, shaking it.

"And on that exciting note," Toby says, wiping his nose on his finger, "I shall make my dramatic exit. I've got this new plate with a face on it and Mum's made spaghetti so I'm eager to get home while it's still hot and malleable enough to form realistic hair."

Then Toby promptly waves and scoots back out of the door. We all try to pretend that we can't see him immediately crouch down behind the hedge right outside.

"I didn't know you were coming." I look at my parents with round eyes. Does nobody tell me *anything* these days?

"Well, if somebody needs to take you abroad it might as well be somebody who spends most of her time there, right?"

I stare at her, then I stare at my parents, and then I stare at my grandmother again. *What?*

"Apparently Tokyo is the place to be this summer," she grins. "I think we should check it out, don't you?"

I suddenly don't care that I've probably met my nomadic grandmother a handful of times in my entire life. I don't care that her hair is sort of baby pink, and I don't care that she currently has what looks like a twig stuck in it.

I don't even care that the last time I saw her we had a forty-five-minute conversation about the benefits of wiping your bottom with your hand instead of a piece of toilet paper to 'save the rainforest'.

"Oh my God, I *love* you!" I yell, throwing myself around her neck. "Thank you! Thank you thank you thank you!"

"Now, *that's* the greeting I was looking for."

Then I lob myself at Dad, and then – a little bit more carefully, in case I squish my sibling – at Annabel. "Thank you! Thank you thank you! You've *saved* my summer! Totally saved it!"

Dad laughs. "How could we argue with a Powerpoint presentation of such quality, Harriet? We're not *monsters.*" He puts his hand over his mouth. "*She's* a monster," he pretends to whisper, pointing at Annabel. "But *I'm* not."

"Go upstairs and get your things packed for tomorrow, Harriet," Annabel says calmly, ignoring Dad. "I imagine your grandmother will want to help you write a brand-new Summer of Fun Flow Chart."

"What's a flow chart?" my grandmother asks. "Does it rank rivers?"

Good Lord. I'm going to have to start training her immediately. "We have new plans to make!" I shout, running up the stairs. "Itineraries! Schedules! Lists! Lists and lists and lists and—"

"Look, Harriet," my grandmother says as she follows behind me, pointing at the garden. "A squirrel!"

"Make sure she has everything she needs," Annabel calls after us.

"My darling daughter," Bunty calls down the stairs. "That's the beauty of foreign travel. You don't need anything but yourself."

"And a passport, Mum," I hear Annabel say tiredly. "And tickets. And a visa. And clean clothes and quite a few changes of underwear."

Uh-huh.

If you thought you saw a marked family resemblance between my maverick grandmother and my maverick father, you would be wrong.

Bunty isn't Dad's mum.

She's Annabel's.

21

My entire summer has just turned around.

And, as I start jubilantly packing all the important things into a suitcase – paper, dictionaries, pens, etc – I suddenly remember that I wrote Nick's email address on an old bit of paper and tucked it into an ancient copy of *Anne of Green Gables* months and months ago. *Ha.* I am so much more cunning and better organised with contact details than Nat gives me credit for.

As *if* I'd let go of Nick that easily.

Mentally high-fiving myself, I think about it carefully and then write the following email on my phone:

Dear Nick,

Got your message. Would love to talk. I've been thinking about you lots! Of course I have! Am going to Japan for a few weeks for a modelling job but taking my phone with me. Send me another message or ring me? Or ask Wilbur and he can give you my new address?

I'VE MISSED YOU SO MUCH. :)
Harriet xxxx

I look at it happily – he *definitely* can't misread or misinterpret that in any way – and then press SEND. Now it's just a matter of time before Nick tracks me down and I have the best, most romantic summer *ever*.

I spend the next twenty minutes contentedly bouncing around my room as if I'm on an enormous imaginary Spacehopper: scanning travel documents, printing them out and arranging them carefully in alphabetical order. I make a list of all the lists I need to make. I sit Bunty on my bed, and read her fascinating snippets from a Visit Japan website: "Did you know that the word *karaoke* means *empty orchestra*?" and "Can you believe it used to be customary in ancient Japan for women to blacken their teeth with dye to make them look less toothy!"

My grandmother, in the meantime, sits on the windowsill and makes comments like: "Oooh – your glasses are making a rainbow on the wall, Harriet, isn't that just *magical*?"

I'm so ridiculously happy, I don't even feel the need

to explain the difference between 'magic' and 'refraction'. I bounce around hysterically until I remember I left my laptop downstairs. I'm probably going to need it at some stage so I can look up additional facts *in situ*.

With an unprecedented degree of physical dexterity, I bound down the stairs to get it.

"Annabel?" I chirp. "Dad? Did I leave my laptop in—" Then I stop, because they're sitting at the kitchen table with their heads together, talking in low voices.

And all I can hear is the word 'Harriet'.

22

Here's the thing: my parents *never* talk in low voices.

Especially not to each other.

Now, obviously everybody knows that listening in on other people's conversations never comes to any good. You usually end up hearing something you're not supposed to hear or getting stabbed to death like Polonius in *Hamlet*. So the most sensible thing to do right now is interrupt my parents immediately, or leave before the conversation goes any further.

I have no explanation for why I duck behind the living-room wall and breathe as quietly as I can.

"I'm just so *exhausted*, Rich," Annabel continues. "It feels like I'm wading through a thick river of treacle all of the time."

"You're not," Dad says reassuringly. "Judging by the state of our cupboards, I'm pretty sure you'd have eaten that too."

Then I hear the sound of a gentle smack round the head. "Seriously," Annabel says, "I had no idea

101

reproduction would be so much work. I would pay really good money to be a reptile or a chicken right now."

Dad laughs. "You're not doing this alone, Bels." There's a *swoosh*, which sounds like a shoulder being rubbed. "I'm not going anywhere. I'm tying myself to you like a mitten to its other mitten."

"Thank you, sweetheart."

"Through the coat sleeve of life. With the string of love."

Annabel laughs. "OK, I think that's enough of the mitten analogy."

There's the sound of a long, sloppy kiss, and I can feel myself making a *blurgh* face. According to statistics and what I overheard while waiting outside Parents' Evening, everyone else has parents that are only together For The Sake Of The Children. It makes me feel a bit awkward, knowing that mine have a relationship that is so flagrantly nothing to do with me. They could at least *pretend* to have no interest in each other.

I'm just getting ready to interrupt when Dad says, "But it still doesn't answer the question. What about Harriet?"

I abruptly stop breathing.

Annabel sighs. "I don't know, Rich. I just don't know. After today" – I can hear her tapping on the table anxiously with a biro – "She can be such hard work sometimes, you know. I don't think I can handle any more. It's my first baby, and you know I love her to pieces but..."

My whole body goes numb. But? *But?*

There isn't supposed to be a 'but'.

I poke my head around the edge of the door just in time to see Annabel put her head in her hands as Dad gently kisses the top of her head. "I just think it's best for everyone if she's not here."

23

The human brain consists of 200 billion nerve cells. In the cerebral cortex alone there are 125 trillion synapses, which is roughly the amount of stars as in 1,500 Milky Way galaxies. It feels like every single one of them is exploding simultaneously.

They're not sending me away for me. They're sending me away for *them*.

Suddenly every thought I've been pushing out of my head for six months is roaring in, the way air rushes into a vacuum. *This* is what I've been scared of. This is what has been building and building, and squashing my excitement about the baby. That the mother panda would choose, and she wouldn't choose me.

And this is just the start, isn't it?

In a year or two, it will take my room.

It will take my bed and my dog.

It will take the slice of sunshine by the window where I sit when I'm reading.

It'll take the bit at the back of the cupboard where I keep my old train set and the loose floorboard where I hide my poems and the shelf where I keep my dictionaries.

It'll take my hook in the bathroom and my time slot in the shower and the pencil lines on the side of the door that have taken nearly sixteen years to draw.

It will take my dad throwing them about in a swimming pool and messing up their hair and being an idiot.

It will take all of Annabel.

And nudge by nudge, I'll be pushed further and further away. Until I'm all on my own.

I lean against the hallway wall, breathing hard through my mouth. Then, quietly, cautiously, I open the box in my head that I haven't touched in six months.

Carefully – one by one – I start putting people inside. I put in Annabel and Dad. I put in the baby. I put in Nat. Finally, I close the lid of the box and sit on it.

It's just best for everyone if she's not here.

If that's how they feel, I'll go somewhere else. Somewhere better. Somewhere more exciting. I'll see the world, and I'll do it by myself.

Because that's the thing about a transformation: there's no stopping it. Once the tadpole has legs it jumps out of the pond. Once the caterpillar has wings, it flies away.

And once you've metamorphosed, you can't go back. Even if you want to.

24

Agreement of Responsibility

THIS AGREEMENT is made between Annabel Manners and Bunty Brown, with reference to the guardianship of Harriet Manners as agreed to by Richard Manners, witness and father.

THEREFORE, intending to be legally bound hereby, the parties agree as follows:

- Bunty Brown will act like a mature and responsible adult, regardless of how fervently she believes that 'age is just a number'.
- Bunty Brown will acknowledge the fact that Harriet Manners is a minor and will accompany her AT ALL TIMES. She will not wander off because she sees something sparkly or rare or 'feels like it, darling'.
- Bunty Brown will not discuss with Harriet

Manners anything she did or did not do in the sixties.

- Or the seventies.
- Or the eighties.
- Bunty Brown will not attempt to convert Harriet Manners to: Druidism, Paganism, Zoroastrianism, Baha'i, Prince Philip Movement, Scientology, Buddhism, Taoism, Sikhism, Islam, Hinduism, Confucianism, Christianity, Shinto, Judaism, Wicca, or any other belief system that Bunty Brown is currently devoted to.
- Bunty Brown will not pierce, henna, tie-dye or attach flowers, feathers or sequins to any part of Harriet Manners.
- Bunty Brown will put Harriet Manners first.

Signed:

ANNABEL MANNERS

Bunty Brown

~~SpiderMan Brad Pitt~~ Richard Manners

25

The next seventeen hours can be summarised thus:

- I avoid my parents.

And that's it.

By the time Annabel and Dad have waved goodbye with the happiest facial expressions I've ever seen on adults, I'm so desperate to go I don't even care that they can't take me to the airport because of a hospital appointment.

Even though we all know that by *hospital* they mean *Harriet leaving* and by *appointment* they mean *massive party*. And by 'tidying up' they mean *blowing up balloons and turning my bedroom into an impromptu home cinema.*

I promise to ring them as soon as I arrive and then focus on:

a) Studying for the entire car journey.

b)   Trying not to get knocked out by Bunty's pink
     dream-catcher, swinging merrily from the rear-
     view mirror.

By the time we reach the airport, I've managed to distract myself completely by acquiring a good ten to fifteen Japanese words *and* working out a detailed itinerary. Shrines I want to light incense at and theatres I want to visit and food I want to eat and parasitological museums I want to take photos of and show to Toby.

So when my grandmother and I walk into the airport departures lounge and there's a high-pitched squeal, I don't even turn around. That's how much I've forgotten what it is I'm actually supposed to be doing here.

"Co-eeee, my little Monster Munches!" a voice shouts. A man in a leopard-print onesie and pink wellies starts stomping enthusiastically towards us. "I've been waiting for minutes and minutes and I was spectacularly bored so I went to the Duty Free. *Smell me!* Close your eyes and I'm unwanted Christmas soap!" He wafts in a jutting, pigeon-like circular motion, and then holds his hand out to my grandmother. "*Enchanté*," he adds, curtsying deeply. "Which is French for *enchanted* because they obviously stole it from us, the naughty little Munchkins."

I stare at Wilbur in bewilderment. "Erm, they didn't," I say. "Both *enchanté* and *enchanted* come from the Latin verb *incantare*, which means *to cast spells*. Hello, Wilbur. Are you coming with us?"

I can't decide if I'm delighted or not. I love Wilbur, but in combination with my grandmother?

"Wilbur," he says, pushing me aside and kissing Bunty's hand. "That's with a *bur*, and not with an *iam*. I'm agent to this little chicken-monkey." He points at me, just in case anyone gets confused with all the other chicken-monkeys in the immediate vicinity.

"Bunty," my grandmother smiles, totally unfazed.

He points to my grandmother's pink floral dress with lace trim, beige, fringed blanket and mirrored waistcoat. "I am *loving* this. What are we calling it?"

My grandmother's eyes twinkle. "Spangled Nepalese goat-herder disco-dances by river in moonlight?"

"Oh my *holy dolphin-cakes*!" Wilbur shouts at the top of his voice. "That is superlatively *fantabulazing*! Could I borrow the waistcoat one day?"

"You can have it now, if you like," Bunty says, taking it off and handing it over. "I have dozens."

"*You!*" Wilbur squeaks, putting it on over his onesie and spinning around in little circles. "If you were liquid I would just pour you all over ice cream and sprinkle

you with hundreds and thousands and gobble you up!
You would be *hell* on my waistline and *laden* with
calories but *I just wouldn't care.*"

See what I mean?

"Are you coming with us?" I repeat politely as my
grandmother beams and then wanders towards some
fluffy key rings in a nearby shop.

"No, my little Turkish delight. I'm just here to prep
you."

I frown. "Wilbur—" How do I put this nicely? "At
no stage at any point in my entire modelling career
have you ever prepared me for anything. Ever." I pause.
"Like, *ever.*"

Wilbur's eyes open wide. "I am *hurt*," he says with
his hand on his chest. "Nay, *wounded*. Nay – what's
another word for hurt, my little Carrier-bag?"

"Offended? Stung? Aggrieved?"

"*Précisement*. How can you say I am ever anything
but one hundred per cent professional?"

"For my last photo shoot you sent me to your
dentist."

"They had *very* similar business cards and I thought
I'd just seen Sting walk past and it was all very
confusing." Wilbur tries to look indignant, and then
sighs. "OK. I'm a terrible, terrible agent. But this time

it's mahoosive, Sugar-plum. Like, Calvin Klein mahoosive. Like, *mamoosive* mahoosive. Yuka's broken away from Baylee to start up her own label. It's huge, Peach-plum, and I need to make sure we're all on the same page."

I suddenly feel a bit sick. You can look at it any way you like, but last time I attempted to model I ended up covered in gold paint and attached to a curtain rod. "She's launching her new label with me?"

Wilbur starts giggling. "Oh, bunny, you *do* crack me down the middle. Can you imagine?"

I patiently wait for him to stop being so insulting.

"No: the main" – he pretends to cough – "*taller* models are being flown out today to China, Hong Kong, Macau, South Korea…"

"Mongolia and Taiwan?"

He abruptly stops laughing. "How do you know that?"

"They're the seven countries in East Asia, excluding North Korea." Wilbur's gone a strange, pale shade of mustard. "It was just a guess. Are you OK?"

Wilbur breathes out hard. "This is all top secret, Moo-noo. We need to get the campaign done before Yuka tells Baylee she's leaving. If I can just organise it" – he leans forward slightly and grabs my shoulders – "Poodle, it might be my way out of here."

"Yuka won't let you out of the *airport?*"

Wilbur starts giggling again. "Out of *agenting*, my little Nutmeg. She's *finally* going to give me a position with her new label."

I don't know why I'm so surprised. Adults almost never like doing their jobs from what I can tell.

"I like being an agent, but I'm shockingly bad at it, Muffin-top. Anyway, I didn't get a degree in fashion so I could sit at a desk, trying to talk to pretty women. If I wanted to do that, I'd have got a job in a normal office."

Wilbur straightens out the waistcoat. "This is our chance, Bunny. Yours, and mine." He pauses. "Mostly mine, because let's be honest: I'm an adult with a proper career and I'd imagine your shelf life as a teen model is almost over."

For the last twenty-four hours, I've thought about a lot of things. I've thought about how far away Japan is (5,937 miles), and how bad I am at eating with chopsticks (very) and my chances of dying in an air crash (1 in 10.46 million). I've thought about how many Hello Kittys I'm going to buy for Nat (zero: they creep her out) and how many vending machines there are for every person in Japan (23).

But it hadn't occurred to me that I might actually have to *model* when I got there. That it would be important to a lot of people. Or that I would be totally out of my depth. *Again.*

"OK," I stammer nervously. "I'll try my very hardest."

Wilbur sighs. "I know you will, Baby-baby Panda," he says, pinching my cheek. "And that is *exactly* what I'm worried about."

26

By the time we get through the security gates, I'm so excited and nervous, I feel like a shark. As if I can't stop moving or I'll die.

Or talking, for that matter.

Which is less like a shark, but does a similar job in making people try to get away from me as fast as possible.

"I'm going to Japan," I tell the man standing by the electric buggies. "I'm going to Japan," I tell the lady behind the counter at Boots. "I'm going to Japan," I tell the man who gives me a sandwich at Pret A Manger.

"I'm going on my lunch break," he replies, immediately entering into the spirit of things.

Everything is suddenly fascinating. The air-hostess uniforms. The scarily round bread rolls. The little packs with free socks and toothbrushes. The fact that you can pop the edges of the headrests out. Even the in-flight safety procedure brochure is – you guessed it – fascinating.

I think I may be over-stimulated.

"Haven't you been on a plane before?" Bunty laughs when I finish breathlessly pointing at random landmarks below us so that I can click the cup holder in and out of the seat in front of me repeatedly.

"I have, but never without—" I swallow. *My parents or Nat.* "Not long distance before. Did you know that the chances of being in a plane crash are less than 0.00001 per cent? That means that you're more likely to be killed by a donkey or to naturally conceive *identical* quadruplets."

Bunty pulls a blanket over her knees. "Is that so?"

"Uh-huh." The lights of London are starting to melt below us into a large, sparkly neon puddle. "They test plane windscreens by throwing chickens at them at five hundred miles per hour so they know they can resist errant flying birds. Once a chicken went *through* the window and smashed the pilot's chair in half. They realised afterwards they'd accidentally catapulted a frozen one."

Bunty chuckles. "You're so much like Annabel was at your age, darling. Fascinated by the little things."

I immediately look out of the window so Bunty can't see my expression. "Actually, everyone likes facts.

117

Apparently three million people Google the words 'interesting facts' every single month."

Bunty looks at me then twists up her nose and closes her eyes. "Funny," she says. "That's just what she would have said as well."

And before I can respond, my grandmother is fast asleep.

I fully intend to stay awake for the next fourteen hours. I have a special Flight Bag I put together to keep me entertained: maps to study and crosswords to fill in and quizzes about the flags of Asia (you never know when somebody abroad is going to test you on something like that).

But I get over-excited about the little butter tubs at dinner, peak early and pass out before we've flown over France.

And the next thing I know…

I'm in Japan.

27

Places I Want to Visit
Japan
Burma Myanmar
Russia

I've wanted to come here for so long that when I get the list out of my satchel I can see where I struggled to join up the *a* and the *n* and there's blue glitter in the creases from when Nat threw it over everything for a term at primary school.

I'm finally here.

Within minutes of landing, it feels like I have new eyes, new ears, a new nose, a new tongue, new skin. People are talking in a language I don't understand, making gestures I've never seen before and eating food I don't recognise. There are signs I can't read, and smells I can't place, and a hum that sounds entirely different to England. Even the colours look different: there's a slightly golden glow to everything, instead

119

of the silveriness of a summer in England. I may as well have landed on the moon.

Apart from the whole gravity element. Or I'd just be floating through the airport and it would be really hard to hang on to my suitcase.

"Enormous fun, isn't it?" Bunty says as I stand, blinking, in the middle of a tiny shop. She waves a couple of bright pink snacks with angry cartoon octopuses drawn on them at me. "Have one of these. It will blow your mind."

I've just seen a sandwich filled with whipped cream and strawberries, a drink called 'Sweat' and an entire dried squid vacuum-packed into a bag. The inside of my head has already exploded.

In a daze, I take the snack from her – it's like an enormous, fishy Wotsit – and then watch a group of schoolgirls roughly my age, standing in a little huddle in a corner. They're all wearing *exactly* the same outfit: the same skirts at the same length, the same socks, the same shirts, the same shoes, the same backpacks. They have no make-up on and one of two hairstyles: black, with a fringe in a ponytail, or black, cut short and pushed behind their ears. There's no cunning personalisation; no fashionable editing or skirt-rolling or high-heel wearing or lipgloss sneaking. It's stupidly disorientating, considering it's the precise definition of the word *uniform*.

They're all studying maps and staring, wide-eyed, around them, so I don't think they're from Tokyo. Then they spot me and their eyes get even bigger. A few start squeaking *kawwaaaaiiiiiiii* and giggling. I promptly fall over my suitcase and am met with a collection of even louder giggles, and a few squeaks of *chhhoooo kawwaaiiiii, ne*?

I have no idea what they're saying, obviously, but it doesn't feel mean.

I blush slightly and give a little shy wave. They blush and start waving shyly back. Then I notice that one of them has a little dinosaur key ring hanging off their satchel. Another has a little Winnie the Pooh, and a third a small fluffy duck.

Oh my God: is *this* where I belong? I have spent an entire lifetime struggling to fit in only to discover that all the other tidy, shy teenage girls with neat ankle socks and no make-up and a fondness for satchel accessories live on the other side of the world.

Maybe I'll ask if one of them can adopt me.

I give another shy wave and then follow Bunty outside.

We walk through a wall of intense, pulsing, dense

heat and climb into the back of a taxi.

Then we start the slow, winding drive into the heart of Tokyo.

I have literally never seen a city more *awake*.

Lights are flashing. People are everywhere. The smell of frying is coming from all directions. Everything is pushed together and jumbled up: streets and paths and roads, winding up and down and over each other like an enormous Scalextric set. The buildings get taller and taller, and – tucked away like secrets – there are tiny wooden temples and flowers and trees, peeking out like grass between pavement slabs.

Everything is moving and glowing and beeping: signs, shops, restaurants, T-shirts, pedestrian crossings, all flickering and lit up and coloured and singing.

It's as if the entire city and everything in it has just drunk eight cups of coffee and is going to spend the rest of the night shaking, feeling really sick and staring at the ceiling. (I did this with Nat a few months ago. It wasn't as much fun as we thought it would be.)

As I stare out of the window to my left, there's a shop display with a purple unicorn in it, wearing tiny orange trainers and a rhinestone saddle. A few minutes later there's a car covered in thousands of diamonds. To my right, ballerina mannequins hang from silver threads.

A group of men wearing grey suits walk past, with a man wearing red tartan in the middle.

A woman dressed as a rabbit waves at us.

And every time the taxi stops at a light, it's all I can do not to open the car door, jump out and swirl around the middle of the road with my hands stretched out, like Julie Andrews in *The Sound of Music*. Except with a much greater chance of being hit by a car and a much smaller chance of falling off the top of a mountain.

I've researched Japan for an entire decade. I've looked at photos and memorised facts and stuck maps on my wall. I've printed things off the internet and ripped pictures out of calendars. But for the first time in my life, studying has let me down. Not a single thing I've read or looked at or studied has ever come close to what it's like actually *being* here.

I stare out of the window in total silence until the car finally pulls into a smaller street with large, grey, grubby concrete blocks and stops halfway along the kerb. The windows have bars across them and there are wooden sticks strewn on the floor with bits of dried chicken still attached to them.

"Ta-da, darling," Bunty announces, flourishing her hands, as if she just pulled a grubby Tokyo suburb out of a black top hat. "Out you hop."

I go to open my door, and then pause. My grandmother looks very seated and her invitation sounds nowhere near as plural as it should do. "Me?"

"No, I'm talking to the cab driver," Bunty laughs. She playfully grabs my arm and shakes it. "Yes, *you*, silly bean."

"Where are *you* going?"

"I thought this would be so much more fun on your own, sweetie. It'll be a real, grown-up adventure. We won't tell your parents. Deal? I'd only cramp your style anyway."

The driver opens my door for me and then starts pulling my suitcase on to the pavement. I climb out with my mouth flapping in confusion. What is she *talking* about? I don't have any style *to* cramp. Does this woman know anything about me at *all*?

"B-but—" I stammer through the gap at the top of the window as the driver gets back in and the engine starts. "What about the contract you signed with Annabel?"

"What's my daughter going to do?" Bunty grins, raising an eyebrow. "Sue me?" And I'm suddenly not at all sure she knows anything about Annabel either.

The car starts moving away.

"W-wait," I shout, unsuccessfully attempting to jog after it. "I don't think that this is... this is a really big... please... I won't... I can't." I swallow. "You can't just *abandon* me on the other side of the world!"

"I'm not abandoning!" Bunty shouts through the window as the car starts driving back up the street. "I'm setting you free! Have a tremendous time, darling! Flat 6B!"

28

According to my guidebook, Tokyo is 2,187 km in area. It has 12.6 million people, twenty-three wards, sixty-two municipalities, 168 tube stations and nine train lines. There are 6,029 people for every square km, and it's the largest metropolitan area in the world. By any stretch of the imagination, it's a pretty big city.

In the last few seconds it just got a whole lot bigger.

I watch the taxi get smaller and smaller until my grandmother disappears completely. Then I take a deep breath, collect whatever enthusiasm I have left and start dragging my suitcase anxiously up the road.

The wheels keep getting stuck in the pavement, it keeps falling over, and by the time I've worked out that the sign for 6B looks like 5E I've walked past it six times and most of my excitement has been left in a sticky trail up and down the road, like a big sad snail.

Finally I clear my throat and press one of the buttons

lined up in two neat rows, like the buttons on a dinner jacket. It crackles, and a fuzzy voice says, "Yes?"

"Umm. My name is Harriet Manners. I think I'm staying here?"

"I'll be right down. Wait there." The crackling abruptly stops, and a few floors above me a door slams.

This is *ridiculous*. I've done exactly as I'm told all my life. Fifteen *years* of not taking sweets off strangers, running with scissors, playing with matches, jumping off swings, petting stray dogs or accepting lifts from people I don't know, and this is how it ends: knocking on the door of a stranger in a darkening alley on the other side of the world with nobody to hear me scream.

If I knew I was going to die like this, I could have relaxed and actually enjoyed my childhood.

I start rifling through my satchel for something to defend myself against my imminent attacker. I'm just tentatively wielding the Pocahontas pen I got from Disneyland in front of my face when the door swings open.

"Oh," the axe murderer says, inhaling sharply, and I drop my weapon.

Because standing in front of me, in black jeans and a grey vest, is the most beautiful girl I have ever seen.

29

When Nat and I were seven we realised we would never be princesses.

I had thousands of freckles and ginger hair, and everybody knew that nobody with either of those things ever got rescued from a tower. They got left there for all eternity, and thus ended their royal bloodline.

Nat had unruly black hair, dark skin and the beginnings of what her mother would later describe as a monobrow. It was generally acknowledged that princesses had complexions like fruit and two eyebrows, clearly distinct from each other. So that excluded her as well.

The tall girl standing in front of me now is precisely what we concluded princesses should look like. Huge mesmerising blue eyes, flawless skin, a pouty mouth, pale golden hair in waves down to her waist. An aura of goodness and an ability to engage in conversation with animals. A ray of sunshine, hitting her head like

128

a halo. (I have no idea how she's found one, it's almost totally dark outside.)

Any second now, rabbits are going to start leaping around her feet in pairs and a bluebird is going to land on her shoulder.

"Hello," she says, sounding utterly delighted, and I realise that she's even more English than I am. "I'm Poppy. You're *so* not what I was expecting."

"H-Harriet Manners," I stutter, taking her hand. "It's nice to meet you, umm…" and I finish the sentence by fading into silence and staring rudely over her shoulder. Part of me is still expecting to see seven miniature men wandering around the hallway.

"I'm *so* happy to finally meet you," she says, taking my suitcase and wheeling it into the hallway. "My boyfriend's always so busy. Anyway, it's just not the same, is it? They just don't want to talk about girly things."

Oh, God. I suspect I'm about to prove an enormous disappointment.

"Umm…" I desperately start racking my brain for a subject that will make this girl like me. "Did you know that high heels for women in the West are believed to have originated with Catherine De Medici in the sixteenth century? She was about to marry King

Henry of France and wanted him to think she was taller than she actually was."

Poppy looks at me with wide eyes, and I remember why in fifteen years I have only managed to make one female friend.

"But in the Middle East," I continue nervously, "heels were used to lift the foot from the burning sand."

"How adorable!" Poppy giggles. "What else?"

What else?

That's not an answer I'm usually prepared for. I've pretty much run out of shoe-based facts. "Did you know that Neil Armstrong took his boots off and left them on the moon to compensate for the weight of the moon rocks they took?"

"Amazing!" Poppy claps a few times, and then pulls my suitcase across the hallway towards a bright green door.

She beams at me – a genuine, open, beautiful smile. I blink and look down at my battered suitcase, crumpled dinosaur T-shirt and tracksuit bottoms. I'm sticky with sweat from dragging my suitcase about, and even without lifting my arms I can tell that I smell a bit like Hugo when he's been out in the rain. This must be how Regan and Goneril felt around Cordelia in *King Lear*.

I think I'm starting to understand why they put her in prison.

"Rin?" Poppy calls, pushing the door open and manoeuvring my suitcase through the doorway with a graceful flick of her wrist. I try to hop over it and smash my ankle against the wheel. "*Harriet* is here! Come and say hello."

There's a clatter, and an incredibly pretty Japanese girl runs out of one of the rooms. Her hair is massive, waist-length and elaborately curled. She's wearing a pink flowery dress with lace trim and buttons all the way down the front, and white ankle socks with pink ribbons. A large, pink toy duck is attached on a clip to a belt covered in sequins. Her face is perfectly matt with round sparkly cheeks, huge eyelashes and glittery lipstick.

She looks exactly like one of the china dolls Granny Manners used to have on her mantelpiece, except slightly bigger and without a sign in front that says DO NOT TOUCH, HARRIET.

Rin stops in the hallway, breathless. "I go for gift, but I'm not finding it. It has gone walkabouts." She drops into a low bow. "My name is Rin. I am delight to meet you."

"Deligh*ted*," Poppy corrects sweetly. "It's deligh*ted*, Rin."

Rin looks bewildered. "Who is Ted? He's coming later? I have no present for Ted."

"It's… oh, never mind." Poppy gestures at me to take off my shoes and starts leading me through an incredibly narrow hallway. "We're both models too. This is a model flat, but you probably know that already."

I've suddenly realised why Poppy looks familiar: she was one of the girls I cut out of Nat's magazine. I distinctly remember putting her face in the bin.

"Me also," Rin beams, nodding happily. "Modelling sometime, then and now." She grabs my hand with her tiny, dainty fingers and starts leading me through the minuscule flat. "This is kitchen," she says, pointing to a bathroom with the smallest bathtub I have ever seen. "This is garden." She points to a kitchen. "And this is alive room." She gestures to a room with a very low table and four round cushions.

"Living room," Poppy corrects gently.

"I am very apologising," Rin says, blushing slightly and bowing again. "My English is so bad. I study super hard, but it is not sticky. I – *nandakke* – slurp."

"You don't *suck*." Poppy laughs. "Rin's obsessed with Australia so she's learning English as quickly as possible so she can move there. My boyfriend says she must have been a koala in a past life."

"One day," Rin says in a dreamy voice, "I move to Sydney and get Rip Curls and big BBQ and burn sausages. I shall be a little ropper."

"Ripper," Poppy says automatically, leading us into a teeny tiny bedroom.

Unlike the rest of the flat, it's not Japanese in style at all. There are no sliding doors and soft rush tatami mats: just a solid grey carpet, one set of bunk beds pushed against the corner and an enormous double bed with a mountain of pillows. In the middle of it is a large black cat, wearing a pink flowery dress, little white socks and a pink toy duck, attached to a sequined collar.

"My cat," Rin says unnecessarily, pointing proudly. "Kylie Minogue." The cat assesses me haughtily, licks a sock and goes back to sleep.

"She's on your bed," Poppy says, trying unsuccessfully to push her off. Kylie clearly doesn't agree: she opens one eye, glares at Poppy and tries to dig her claws through the socks into the duvet. "The big one's yours. Rin and I share the bunks."

That doesn't seem fair. I've only just got here. "I can move," I say quickly. "Or we can take turns?"

"No, Harry-chan," Rin says, shaking her head. "You have big VIP job." She says VIP as it looks: *vip*. "You stay here. Super cosy."

Rin picks Kylie up and the cat lets out an enormous disgruntled *squark*.

"I really don't care either," Poppy says, shrugging. Then she catches her reflection in the mirror behind me. "Oh my goodness, my hair. I'm going out with my boyfriend tonight, I should go and start getting ready."

I stare at one maverick gold strand, misbehaving by less than a centimetre, and then at my own rumpled reflection. There are still remnants of aeroplane gravy on my chin.

Poppy starts heading towards the bathroom, and then abruptly turns just in time to catch me surreptitiously trying to reach a splodge with my tongue stretched out.

She grabs my hand. "Harriet?" she says. "I really want to get to know you better."

I can feel my eyes open even wider. "Really?"

"Yes. You're… like a little piece of home."

"*Hai*," Rin agrees. "Home like hamster."

"Hampshire," Poppy corrects.

"Where hamsters come from," Rin says, smiling.

"Umm…" I stammer. "Th-thank you."

Poppy says, "I can tell already we're going to be inseparable."

And with that beatific smile – the kind that makes princes climb towers and fight dragons – Princess Poppy kisses my cheek and glides into the bathroom, locking the door firmly behind her.

30

OK. Something is wrong.

I blink a few times and sit heavily on my suitcase. I've just met two girls, and as of yet they haven't:

- Looked me up and down and then pretended they can't see me.
- Stood behind me, making faces.
- Said something as if they clearly mean the opposite.
- Rolled their eyes while I'm talking.
- Told me that my hair is "awfully bright for hair, isn't it?"
- Written an offensive yet painfully accurate observation about my personality on my suitcase.

They haven't pointed out sweetly that I'm quite short, for a model, or quite freckly, for a model, or quite weird-looking, for a human being. I quickly check my

back with my fingers. There isn't even a sign attached. Are these girls trying to be *friends* with me?

"I search gift under bed," Rin says enthusiastically as I desperately try to orientate myself. "You will like very much, Harry-chan. It is to speak welcome to Japan." She scampers towards the bunks and then stops and turns around. "Harry-chan, where are you come from?"

"England."

"England!" Rin looks absolutely delighted, as if I've just whipped off my T-shirt and revealed multi-coloured wings. "What language is speaken in England, Harry-chan?"

"Umm." I never, ever thought I would have to answer this question. "English. Just like Poppy."

"Like in Hamster also!" Rin couldn't look more astonished. "English everywhere! Super handy!" And then she drops to her knees in her pretty dress and starts trying to fit under the bed with her bottom wagging, like an over-excited puppy.

I can feel a warmth starting in my chest: the kind I haven't felt since I crawled under the piano ten years ago and found Nat there.

You know what? This is *exactly* what I needed. Adventure. Excitement. New girlfriends, for the first time since I was five years old. A chance to start again without my parents, without Nat, and without Toby. A chance to be me, with a totally clean slate.

Plus I'm in my perfect environment, because every time I turn around there's something new to learn about. It's like being in school, except all the time and without Alexa.

I'm going to have the best summer *ever*.

There's a loud knock at the front door, and I stand up and bounce over to answer it. Honestly, I can't remember the last time I felt this happy.

And then I open the door and remember.

Because standing in the hallway is the last thing that made me feel this way.

Nick.

31

February 13th (132 days ago)

"You know," I said sleepily. "I'm not a dolphin or a duck, Nick." I had flu, and was holding the phone away from my face so my nose didn't leave little slug trails all over the glass.

"You're not?" I could hear him smiling. "Are you totally sure?"

"Hang on—" I sneezed and reached for a tissue with my eyes still shut. "Yes. And that means I don't sleep with one half of my brain still awake so that I can surface periodically for air or keep an eye out for predators, so when you ring me at" – I held the phone a little further away – "6.34am on a Saturday, I am one hundred per cent asleep."

"Gotcha." Nick laughed. "If only you were a giraffe. They only sleep for about five minutes at a time, so you'd probably be awake."

Huh. That was totally one of my facts. I couldn't

139

believe he was stealing them already. Did boys have no shame?

"Actually, giraffes have neither hands nor vocal cords, so I don't think that would help me much with the whole answering the phone conundrum." I smiled and sat up, rubbing my eyes. "Have you finished the Dolce & Gabbana shoot? How's Paris?"

"Cold. But not as cold as here."

I blinked. "Here? As in England?"

"As in *here*." Something hit my window.

My stomach flipped, and I bolted out of bed and pulled open the curtains. There he was: lit neon yellow in the early-morning lamplight. The only person on the entire planet who could look beautiful the same colour as a Simpson.

We beamed goofily at each other, and then he flicked his wrist and something else hit my window. "You can stop throwing pebbles, Romeo," I laughed.

"They're not pebbles," he called up. "They're mints. Something to eat on the train journey and fresh breath all in one go. A multi-purpose tactic. Or a multi-purpose Tic Tac. Catch." He grinned and lobbed another one.

(It landed in the front garden and would result in an hour of my father wandering around later, saying

"Annabel? I think the birds around here have got some *really* regularly shaped constipation.")

"Wait there," I said, and then tore around my bedroom, desperately trying to make myself look presentable. My nose was bright red and flaky, there was yellow crust in the corner of my eyes and when I licked my hand and sniffed it, there was the sick, flu-y aroma of damp curtains.

I'd have to start sleeping with a toothbrush and little bowl of rose water next to my bed, or maybe just a pre-emptive paper bag to put over my head for moments like this.

I quickly swilled a bit of cold, sugary tea around my mouth, spat it into a pot plant and sprayed some perfume in my general direction. Then I took a deep breath and flew down the stairs with my dressing gown fluttering like a superhero's cape.

"Yo," he grinned as I flung open the door. I was flushed and shaky and hot all over and it had nothing to do with my viral infection.

"Hey," I mumbled, suddenly shy.

"How are you feeling?"

"A bit snotty and gross, if I'm totally honest."

His hair was all pointy, his eyelids were sleepy, and he had his big blue army coat on: the one with pockets so big they could fit both our hands in it at the same time. He looked so handsome it took every single bit of energy I had not to dance a smug little MINE-MINE-MINE jig right in front of him on the doorstep.

"You look ridiculously cute," he said, wrinkling his nose. "Have you considered accessorising with a bug more often?" I stuck my tongue out. "On second thoughts, I wouldn't put that back in if I were you." He grinned as I play-punched his arm and pulled out a flask from behind his back.

"So, Sick Note, I've brought you a honey and lemon and paracetamol drink that shall remain unbranded for the sake of impartiality." He dipped into his huge pockets and pulled out a little box of tissues. "These, for your runny little nose." He took his stripy scarf off. "This, for your normal-length, non-giraffe neck." Then he made a little flourish and pulled out a tiny toy lion.

I went even brighter red. "Umm," I said, clearing my throat awkwardly. "I have absolutely no idea what this is referring to."

He leant forward and kissed me gently, like some kind of brave, flu-impervious Arthurian knight. "I've seen what's written all over the history exercise book that you've been sadly neglecting of late, Manners. I was going to try and bring a real one for you, but they wouldn't let both of us out of the zoo."

I kissed him back, and having the flu was suddenly the best thing that had ever, ever happened to me. I was going to look into having it forever.

"I didn't think you were in the country until Tuesday," I said when I finally caught my breath. (And sneezed into my dressing-gown collar.)

"And let you hog all these disgusting germs to yourself?" Nick brushed a strand of hair away from my face. "I needed to talk to you about something."

I tried to steady myself surreptitiously against the doorframe so my boyfriend wouldn't see that kissing him had made me dizzy. After two months, I was pretty sure that was supposed to have worn off. If anything, he was getting more and more handsome and it was getting worse. "Talk to me about what?"

"Anything," Nick grinned, tapping the end of my nose. "I just wanted to talk to you, Harriet. About anything."

And he kissed me all over again.

32

Scientists say that the earth spins on its axis at nearly 1,000 mph, and if it suddenly stopped everything would be swept away in a moment; torn from the surface and swept into oblivion. Trees. Rocks. Buildings. People.

That's exactly how it feels now. As if the world has come screeching to a halt and I'm being launched from the top of it.

"Yo," Nick says, leaning against the doorframe. "How's it going?"

His skin is darker, and his hair has been cropped. The big black curls have gone, and it's changed the proportions of his face: his cheekbones look sharper, his eyes more slanted and his lips more curved. He still looks like a lion, but now he reminds me of Aslan in *The Lion, The Witch and The Wardrobe*, just after he gets shaved and dragged to the slab. In a more modelly, less representing-Jesus kind of way, obviously.

Early Egyptians believed that the heart could literally

move around inside the body. I think they had a point: mine feels like it's lodged in my windpipe somewhere.

I blink in silence, and then realise that it's my turn to talk. I'm still looking at Nick in the blank-yet-fascinated way that Hugo stares at the television.

"H-h-hey," I finally stammer, unable to breathe. "It's g-going… erm…" *Nice one, Harriet.* That's fifteen years of studying a dictionary, totally wasted.

"*Erm,*" he grins. "Not as good as *umm* or *err* but still one of my favourites."

"Actually," I say, starting to beam with my whole body. "I was trying to say erm-mazing, but you interrupted me."

"I'm umm-believable, aren't I?" He wrinkles his nose. "Awesome new T-shirt. I think I recognise that one. Diplodocus?"

"Uh-huh." I stretch it out. "Except that it's actually anatomically incorrect because this version has his head held up like a giraffe. Experts now believe it was held horizontally and they used to just *sweep* it across the foliage."

Before I can stop myself I feel my neck do a nervous little swooshing action to illustrate the point.

As if I'm a diplodocus.

*

I blush and his nostrils flare slightly.

"You should write to the T-shirt company and tell them."

"I already have," I admit, going even pinker.

Nick shouts with abrupt laughter, and – just like that – we're back to the beginning, and I have flu, and he's waking me up to kiss me all over again.

"So…" Lovely as this is, I don't really have the lung-capacity for any more small talk. A crocodile can hold its breath for up to fifteen minutes, but I am not a crocodile. If I don't start breathing soon, I'm going to pass out. "What are you doing here?"

Nick rests his head against the wall and looks at me for a few seconds through beautiful, lowered eyelids. "I'm doing a couple of modelling jobs and helping out behind the scenes of Aunty Yuka's new campaign."

"Oh." I feel a bit punctured. "But what are you doing *here*?" I point at the doorstep. "Did you get my email?"

"I did." He takes a step towards me. "And I need to talk to you about something."

Yesss! You see? I don't want to sound smug, but this is *exactly* why I wasn't worried. Nat was wrong, and I was right. All a girl really needs is a bit of faith in the romantic narrative arc that's been proven by countless films, books and TV dramas.

Nick's finally realised that the stars don't shine without me. That the sun doesn't burn, and the moon doesn't glow. (Metaphorically, obviously, or we'd all be dead.) That his world just doesn't make sense without me in it to explain everything in unnecessary detail every thirty seconds.

And OK, so he took a bit longer than I'd have liked, but if two months is what Nick needed to make a nice dramatic entrance and woo me back, then who am I to deprive him of it?

I'm *so* telling Nat that I understand boys better than she does when I get home. *She* can start taking relationship advice from *me*, henceforth.

I might even run some kind of classes.

I take the deepest breath I can find. *Stay cool, Harriet. Stay calm. Stay sophistica—*

"Oh, Nick," I blurt happily, fizzing and popping all over. "I knew I was right and you'd come ba—"

The bathroom door opens.

"Hello," Poppy says, swishing towards us with her hair pinned into a braid and bright red lipstick on.

"Hey," I smile. She looks even more ridiculously

beautiful than she did five minutes ago. "Poppy, this is—" and then all words fail me as she keeps walking and slings her golden arms loosely around Nick's neck and kisses him on the cheek.

"Hello, handsome," she says softly into his ear. "You're much earlier than we agreed." And I'm suddenly falling very slowly, like Alice through the rabbit hole.

"Am I?" Nick says stiffly. He's not looking at me. "Sorry. Are you ready to go?"

No.

No.

NO.

"With you, Nick Hidaka?" Poppy says, grabbing her handbag, beaming prettily at him and swishing into the hallway. "Any time and anywhere, baby."

I'm not falling any more.

Every part of me has just slammed into the ground.

The front door swings back behind her and Nick finally looks at me.

"Now's probably not the best time," he says quietly, as if there are other, more appropriate times for having your heart shattered into a billion pieces. "Can we talk later?"

I open my mouth to reply, but I have literally nothing to say and even fewer words with which to say it.

Nick waits patiently, and then takes a few steps backwards. "I'll see you soon?"

I open my mouth, but it's still empty.

He frowns and flushes slightly. "Have a great first night in Tokyo," he says quietly, grabbing the door handle. "Sleep well."

And then he closes the door between us.

33

Reasons Not to Think About Nick

1. He told me not to.
2. I have much more life-changing things to think about.
3. It's all I do.
4. He's an idiot.

I don't know how long I stand there for.

It could be minutes; it could be hours. It could be a thousand years and vines have started to grow up the back of my shins and moss has started to sprout out of my shoulders and squirrels and birds have set up home in my hair and I don't notice.

I have been so incredibly, unbelievably stupid.

Nick didn't want to talk to me so we could get back together. He wanted to tell me he had met somebody else. He wasn't trying to woo me.

He was trying to *warn* me.

150

Snippets from my happy little email are starting to bounce around inside my head, and every time a line makes contact I sink further towards the centre of the earth.

I've been thinking about you lots! Five hundred miles.

Of course I have! Another five hundred.

Send me another message or ring me? Three hundred miles down.

I'VE MISSED YOU SO MUCH. Another thousand.

Four kisses, and a needy, keen smiley face: **:)** And I'm right in the middle where there's nothing but flames and molten lava and hotness forever and ever and ever.

Oh my God. This doesn't happen in *any* of the stories I love. Except maybe in the Hans Christian Andersen version of *The Little Mermaid,* and that doesn't bode well for my immediate future.

No wonder I can't find my voice any more. I probably sold it to a Sea Witch in return for legs.

"Harry-chan?" A soft hand lands on my shoulder. "You OK, Harry-chan? You are very paling, Harry-chan. Perhaps you are lagging jet now?"

I turn and look blankly at Rin's pretty face.

"I-I-I…" I swallow. "I – umm – think I'm suddenly quite tired." I turn around and start wobbling on jelly legs into the bedroom. "It's been a really long day."

I push Kylie-cat aside, crawl into my new bed fully dressed and wrap my arms around my legs. Today is starting to feel like one of those confusing nightmares where you wake up crying and sweating and hurting and you don't quite remember why.

"Yes, you sleep," Rin says, sitting on the edge of my bed and carefully tucking me in. The cat jumps up and starts kneading my legs, but Rin picks her up. "No, Kylie Minogue. Bad cutey. No making biscuits on Harry-chan while she sleeping."

Then she follows my blank, shattered gaze to the door. "Nick is super handsome, *ne?* He is like prince or movie star or man in Abercrombie advert. One day I am hoping I will be in romantic twosome with Australian. Is it not perfect, Harry-chan? Like fairy tale?"

I can suddenly see Nick and Poppy: all cheekbones and glowing skin and perfect, magazine-approved beauty. Matching perfectly. Fitting perfectly.

"Yes," I agree. "Exactly like a fairy tale."
Just not mine.

And then I close my eyes and wish – with every part of my eternal mermaid soul – that I was at home, in England.

34

Now, I know many things.

I know that caterpillars have 4,000 muscles. I know that one in twenty people have an extra rib, and that astronomers have discovered that sometimes on Uranus it rains diamonds. I know that camels originated in North America, that killer whales breathe in unison when travelling in groups, and that there are more receptor cells in a single human eye than there are stars in the Milky Way.

But I clearly know nothing about boys.

And right now I'd trade in every single thing I've ever learnt for just the faintest idea of what it is I'm supposed to do next.

I can't sleep, so I wait until Rin is softly snoring, drag my duvet into the bathroom and curl up in the empty bathtub with my phone. It takes Nat a while to work out what's going on. This is because I'm crying so

hard all she can make out for the first three minutes is "S-s-s".

"Spots?" she guesses, peering down the webcam. "Sausages? Socks?"

I shake my head. "S-s-s…"

"Sun cream? Scissors?" I can see Nat's brain scanning through her vocabulary for anything that starts with an S. "Caesar Salad?"

A little bubble of unexpected giggle-snot comes out of my nose. I try something different. "N-N-N…"

"Nipples? Nits? No offence, Harriet, but it's starting to feel like I'm trying to communicate with a penguin. Calm down and try to finish a word."

I obediently wipe my nose on the duvet (oh, come on, as if everybody in the world doesn't do that when they're heartbroken). Then I take a few deep breaths and finally manage to hiccup: "S-sorry. I'm s-s-so s-s-sorry, N-nat. Y-you w-were r-r-right and I-I was wr-wrong and N-Nick d-doesn't c-care about m-m-m-me and h-he h-has a n-n-new girlf-f-friend and sh-sh-she lives in m-my flat in T-T-Tokyo and sh-she's b-b-b-beautiful and I-I d-don't know w-what to d-do and I h-hurt a-all ov-v-ver a-and I j-just w-want to g-g-go *h-h-home*." And I promptly burst into tears again.

Nat sits bolt upright. "*What*? He's in Tokyo? *You're* in Tokyo? Are you freaking *kidding* me?"

To say that I am not in the mood for kidding anyone right now is the understatement of the century. "I j-just s-saw him."

Nat's face disappears, and somewhere in the background I can hear things being zipped. I sniffle and wipe my eyes on a separate bit of soggy bedding. "Nat? Are you listening?"

"No." Her head pops back into the screen. "I'm packing my bags and coming to get you."

I smile. Toby was right: Nat is my non-kissing soulmate. I want things to stay exactly how they always have been: like salt and pepper, strawberries and cream, cheese and Marmite. Two halves of the same teddy-bear-shaped friendship necklace.

Although Nat might be being slightly optimistic. She has no transport and no money and she's in deepest, darkest France. At 11 mph it's going to take the poor pig nearly a month to get here.

"D-don't be silly," I hiccup, feeling a little bit calmer already. "Your mum will ground you for the rest of your life and then she'll ground your ghost. I'll be OK."

Nat pauses, and then throws her passport on the

floor with a frustrated growl. "Ugh. Seriously: what is *wrong* with boys?"

We both ponder this important question. It feels like one of the ancient, unanswerable ones. You know:

Why Are We Here?

How Big Is The Universe?

Is There A God?

What Is Wrong With Boys?

"S-s-so…" I sniffle on to my hand. "What do I do, Nat? Tell me, and this time I promise I'll listen."

We sit in comfortable silence while my Best Friend thinks about it. When we were little we would do this every time one of us fell over and scraped a knee, until it didn't hurt any more. As if – just by being together – we could somehow share the pain. As if in some way we still can.

Finally, Nat makes a decision. "Pretend you don't care, Harriet. Pretend you never have."

I frown. "Nat… I didn't even have the thespian skills required to play a tree in our Year Two performance of *Snow White*, remember?"

Nat laughs. "You fell off the stage and just lay there, waving your branches around until your dad came and stood you back up again. It was hilarious."

It really was not. I couldn't look Miss Campbell in

the eye for months. She said I ruined the entire performance and maybe she would take that Drama job in Scunthorpe after all. "I don't think I can do it," I admit quietly. "It's…" How do I even put this? "It's *Nick*."

"Which is why it's even more important." I can see Nat's furious rash climbing up her neck again. "We can't let him win. He's not ruining this for you. Let me remind you, Harriet, YOU ARE MOD-EL-LING IN TOK-Y-O. You're the luckiest girl ever. EVER. You pretend, and you pretend as hard as you can."

This is all so confusing. One minute I'm being taught that lying is bad and I should never do it, and the next I'm being told to do it as convincingly as possible. Clearly when it comes to boys, every lesson I've ever learnt is supposed to be inverted. Why wasn't there a class in this at school?

I cannot believe I wasted three years of my life doing woodwork.

"Harriet, listen to me. Will you please just trust me?"

I look at the floor and nod. If I had listened to Nat in the first place I'd now be two months into getting over Nick. I'd be much, much closer to being fine. "OK," I agree. "I'll pretend."

"Good," Nat says. "I didn't want to be right, Harriet. I just didn't want *this* to happen. I didn't want him to hurt you."

I'm so glad I don't have to do this on my own.

"I miss you, Nat," I say in a tight voice. "Can we never, ever fight, ever again?"

Nat laughs. "Of course we're going to fight again. That's what we do. I'm going to kick your skinny butt for the rest of eternity." She looks at her nails. "Call whenever you need me. All I'm doing is trying not to milk cows."

"Really? What's it like? Is it all squidgy?"

"No idea. I keep telling people I'm not touching a cow's boob like a big cow lesbian so I have yet to find out." Nat grins and blows me a kiss. "This feels weird to say because it's totally broad daylight here, but: go to bed, Harriet. Things will look better in the morning. They always do."

I yawn and nod, suddenly feeling exhausted and drained. But also as if I've abruptly let go of something heavy. Or maybe something heavy has let go of me. By the time we say goodbye and I crawl back into my enormous bed – puffy but totally dry-eyed – I know exactly what my New and Infinitely More Glorious Summer Plan 3 (NAIMGS3) plan is:

Lie. Again.

This is my big adventure. I have travelled 6,000 miles and fifteen years to get here. I came to Japan to have the best summer of my life, and I am going to have it.

And no *boy* is going to ruin it for me.

35

Experts say that people with abnormally high IQs often have problems sleeping. Which is no doubt why I'm snoring within thirty-five seconds.

"Harry-chan?"

Something tiny and soft prods my face. I roll over, open my eyes and promptly shoot straight into the wall behind me. It's almost totally pitch-black, but I can vaguely see the outline of Rin's face, two centimetres from mine. She leans slightly closer and inexplicably prods me with her finger again. "Harry-chan," she says. "You are squeaking like tiny mouse. Bad dreaming?"

"Mnnneugh," I mumble. "Whatimezit?"

"Four am." Rin says this as it looks: *4am.*

"M'so sorry," I yawn, sitting up straighter. "Did I wake you up?"

"No." Rin perches on the end of my bed, picks up a still-sleeping Kylie and points to the huge earphones hanging around her neck. "I sleep super soundly. I listen to *nandakke*... Scotlands. Whales. But battery

passes on and man wakes me. For you, *boom boom boom* at door."

I sleepily try to rearrange the sentences. "There's a man at the door for *me*?"

"Yes. So I came to awaken you up." Rin beams proudly and prods my face again. "I did good job, *ne*?"

Blinking, I grab my blue dolphin hoody and press the light on my Winnie-the-Pooh watch. It's just after 4am. I can't count out the possibility that I might still be dreaming. Although – if I am – I'll have to reassess what I eat before bedtime. It's certainly not one of my better ones.

In a daze I stumble through the corridor, open the front door and stare in bewilderment at the man standing there. He's wearing white gloves, a black suit and a black hat. I peer down at his little white socks. "Michael Jackson?"

"No. My name is Shinosuke. I am your chauffeur. The car is waiting outside to take you to the first photo shoot. You have five minutes to get ready."

I look at my watch again. "*Now*?"

"Not now," Shinosuke says, frowning. "I just told you. In five minutes."

OK: are they kidding me? Yuka wants me to do my first shoot at 4am? When I landed in the country nine hours ago? After a fourteen-hour flight? On four hours of sleep? With jetlag and a badly broken heart?

On second thoughts, I don't know why I'm surprised. This is the heartless world of fashion: I'm actually quite touched Yuka didn't drag me there straight from the airport by my eyebrows.

I nod briefly, race into the bedroom and grab my suitcase. I still haven't unpacked, so I drag everything into the bathroom so I don't wake up Poppy or Rin (she's already back in her bunk, snoring quietly with Kylie lying across her stomach). I quickly dress in whatever's at the top of the pile – my black and yellow stripy leggings and my Batman T-shirt – and tie my hair in a ponytail. Then I rally my inner model and glance briefly in the mirror.

Flaky skin, swollen eyes. A red dent from a pillowcase button on my cheek, an ink blob on the end of my nose and two enormous stress spots erupting by my mouth. And I still haven't cleaned the gravy off my chin.

Yet again, my inner model has clearly decided to stay there.

A couple of seconds later I'm running through the flat while brushing my teeth then out of the front door while cramming a chocolate biscuit into my mouth (I realise I got the biscuit and the toothpaste the wrong way round).

There's a huge black limousine waiting outside, and as soon as I appear it moves forward ominously by a couple of centimetres and the door swings open.

"Four minutes fifty seconds," I mumble through my mouthful, looking at my watch and clambering into the back seat. "Totally nailed it!"

"Congratulations," a cold voice says from a metre away, wiping a spray of chocolate crumbs off her face. "If only we could say the same for your personal hygiene."

A light switches on over my head.

And there – staring at me -- is Yuka Ito.

36

Believe it or not, the last time I saw Yuka Ito is actually the last time you saw Yuka Ito.

After I humiliated her on national television, kissed her nephew and nearly destroyed the entire Baylee brand, I haven't run into her since. She's stayed in what I would imagine is a tower made out of fairy skulls, surrounded by molten lava and the bodies of aged models, and I've stayed buried under books in a semi-detached, three-bedroom house in Hertfordshire.

Which – I'll be totally honest – is exactly how I like it.

Swallowing my biscuit as quickly as I can, I squint upwards at the spotlight and then back at Yuka. She's so tiny, and so pale, and so completely dressed in black from head to toe that she totally disappears into the car seats, and all you can see is a small white face, hovering in the air. There's a faint iciness around her, and I'm not entirely sure it's all down to the air conditioning.

Yuka Ito looks at me, and then switches the light off. I think this might be going quite badly already.

"Harriet Manners," she says in a clipped voice, looking straight at my spots. "I thought we had agreed that you were to stop producing pus. It was part of your new contract."

I try to cover as much of my face with my fingers as I can. "I'm really sorry." The apologies have started already, and I haven't even properly sat down yet. "I don't really know where they come from."

Yuka looks pointedly at the remnants of the chocolate biscuit in my hand. "I can offer a few suggestions."

"Actually," I say, "there are numerous scientific studies that show that chocolate isn't actually a cause of acne and that it comes from hormonal—"

Yuka narrows her eyes and my survival instinct finally kicks in. I shut up, put the rest of the biscuit in my satchel and anxiously clear my throat. *Change the subject, Harriet.* "I – umm – didn't think you would be here, Yuka. I thought you would be" – *arranging your winged monkeys* – "with the other models. In one of the other countries."

"Everybody else I employ knows how to organise themselves," Yuka says, folding her hands neatly in front of her. "That's why I employ them."

I try not to notice the implication now hanging in the air. "Well, it's very nice to see you again," I lie. "How is your… umm…" *Think fashion. Think emotional connection. Think mutual interests.* "… hat feeling?"

How is your hat feeling? It's not one of the all-time great conversation starters.

"Harriet. What is a model?"

Oh, God. She's testing me already. It's a good thing I've looked it up in the dictionary quite a few times over the last few months, just to check what it is I'm supposed to be doing. "A standard or example for imitation or comparison?"

"Precisely." Yuka lowers her eyes. "The world's female population does not want to look like a crime-fighting bumblebee."

I glance down at my outfit. I look like I'm about to don a black face mask and start karate-kicking wasps and possibly grasshoppers. "I was in a hurry and it was at the top of my suitcase?"

"Then don't pack it."

In China there is a dish called 'Drunken Shrimp', which involves little shrimps being put into a hot broth of strong liquor and then eaten while still alive and wriggling. I'm starting to understand how they feel.

"Yuka," I say, taking a deep breath: "I just want

to take this opportunity to say how grateful I am to be given a chance to come to see Tokyo, and to be a part of—"

"Gratitude is not necessary," she interrupts, holding up a hand. "I want your face for my new brand. That is why I am paying you."

I flush with pleasure, even though it does sound a bit like she's about to slice it off and attach it to some kind of elaborate necklace. "What's the label called?"

Yuka looks at me as if she's already regretting her decision. "*Yuka Ito.*"

"Ah."

"However," she says, leaning back in the seat slightly, "I would like to make three things clear."

I quickly scrabble in my satchel for a pen and a piece of paper. "Shoot," I squeak, and then clear my throat in embarrassment. "I mean, please go ahead, Yuka Ito. Please. Thank you very much. Please."

Yuka looks at me in silence and a line appears between her eyebrows. "Wilbur explained to you that the next few weeks require your complete discretion. Understood?"

I nod enthusiastically, and write *1. Discretion.*

"I have not flown you to Tokyo to party. This is a job, and you will be working extremely hard. Clear?"

I nod, slightly less enthusiastically, and write 2. *Not a holiday.*

I guess that means I can wave goodbye to my planned trip to the Meguro Parasitological Museum, then.

Yuka narrows her eyes. "This launch campaign is a unique blend of Western and Eastern ideology. Every shoot will take stereotypical images and pull them apart: question and celebrate them. It will be powerful, fragile, feminine."

"That sounds—"

"This is not Baylee. There is no four-hundred-year heritage and enormous profit margin to fall back on. It's my designs, my name, my career. I do not have the luxury of tolerating maverick behaviour this time. Is that *perfectly clear*?"

I swallow, suitably chastened. I've never been described as a maverick before. Maybe I'm turning out more like my father than I realised.

It's a sobering thought.

"I understand," I say solemnly, and write 3. *Just behave.*

"You are being paid a *lot* of money," Yuka says as I underline the last point three times for good measure and draw a series of stars next to it. "If you cannot meet those three simple expectations, there are many models who can."

I redden. Annabel made it part of my initial contract that I don't find out how much money I'm making until I'm eighteen. But – honestly – I'm a little bit intrigued now. I might be able to afford a piano, and then I can be just like Beth in *Little Women*, without the dying of typhoid part.

"OK," I agree.

"Good," Yuka says, turning to the window and making it clear that the conversation is over.

I watch the huge lights of Tokyo flash past in meek silence. You can say what you like about Yuka Ito – although obviously no one actually does – but she doesn't mince her words. She's terrifying, but at least you always know where you stand.

About four centimetres from decapitation, usually.

I clutch my new modelling list nervously in my hand until the car starts slowing down. I'm hit by a powerful salty, tangy smell that I recognise immediately. It comes from a chemical compound called *bromephenol*, which is found in algae and seawater.

I lean forward in excitement. "Ooh – are we at the seaside?"

Yuka snaps, "Tokyo is not a coastal destination."

"But the smell," I explain. "It smells like—"

"This is Tsukiji, the biggest fresh-fish market in the world."

We're pulling up outside one of the most enormous warehouses I've ever seen. It's immense, and industrial, and the fishy smell is so strong, the chocolate biscuit in my stomach is threatening to make a reappearance.

"But…" I frown. "I thought we were doing our first shoot today?"

"We are," Yuka says, opening the limousine door. "We're doing it here."

37

Whoever says that modelling is glamorous is totally fibbing.

There's blood *everywhere*. Shining at the bottom of boxes. Dripping off tables into buckets. Casually staining mounds of crushed ice, the way strawberry sauce stains a Slush Puppy. And – in the middle of all the redness – are fish. Big fish, little fish. Oysters, lobsters, squid, prawns, scallops, eels. Thousands and thousands of sea-life, piled on top of each other or laid out in rows. Whole, headless, finless or chopped into tiny pieces. Some that have already shuffled off this mortal coil, and some that are clearly in the process of desperately trying not to.

It's 4.40am and I'm standing in the middle of a Quentin Tarantino version of *Finding Nemo*.

"Problem?" Yuka says sharply.

I swallow. "Nope."

"Then find something prettier to do with your face." Yuka turns on her sharp black heels and starts clicking

violently across the enormous concrete warehouse. I follow meekly behind her: smiling as hard as I can at everyone. They ignore me completely. I guess fishermen in Japan have even less interest in fashion than I do.

A corner of the warehouse has been set aside for the shoot, in the most temporary way possible. A 'changing room' has been propped against a wall with a mirror leaning next to it, and a fold-up table covered in make-up/hair accessories is standing right next to a bucket of eels. Fashion people are running around: talking loudly and plugging in hairdryers and curling tongs. It's a whirlwind of activity and noise, yet as we approach it goes strangely silent.

I'm 6,000 miles away from school, but it feels like I've just entered the classroom with the headmistress standing behind me.

"Not there," Yuka snaps at a woman who just put a chair by the wall. "Move them," she says, pointing to a pair of shoes on the floor. "Stop that," she says to a man brushing a coat with a clothes brush and wiping terrified sweat from his forehead.

Any second now she's going to demand that everyone sits up straight before she asks for their homework.

Then Yuka reaches behind a curtain and retrieves a blue plastic suit bag. Slowly, she slides it open and pulls out the contents. It's short and pale orange and frothy, made of layers and layers of delicate, transparent material: tight, rigid and wired at the top and puff-balling out at the waist into a stiff bell shape. There are tiny embroidered red circles scattered through each layer – stitched in an immaculate, intricate spiral – and at the hem and around the neck are thin tendrils of orange material, floating upwards and outwards.

It's a dress. Or perhaps I should say: it's related to a dress the way a fat ginger cat is related to a tiger, or a mural on the wall of McDonald's is related to the Sistine Chapel.

"Oh my goodness," I whisper, reaching out to touch it. "It's so beautiful."

Yuka immediately knocks my hand away. "Of course it is," she says stiffly. "I don't make things that aren't." She raises an eyebrow. "This is *haute couture*. Do you know what that means?"

I quickly scan my brain for anything I can remember from French GCSE. *Couture* = scar. *Haute* = tall.

"A huge trauma?" I guess tentatively.

"No." Yuka's lips are getting thinner by the second. "It means *high fashion*. It means there is only one. I made it, by hand, specifically for you. It is more valuable than the car we just came in. These, therefore, are your dressers." Yuka gestures to a couple of young Japanese women wearing black, who've just appeared on either side of me like twins in a creepy old horror movie.

I blink then start feeling a little bit indignant. *Dressers*? Exactly how much of a child does Yuka think I am? "I'm very nearly sixteen years old," I tell her in my most aggrieved-yet-still-respectful voice. "I think I can dress myself."

Yuka lifts her eyebrows. "This time I do not want you accessorised with stickers. Gold or otherwise."

And I think she's made her point.

38

I am a creature of maturity and elegance, maturity and elegance, maturity and elegance.

It doesn't matter how many times I say it: I'm not convincing anyone. I'm certainly not convincing Yuka. She won't let me touch anything. I'm dressed enthusiastically by strangers, with my hands stuck in the air and my feet apart like some kind of rigid, overly affectionate teddy bear.

When they've finally finished zipping and prodding and the make-up artist is done poking and colouring me in – thick white foundation, black eyeliner and red lipstick – I'm finally led over to the mirror.

It doesn't matter how many times this happens: I'm totally shocked at the transformation. My hair has been smoothed into a shiny red bob, my skin is glowing and spotless and my eyes have actual, visible eyelashes so I don't look like a rabbit. I'm totally unrecognisable. My own family couldn't pick me out of a line-up. Every

single time I model, I start off as a normal schoolgirl and end up looking like somebody else. Like *somebody*.

It's like being Superman, except I only transform temporarily every few months with the help of a lot of very highly paid professionals and an enormous quantity of expensive cosmetics.

The team tweak the dress until they're happy, and then finally lead me – unable to see or walk very well – round the corner into a different part of the warehouse. Where I stop, startled.

On the floor there are fish.

Thirty or forty *enormous* dead silver fish glittering under huge temporary lights, lying nose-to-tail in perfectly straight lines like a sort of camp, aquatic military school. Faint steam is rising into the freezing air and between the fish are two men, arranging fins and spraying water to keep the fish shiny.

It's impossible to look away. Which – considering it's an advertising campaign – I'm guessing is sort of the point.

"Fresh tuna," one of the stylists whispers. "They'll go on sale in an hour to every sushi restaurant across the country. The shoot needs to be finished before the fish have to be cut up and carted off."

I nod, totally speechless. Only Yuka would shoot a fashion campaign this horribly beautiful.

Humans eat 100 million tons of fish every year and a single Brit alone consumes an average of 20kg. I can't get judgemental and weepy just because I can see their faces and they're not mixed with mayonnaise, put between two bits of bread and wrapped in a nice, bar-coded package for M&S.

A small, neat Japanese man in a dark suit with stiff, waxed hair walks over to me and bows politely. "Halloo," he says.

"Halloo to you too," I say, accidentally doing a little curtsy and then trying to turn it into a confused bow. I get sort of stuck halfway between and end up bobbing up and down as if I need the toilet.

"Halloo," he says again, a bit louder.

This is obviously some kind of Japanese custom I haven't come across yet. "*Halloo.*"

"Halloo."

We could be here all day. "Halloo. I am Harriet Manners." I quickly race through some of the phrases I've studied, and convert it to: "*Wa-ta-shi-wa Har-riet Man-ners desu.*"

"His name is Haru," a woman says from somewhere behind me. "Spelled H-A-R-U."

Ah.

I blush bright red and spin round to face a pretty Japanese lady with a straight black fringe and pouty, pillowy lips. "Oh my God, I'm so sorry." I turn back to Haru. "I didn't really get much sleep and I don't really know what I'm doing and when I get nervous I can't stop talking and I'm doing it now aren't I and I should probably shut up but this is all so exciting and—"

"He doesn't understand English," the lady adds.

"*Watashi wa kameraman desu,*" Haru says in a tone that indicates he already thinks I'm an imbecile.

"Haru is the photographer for this campaign," the lady explains, smiling. "One of the very best in Japan. I'm Naho, his translator."

I look at Yuka standing at the edge of the room, watching us with her usual expression. "Well, it's really lovely to meet you both," I say, holding out my hand nervously.

Haru looks at it. *"Kimiwa omoinohoka sega hikuine,"* he says flatly.

"You're shorter than he thought you'd be."

"Right." I can feel my cheeks getting even hotter. "Umm – sorry about that. My father's quite small as well. He claims our genes would be too overpowering for the world in larger quantities, and possibly hallucinogenic. Like nutmeg."

"*Hayaku hajimeruyo,*" the photographer says sharply, turning to his left and nodding at one of his assistants. "*Kono gaki no tameni wazawaza jikann wo saku hituyouha naikarane.*"

"Haru says—" Naho pauses just long enough for me to realise she's editing his words as well. "We don't… have time for this delightful talk. Let's begin."

She points at a small white chalk cross on the floor in a gap between two particularly shiny fish. "You stand there."

"*Isoi de,*" Haru barks.

Naho looks embarrassed. "Erm – quite soon, please?"

"Right. Sure." I start cautiously tiptoeing between enormous fish without treading on noses or fins as if I'm playing a particularly tricky game of fish-death Hopscotch. Then I stand, wobbling slightly, on top of the cross. "OK?"

"*Koitsu, baka ka?*"

"Umm…" Naho says, closing her eyes briefly. "Fine."

According to what I've gathered thus far from my epic modelling career, all I have to do is move my arms and legs occasionally with my most bored, lifeless expression on my face. How come after all the life-changing exams I've done in the past month, *this* is the one that feels the hardest?

Haru looks sternly through his camera with his eyebrows furrowed, fiddles with a few buttons and then nods.

I blink. "Did you want me to do something else?"

"*Nande gaikokujin moderu tukaunnda, nihonjin demo iijyanaika?*"

Naho frowns.

"Charlie," she says to the room in general. "Somebody grab him."

Charlie? I'm working with *another* male model?

Sugar cookies. I don't think I'm ready for this. I'm nowhere near as impervious to beautiful boys as a female model probably should be.

One of the assistants wheels an enormous tub next to me, and I blink at the very-much-alive and squiggling bright orange and red contents. I stare at the tendrils and embroidered sucker-style circles on my red and orange dress and everything slots into place. "Charlie, the *octopus*?"

"Yes," Yuka says in a clear voice from across the room. "Try not to let him outshine you."

I studied the domain of *Eukaryotic* for a project in biology last year. Did you know that an octopus has three hearts: two to pump blood to the lungs, and one to pump blood around the body? Or that they have special cells called 'chromatophores' that change colour so they can blend into any background?

And did you know that octopi are generally acknowledged to be the most intelligent of all invertebrates and have been known to steal cameras, defend themselves with weapons and unscrew lids to get at prey within containers?

This is my first ever encounter with a real-life octopus. I've always wanted to see one up close. They're the geeks of the sea world.

I lean forward to get a better look.

"*Furenaide kudasai,*" Haru shouts. "*Kare wa junbi ga dekite naikara.*"

"Please," Naho squeaks. "Don't touch the—"

My finger makes contact with an arm. Charlie makes a sudden thrashing motion.

And – in one swift arc – sprays dark blue ink all over my dress.

39

IQ tests on the internet can say what they like; it's not a great sign when you're outwitted by an octopus. Never mind invertebrates, Charlie's clearly smarter than at least one animal with a spine as well.

My co-model isn't ready. That's what Haru was telling me. Charlie needed a few minutes out of water first so he wouldn't panic. Nobody expected me to try grabbing him straight away; they expected me to categorically refuse to touch him, like a normal fifteen-year-old girl.

The dark ink doesn't just hit the dress: it goes everywhere. All over my face and hands and legs. All over the floor. All over the expensive tuna fish. It's like the world's biggest, most explosive, broken biro.

"*Baka!*" Haru yells as I stand there in shock, quietly dripping deep purple everywhere. "*Bakayaro!*" He throws a plastic lens cap on the floor.

"Umm…" Naho says, but this time there's no need for translation.

He's right.

I'm an idiot.

I apologise earnestly and repeatedly, but by the time they've wiped me down with half a dozen paper towels and sponged the ink off my hair, I realise the situation can't be saved. The one-off dress is ruined. The fish that aren't blue have been sold; the rest are being hosed down in a corner. The photographer is smoking outside and throwing sporadic Japanese words at me through the door. Naho is politely refusing to translate them.

And Yuka has gone.

40

For the second time in a week, I am totally the wrong colour. All I need now is a little gold lamp and a curly black beard and I'll look exactly like the genie from *Aladdin*.

What is *wrong* with me?

"For the love of dingle-bats," Wilbur sighs down the phone as I clamber back into a taxi and sit carefully on a towel. "This is exactly what I was talking about, Honeytoes. Do I need to get a portable naughty step sent with you everywhere?"

I rub my nose guiltily and then look at my finger. It's faintly purple. "I'm so sorry, Wilbur. I honestly don't know how it happens all the time."

"Really, Plum-pudding? No idea at all?" He sighs again. "I suppose I'd better ring Yuka and try to calm her down before we both get fired. But *please*, my little Carrot-cake. If we speak again this week I want it to be because you've found a sparkly pink unicorn roaming the streets of Tokyo and you'd like to gift it

184

to me as my new steed, OK? Not because you've mucked something up again."

There's a silence.

"Are you thinking about a sparkly pink unicorn now?" Wilbur asks sternly.

"What if it's purple?"

He sighs for the third time. "I think, Kitten-shoes, this may be part of the problem. *Try and focus.*"

Nat's not as surprised about my octopus mishap as I'd like her to be either. According to the poet, Christina Rossetti, a friend is supposed to:

a) *Cheer one on the tedious way.*
b) *Fetch one if one goes astray.*
c) *Lift one if one totters down.*
d) *Strengthen whilst one stands.*

They are *not* supposed to send one a text message that says:

AHAHA u r such a plonker. xxx

While I've been busy turning everything in a ten-metre radius blue, I've also had eleven missed calls from my parents, two wrong numbers, four answer machine messages and nine text messages. Most of which want to know if I've arrived in Japan safely, and four of which want to remind me of what I'm missing:

1. **You left a multipack of Mars Bars on top of your wardrobe. Can I have one? Dad x**

2. **I had three. Hope that's OK. Dad x**

3. **I'm just going to have one more. Dad x**

4. **Harriet, your Dad's made himself sick on an entire multipack of Mars Bars again. Please don't leave sweets where he can find them. Ax**

I begin to smile, and then I remember.

Maybe it's best for everyone if she's not here.

My bottom lip sets, and I glare at my phone. They wanted me to leave: they can't get all clingy now I've actually gone.

I abruptly type:

Am fine. Stop eating my stuff. H

Then I press SEND, turn off my phone and stare miserably out of the taxi window. Tokyo is just starting to wake up: people in suits are swarming in and out of stations and music is beginning to blast out of speakers. The sunshine is bright, and the air is starting to thicken up with heat and smells.

I cannot believe I've managed to screw up already and the shops aren't even open yet. That's speedy, even by my own standards.

All I really want to do is go straight back to bed, pull the duvet over my head and wait for the day to end. Again.

So that's precisely what I do.

41

In my dreams I'm fighting octopuses and pink unicorns and Japanese-speaking seagulls, and finally one lands on my shoulder and starts screeching in my ear. I open my eyes with a start.

It's not a seagull.

A thick wave of dense black smoke is pouring under the door, and the only working fire alarm is having a loud panic attack in the living room.

"Rin?" I yell at the top of my voice, coughing hard. "Poppy?"

There's no response, so I leap out of bed and run straight into the kitchen. I switch the grill off, open a window and pull out the burning toast. Both pieces look just like Hello Kitty, except totally black and smoking. One of them has an ear on fire.

I really hope Rin never takes up arson as a hobby. They'd catch her within seconds.

"Rin?" I shout, running Hello Kitty under a cold tap until she goes soggy and her bow falls off. Then I stagger

into the living room, turn off the alarm and flap my arms around to dissipate the smoke, even though I know that's not actually how smoke or arms or flapping works.

Suddenly I hear a screeching, desperate sound coming from the bathroom, and race to the door in a panic. *"Rin? Are you all right?"*

"Lalalala," somebody is singing at the top of their voice. *"No I won't,* be a Craig, no I-I-I-I won't be a Craig, just as l-oong as you stabby, stabby me. Lalalalalalala *me,* dddddaahly daaahly."

The bathroom door abruptly opens in a wave of steam, and a slim blonde figure pushes past me and past the girl emerging from the bathroom.

Without a word, Poppy slams the door behind her.

"Stabby Me is favourite Australian song," the girl states happily, drying her hair with a towel. "But who is Craig? And why does nobody want to be him?" Then she frowns and sniffs. "Are you smoking, Harry-chan? That is super bad for you. You should reassess this."

"Rin?"

The girl in front of me looks nothing like Rin. The curls have gone, and her hair is straight and in a short, ear-length crop. Her eyes are clean and shaped like a kitten and her skin is flushed pink and pearly. I look down and stare at the huge T-shirt she's wearing:

I AM! Happiness when I eat potato.

"English is magical, *ne*?" she says, beaming at my stunned expression. "Harry Potter. Cute Australian with shiny stick and glasses. Pow pow."

"Rin... I didn't even recognise you."

She looks heartbroken. "*Hai*. Yes. Pretty stuff is back in box. Models not allowed sparkliness. It's *nandakke*... non-professional." She pulls on her T-shirt and makes a vomit-face. "Now I look just like boy."

"You don't." Without all the attachments and plastic accessories, Rin gives Poppy a run for her money in the looks department. "You're so beautiful."

Rin giggles and pats me on the head, reaching up on her tiptoes because I'm considerably taller than she is.

"Foreigns are crazy, *ne*? Don't worry about Poppy, Harry-chan." She looks at the bathroom with a shake of her head. "In the morning, she is – *nandakke*. Mean like God."

"Mean like *God*?"

Rin puts two fingers up to her forehead like horns. "*Meh meh*. Eat grass."

"Goat?"

"Yes. God. Bites and booms with head." Rin taps

her forehead. "Super perfect at modelling, though. Poppy, not God."

She frowns and looks me up and down. "Harry-chan, in English is cute to look like *Avatar*?" She touches my face cautiously, looks at her finger and rubs a little blue ink experimentally on her own face.

I smile awkwardly. "Yesterday's shoot went pretty badly, to be honest."

"Then we must fix this," Rin says. She takes my hand and starts pulling me into the bedroom. "If you are unobstructed today, I will show you Tokyo."

"I think I'm free, actually." Yuka's going to need at least twenty-four hours to calm down, I reckon.

"Free? *Chotto matte.*" Rin gets a little computer out of a pocket in her T-shirt, and a few seconds later says, "Without charge? Will you normally charge me for friends, Harry-chan? Why?"

I laugh and the bathroom door opens. "Are you going out?" Poppy calls. "Can I possibly come too? Chanel's given me the day off so I'm going to be so *bored*." She wanders into the hallway and grimaces. "Sorry for queue jumping, Harriet. I was desperate for a pee and you were kind of standing in the way."

Rin makes goat horns and pretends she's eating grass behind Poppy's back.

I grin, but my stomach's starting to flip anxiously over and over. Poppy's lovely, but I'm not sure I want to spend the entire day with her. She's what Nat calls an MBF-er: a girl who refers to 'My Boyfriend' every twelve seconds, just in case anyone makes the hideous mistake of thinking she's single and unloved and unwanted. Even though people who look like Poppy never are.

I'm not sure I can cope with this. I like to think of myself as existing on the nicer end of the human spectrum, but I'm not Mother Teresa.

"Erm…" I start doubtfully.

"You come," Rin tells Poppy, promptly deciding for me. She sticks her tongue out at a pair of black jeans and a simple black vest and then pulls them on. "We will spend day together as three new BFFs." She says this *biffs*. "I shall show you the many wonders Tokyo and… *Dame! Kono itazura neko!*" She grabs Kylie, who's pouncing around a box in the corner of the room. "*Gokiburi wa tabenaino!*"

"What's that?" I bend down and pick the box up. It's a little cardboard house, with painted roof tiles, tiny drawn bricks, flowers and a little white picket fence. Out of one of the windows, between bright pink curtains, is a smiling cartoon beetle, waving happily. Over the door it says – in English – **WELCOME**.

"It's a Japanese cockroach trap," Poppy explains as I drop it on the floor. "They're huge and sooo gross." I look a little closer at it.

Under the word **WELCOME** it says – in small yellow letters – TO YOUR DEATH.

I guess we have to hope our cockroaches either don't speak English or have really bad eyesight.

"Cockroach climb in," Rin says perkily. "Cockroach pass out." She frowns. "*Nandakke*. Pass on." Then she looks back at me and adds, "Go shower, Harry-chan. You smell of fishes. We will begin Japan from new for you."

She pushes me gently towards the bathroom, and the warm feeling in my stomach starts to glow again. Poppy and Rin start taking photos of themselves holding up Kylie so they look like they have furry beards, and Kylie desperately tries to get back on to the bed again.

Friends, I think as I laugh and close the bathroom door behind me. After fifteen years, maybe I'm finally starting to understand how to make them.

42

I ♥ Japan.

By lunchtime, I am incoherently, head-over-heels in love with Tokyo. As my brand-new T-shirt, baseball cap, pen and pencil, and badge will tell you.

I ♥ the strangeness and the noise and the height of it.

I ♥ the politeness and how simultaneously ordered and manic it is.

I ♥ the two-storey-high televisions stuck to buildings, and the way the shop assistants bow and sing *irrashaimmaasseee*!!! (welcome!), as if you're royalty.

I ♥ the fact that you can throw coins in a ticket machine any way you like and it still counts them properly, and the way people fall asleep on the tubes against the shoulders of strangers.

I ♥ the electric toilets with warm seats that play music and spray water at your bottom and pretend

to flush while you're peeing so that nobody can hear you.

I ♥ people who actually wait on the side of the road for a green light, even when there are no cars coming.

I ♥ the sense that I could never be bored, not if I lived in Japan for a billion years.

And, more than anything:

I ♥ how ignorant I am here.

I can't read, I can't write, I can't speak. All I can do is marvel with wide eyes at just how insignificant and tiny I feel.

Bunty was right: I even feel temporarily free from being me.

"Tokyo's OK," Rin concedes with a casual shrug. She's been racing us through tourist attractions as if there's a twelve-hour deadline before the entire city falls down. We've been up the enormous Tokyo Skytree; lit incense at the Asakusa Kannon Temple; wandered through Ueno Park and watched the jugglers. We've eaten bits of chicken on sticks and coffee jelly and tuna mayonnaise wrapped in rice and seaweed and bits of fried octopus in balls of batter (sorry, Charlie).

We're now in Harajuku, having crêpes on Takeshita Street, and it's taking every bit of my inner dignity not to attempt a joke that – frankly – I'm too old to be making.

I stare at Rin over the top of my strawberry, banana, ice cream and cheesecake pancake. "Rin, Tokyo is incredible."

"Not like Sydney" – Rin shakes her head – "There is no aces beach and BBQ and flaming gallahs."

I laugh. "Did you know that there are more people in this city than there are in Australia and New Zealand put together?"

Poppy sighs. She's picking off bits of strawberry, wiping cream on her napkin and then flicking it on the floor. "I find it all a bit much, really." She points at a tiny, fluffy dog walking by in a green dress with a bright green, lit-up, pulsing lead. "I mean, what exactly is the point of that?"

"But that's what's so brilliant," I say in surprise. "There isn't one."

We watch a couple of Japanese girls wander past. One has bright pink hair with blue tips, a purple tutu, green stripy tights, a camouflage-pattern jacket and yellow shoes. The other is covered – head to toe – in cuddly pink toys, as if she's doused herself in glue and run really fast through a toyshop. I turn back to Poppy with a huge smile. "How lucky are we?"

"I've been a successful international model since I was fourteen," Poppy says, pulling a bit of chocolate off her pancake, sniffing it and then wiping it on the bench. "The world gets boring pretty quickly."

I suddenly feel a pang of pity for her.

Toyshop girl and her friend notice Poppy and I, and stare at us. "*Kaaawwaaaiiiiiiiii*," they squeak. Then they dissolve into giggles and skip down the street, glancing back so that they can collapse in hysterics again.

I turn to Rin. "What does *kaaawwaaaiiiiiiiii* mean?"

"Cute. *Kawaii* mean cute." Rin looks with open loathing at her black jeans and vest. "You are wrong, Harry-chan. There is point. Cuteness is point."

Everything surrounding us is fluffy, or pink, or sparkly, or covered in hearts. Everything has a face: gloves, umbrellas, crisp packets, mascara. Rin's bank card is pink. Even the poles holding up the building works opposite have yellow bunnies drawn on them. "In Japan, all must be cute," Rin explains firmly, "or…"

"Or what?" Poppy suddenly says. "For goodness' sake, Rin. There are more important things in life than being *cute*."

I glance at Poppy in surprise. She's been staring at herself in every reflective surface since we left the house. A few minutes ago she was checking herself out in the pancake spoon.

Rin is appalled. "No," she says belligerently. "Cute is *most* important. Love is cute. Fashion is cute. Flowers is cute. Animals is cute. All good things is cute." She gestures at us. "Friendship is cute. We shall ask BFF questions and do answers now, *ne*?"

I beam at Rin. I *love* questions and answers. Plus, I'm not sure any girl has ever said that to me before. Even Nat tends to avoid Q&A whenever possible. She knows I get a bit too carried away.

"Brilliant," I say, trying not to notice Poppy stifling a yawn. "I'll start. Rin, where in Japan do you come from and what is it like?"

"Nichinan," she says. "It is small fishes town at bottom of Japan. Very hot. Palm trees and chicken and rice and mountains and sea. Pretty but *nandakke...* hushed." She pulls a face. "Me now. Harry-chan, have you always been wanting to be modelling?"

"No," I laugh. "It just sort of... happened."

"You enjoy model much?"

I think about this. "Sometimes. It's fun and exciting, but it can be a bit scary. And I'm a walking disaster in high heels. I guess I'm always waiting for it to end, to be honest."

Rin nods. "And you are possibly here for more Baylee, Harry-chan? I see cute jump jump picture in snow."

"Nope." I wipe cream off my jeans with a bit of pancake and then stick it in my mouth, like the Goddess of Class I am. "Actually it's for Yuka's new campaign. She's left Baylee, and she's setting up her own label. There are quite a few of us working on it in different countries. I got Tokyo, so I'm super happy." I smile at Rin. "Your turn, Poppy."

Poppy throws another strawberry on the floor. "Hit me," she says.

"Nick-kun," Rin replies, and my stomach drops as my ears go totally numb. "How long have you been in awesome twosome with perfect Australian, Poppy-chan?"

"Oh, I don't know, six weeks?" Poppy says, instantly brightening. "Seven?"

What?

He waited less than *two weeks* before moving on?

"We met on a shoot and REALLY hit it off straight away. I could tell he liked me immediately. He'd just split up with somebody else, but that was a total non-issue."

An involuntary twitch has started in the corner of my eye. *Change the subject, Harriet. Quickly. Pretend like Nat told you to.* "Who…?" I hear myself say, and then clamp my mouth together.

Yup. Whatever comes, I've totally asked for it.

"Just some girl," Poppy shrugs, throwing a bit of pancake at a passing scooter. "He must've got bored of her pretty quickly. It was no big deal."

I suddenly want to cry. The only romance of my life was *No Big Deal*?

It was a big deal to me.

No: it was a *massive* deal. Elephantine. Titanic. Megalithic; cumbersome; stupendous; monumental. I feel like I'm a tiny fly that accidentally zoomed into Nick's face: as if he's just wiped me away on a bit of tissue and carried on walking with slightly watery eyes, while I've been totally obliterated.

Boring?

I start getting all indignant and then abruptly stop. Oh, who am I kidding? I hear that insult all the time. It's currently scratched into my pencil case.

Rin is totally fascinated. "You are One for Him, Poppy-chan," she says, her eyes glittering. "I feel it here." She pats her chest. "Everything until you meet is… *nandakke*. Rehearsal."

"I guess," Poppy says, standing up gracefully and throwing the rest of the totally uneaten pancake in the bin. "When it's perfect you just know, don't you?"

No, I realise. *Clearly I do not.*

"Entirely," Rin says cheerfully, hopping off the bench. "I think we will go have *biff* photos taken now. We can ride horse and wear bunny ears together. Amazingballs?"

"Cool," Poppy says. "Can I be in the middle? I've just bought a new lipstick."

As we start making our way to a huge machine with a queue of giggling girls standing outside it, all I can think is if there's anything worse than being dumped, it's knowing that you were just a dress rehearsal.

That a Big Deal for you was just practice for somebody else.

43

Rin drags us around the rest of Tokyo until even my love affair with it starts to feel a little strained.

Finally she decides we've seen enough for one day and allows us to drag our exhausted, aching bodies back to the flat. Poppy goes straight to the bathroom to get ready to go out again.

With her MBF, I think miserably.

"Harry-chan," Rin says, patting a plastic bag containing a puffy sparkly yellow dress and matching yellow shoes. "I must go get dressed up for stay in watch TV. This trousers is making me super sad. Ooh." She bends down and picks an envelope off the mat. "Alphabet for you."

I smile and open the letter. In beautiful, curly handwriting it says:

Ring at 7am. Be ready. Yuka

On the upside: I obviously haven't been fired yet.

On the downside, I have absolutely no idea what Yuka means.

She's never been prone to particularly elaborate sentences, but this is concise even for her. There's an address written in Japanese just below that makes equal sense to me.

What am I supposed to do? Is she going to ring me? Does she want me to ring her? Are we doing a wedding shoot, or something based on horror films? Is it *Lord of the Rings* themed?

Actually, I bet this is the exact letter Frodo got before they sent him out of the Shire.

Tucking the letter into my back pocket, I go straight to the bedroom and pull an alarm clock out of my suitcase: a pretty little plastic bird that plays a genuine recording of a British skylark. I carefully set it to start dancing and flashing its eyes at 6am tomorrow morning and put it on the top of the drawers next to my bed. Then I drag out my rocket alarm clock, set it to launch at 6.10am, and put that next to the bird.

Finally, I get my target shooter clock out and put it on the other side of the room. When it goes off at 6.20am, I'll have to get out of bed, cross the room and shoot it in the middle with a laser gun to stop it beeping. And probably throw it against a wall and stamp on it as well, because even point-blank range is a bit too far for my sporting prowess.

Rin watches the entire process from her bunk bed, and then abruptly grabs Kylie (also now in a little yellow sequin dress), runs into the cupboard in the hallway and climbs inside it. After a lot of rummaging – and a bit of disgruntled yowling – she scurries back over to my bed with an armful of objects I don't recognise.

"Too-doo," she says triumphantly, dumping them on my lap.

"It's ta-da, Rin," I smile. "What's this?"

"This," she says, picking up a big white plastic ball, "shines relaxy picture on ceiling." She picks up a small plastic box. "This measure snoring." She hands me a thin sheet of plastic. "This keep pillow cold. And this" – she pulls out an umbrella – "is umbrella with lights. *Mi-teh*." She presses a button and the whole thing lights up like a Christmas tree.

I pause, trying to find a way to put this without sounding ungrateful. "Umm – what are they for?"

"For help sleep, Harry-chan. For good dream tonight." She pauses. "Not umbrella," she adds. "Umbrella for rain. Or flying, like Mary Poppins."

A lump suddenly forms in my throat. "Thank you, Rin."

"It's *nandakke*… Okily-dokily. Is that right, Harry-chan? I saw on Sampsons."

"*The Simpsons.*"

"Yes. Funny yellow Australians." Rin laughs and claps her hands, at which point we both hear the sound of desperate scratching coming out of the cupboard. "Oh my goat!" Rin cries, standing up and putting her hand over her mouth. "I shut Kylie Minogue in closet!"

As she scampers out of the room, I start merrily setting my new presents up. I plug in the big round ball so it shines pictures of kittens on to the wall next to my bed, press a few buttons on the sleep analyser and stick the cooler into my pillowcase. I'm just trying to work out how I can wedge the umbrella into the corner of my bed as a kind of waterproof night-light when there's a loud knock at the door.

"Harriet?" Poppy shouts. "Can you get that for me?"

I look at the door with a sinking heart and abruptly decide: *no. Actually. Thanks, but I'd rather give myself root canal with a coat hanger.*

So I do the only thing I can think of: I whip my top off. "Sorry, but I'm not properly dressed," I shout back.

Poppy pokes her head round the door and looks at me. "Is that an Eeyore bra?"

I knew I should have listened to Nat and burnt it before something like this happened. "Kanga's on it too, actually," I say with as much dignity as I can muster. "And Roo."

"They never do silly things in my size," Poppy sighs. "It's all boring lace and silk and underwiring." She does a little twirl in a silvery dress. "How do I look?"

"Beautiful," I say, and then look down at the non-event happening on my chest.

Thanks, genetics.

"Wish me luck?" Poppy beams, grabbing her handbag and glittering out of the door in a wave of perfume and curls.

"Luck," I call and – as soon as the door shuts behind her – groan then slowly get my laptop out of my satchel.

Boring, I think as I open my computer and start playing online Snakes and Ladders with a random twelve-year-old in Indonesia.

Silly, I think as I yank my dolphin hoody on over my stupid bra.

No big deal.

44

January 17th (161 days ago)

"It's not going to rain," Nick said firmly. "They're not rain clouds. They're all fluffy and white."

"Is that the technical term?" I said, grabbing my umbrella anyway. I was *so* not taking weather advice from an Australian.

"Of course not. That's 'Clouds Which Look Like Big Sheep'. Not 'Clouds Which Make Water'."

"They're cumulonimbus," I reply. "And that out there's some stratocumulus. There's no nimbostratus but don't let that fool you. British weather is sneaky."

He leant over and kissed my nose. "I love it when you talk meteorology."

"Obviously. Meteorology is awesome. You're not *insane*."

Despite my warnings, both Nick and my dad insisted that we take a picnic. "It's not going to rain," my father said, shoving a French baguette,

207

some cheese and a few apples into my satchel.

Nick raised his eyebrows. "I know, right? Tell that to little Miss Smarty-Pants here."

My dad shook his head sadly. "I'm afraid all the female Pants are Smarty in this house. They won't listen to rightness, and there's absolutely nothing we can do about it."

It was raining before we got to the end of my road.

Nick sighed and pulled his coat over our heads. "It's at times like this I really regret liking a girl with brains."

"At least I have an umbrella," I smiled and let him snuggle under it with me. "Did you know that 6,000 pounds of micro-meteorites hit the atmosphere every day?"

"That sounds incredibly dangerous." Nick grinned and waggled the handle. "Are you sure we're totally protected by this bit of waterproof fabric?"

"They're really tiny. They get caught in clouds and water coalesces around them so that they fall to Earth in rain."

"I should probably stop sticking my tongue out and trying to drink it then."

I laughed. "Maybe, seeing as you're catching tiny bits of shooting star that are billions of years old and have just come from outer space." I put my hand out, caught a few raindrops and showed it to him.

Nick wasn't looking at my hand. He was looking at my face. I blushed and focused on the water in my hand.

"Do you know what I think?" he said.

"Absolutely never," I said, staring at the rain. "Like, literally never. I never ever know what you think."

It was his turn to laugh.

"I think I was right," he said, closing my umbrella and tucking it away. Then he put his arm round me and continued walking us into the rain. "We don't need an umbrella after all."

45

The human body is amazing.

Did you know that the acid in our stomachs can dissolve zinc? Or that in a lifetime, we'll produce enough saliva to fill two swimming pools? Or that we're roughly one centimetre taller in the morning than in the evening?

And – most relevantly of all – did you know that in the hour before you're supposed to wake up, the anterior pituitary gland in the brain releases a polypeptide tropic hormone called *adrenocorticotropin*, which acts as a stimulant and natural alarm clock?

All of my preparation last night was a total waste of my time. After years and years of getting up early for school, my pituitary gland has been honed to perfection and is eerily accurate. It's still pitch-black and none of the alarms have gone off yet, but I'm wide-awake and perky as an otter.

If only I could start trusting my body a little bit more, I could save a huge amount of money on AA batteries.

210

Yawning a few times, I pull on my slippers and rub the sleep out of my eyes. Then I pad through the dark bedroom to the bathroom, then into the kitchen to get a glass of water and a couple of chocolate biscuits, and then into the sunlit living room to switch on the TV. (I love Japanese adverts. I can't understand a single word but they're so incredibly cheerful.) At which point I stop, glass frozen in my hand and a biscuit halfway to my mouth. Sunlit living room. Sunlit living room.

Sunlit living room?

It's not even dawn yet. Unless…

Oh my God.

OH MY GOD.

I run to the window, and there's the sun: emitting its massive solar energy from too high up in the sky.

I look at my watch: 9.25am.

NO.

NOOOOO.

NONONONONONONONO.

I sprint into the bedroom and fling open the curtains. The sun comes streaming in. Rin's snoring in her bunk with her headphones on, Kylie's curled against the small of her back and Poppy has gone out already. I pick up the bird alarm and shake it: its eyes are still closed. I look at the rocket: it's still in its launch pad. Then I stare at the laser alarm. The lights are dead.

None of the alarms worked.

How is that even *statistically* possible?

I need to find my mobile phone, ring Yuka and get out of here. But when I look at my bedside table, my phone isn't there.

So I grab Yuka's letter, sling a yellow cardigan over my penguin pyjamas and run straight into the streets of Tokyo.

Why didn't Yuka ring? Why didn't she send somebody to drag me out of bed by my feet? Where is my phone? Why are our bedroom curtains so thick?

Most importantly: why am I?

I ask the taxi driver all these questions, but he doesn't speak English so I just get a lot of nodding and uncomfortable glances in the rear-view mirror.

Finally – almost precisely three hours late – we pull up outside an immense, low, square building with a pale green roof. I'm so impressed I actually stop talking. The roof slopes to a gradual point in the centre, there are big glass doors at the front and the two white walls on either side of the entrance are covered in huge paintings of enormous, robust-looking men wearing bits of material around their waists, furious expressions and absolutely nothing else.

Ring.

Sumo ring.

I'm in Japan, and this is the only 'ring' that didn't occur to me?

I stare at the doors with my stomach starting to clench and squeeze. I have no idea how much trouble I'm in, but after Monday's disaster I think the answer is: quite a lot.

Focus, Harriet.

Hands shaking, I hand a pile of money to the driver, climb out of the car and start nervously running towards Yuka.

Then I stop, because:

- There's a boy sitting on the stairs.
- He's blocking my path.
- I've forgotten where I'm supposed to be going.

"It's a shame the tables in Japan are so low," Nick says, wrinkling his nose. "Where on earth are you going to hide this time?"

46

<u>Reasons Not to Think About Nick</u>

1. He told me not to.
2. I have much more life-changing things to think about.
3. It's all I do.
4. He's an idiot.
5. I only have finite memories, and I don't want to wear them out.

I have given my heart a number of strict instructions over the last couple of days.

Judging from what it is doing now, it has listened to precisely *none* of them.

My hands are clammy. My throat is dry. My ears are hot and my cheeks are cold; I'm breathing too fast and blinking too slow. Something has short-wired and every function in my body is in the process of swapping over.

I scowl to hide the dolphin-like leaping in my chest

and then remember I'm wearing penguin pyjamas, which sort of undermines my intended impression of fierceness and sophistication.

Pretend you don't care, Harriet. Pretend you never did.

I clear my throat and try to adopt my most nonchalant expression. "Hey! What are you doing out here on the pavement?"

Nick puts his hands to his face. "Sniffing my hands, obviously. Do you want to smell them?"

He gives me a crooked grin and holds out his hands, and I blush all over. That's what I said the second time I ever met him. He's laughing at our romance already. Isn't there supposed to be some kind of... respectful grieving period first? A minute's silence or something?

My temper flares. "Brilliant," I snap. "In that case why don't you just go—" and I promptly run out of imaginative places to send him. So I stick my nose in the air and march past.

Within seconds he's sauntering casually next to me. This is the problem with stupidly tall model-boys: they have a totally unfair stride advantage. Especially when one of us is wearing fluffy, teddy-bear slippers and their noses keep getting caught in the pavement.

I try to pick my feet up a bit, but now I just look like a little child stomping off to bed.

"Harriet..." Nick says. "Look. There's stuff I need to say but I couldn't do it at the flat. Not in front of Poppy. You understand, right? Don't be angry."

I stop walking, and my heart tips.

I don't want to hear it. I don't want to hear how guilty he feels, or how he tried to warn me. I don't want to hear that the heart just 'wants what it wants' or that some things aren't 'meant to be'.

I don't want to hear that he has inexplicably decided he prefers perfect, blonde, supermodel types over freckly, ginger schoolgirls.

I don't want to hear that he never meant to hurt me.

And – most of all – I don't want to hear that he still cares about me, *just not like that.*

As if friendship is the wooden spoon I get for being such a brave champ to give it a shot with somebody like him in the first place.

I hear Poppy's voice in my head. *Silly. Boring. No big deal.*

And I abruptly change my mind.

"Please don't say it," I say brightly, turning to him with the biggest, breeziest smile I can find.

Think mature, Harriet. Think adult. Think suave and cool.

"It's fine. It's lovely to see you, but I'd like to put the vagaries of our mutual past behind us." *Nice. Kind of Henry James-esque.* "It's totally..." *Like having my insides hacked out with an ice-cream scoop over and over and over again*? "Coolioko."

Then I flinch slightly. It's totally *coolioko*?

That's not even a word.

Nick looks stunned, and I finally realise that Nat knows exactly what she's talking about. This is the perfect way to handle the situation. I've never, ever seen a boy look more confused.

"Do you mean that?"

Not even a little bit.

"Absolutely," I say, and am rewarded with an even more shocked expression. I stick my hand out. "Friends?"

Nick stares at me.

I am so nailing this acting stuff. Take that, Miss Campbell. Maybe I shouldn't have quit GCSE drama after all.

Slowly, he takes my hand and frowns. "Are you sure?"

No.

"Definitely," I say, beaming at him and pumping

his hand up and down like a weird stranger at one of my parents' dinner parties.

Then I start quickly walking towards the building as if my insides aren't about to fall out in a heap all over the pavement.

"Right," Nick says flatly, as he catches me up. "Glad that's clear." He doesn't sound very relieved, given that I've just saved him from a really uncomfortable conversation. He should be erecting a plaque to my selflessness and bravery right now. Lighting candles next to my extremely non-confrontational portrait. "Hang on, Harriet," he says, grabbing my arm just as I reach the door.

It feels as if somebody's just stabbed me with a cattle prod. Electricity crackles down to my wrist, up to my shoulder and back again, then somehow spikes into my brain so I can't think, hear or see.

I politely tug my arm away.

Nick's staring at his hand. Then he blinks and looks back at me. "Umm..." He blinks again then shakes himself. I'm slightly worried I may have actually electrocuted him. "What I mean is... don't go through the front door. You need to go through the side entrance before Yuka sees you."

Oh, sugar cookies. I'd totally forgotten about

modelling. *Again*. Wilbur's right, I really need to learn how to focus.

"Sh-she's that angry with me?"

"I've seen her happier," Nick says, pulling a face. "We need to get into the ring pronto. That way you might survive until lunchtime."

Every romantic thought is swept away in a sudden flood of panic. "Did..." My mouth is paper dry. "Did you just say into the ring?"

"What did you think we were doing here?"

I'm going to be sick. *I'm actually doing sumo?* I didn't even have the coordination necessary to take part in last term's Year Eleven Dance. They said I wasn't 'physically equipped to move in public'. "We?"

"I'm doing the shoot too. With you. At a distance, though, I'm just in the background. A boy-shaped prop."

Oh my God. I may not know much about ex-boyfriends, but I'm pretty sure you're not supposed to throw yourself at them. Especially not physically, on a stage.

"Just me and you?" I know, shock is playing havoc with my grammar.

Nick shakes his head, and suddenly I can't breathe very well.

"Not any more," he says, opening the stadium door. "That's what you get for having a lie-in." He points to the biggest crowd that has ever existed in the history of the world, ever. "No biggy."

47

As my PE teacher will happily testify, I am not a very fast runner. But I still manage to get at least ten metres away before Nick catches me. He has to push me back into the stadium like I'm startled cattle.

Actually, I'm shaking so hard that if I *did* contain milk, I'm pretty sure it would now be butter.

"There was supposed to be nobody here," Nick explains when I've finally stopped waving my arms and legs in every direction, like an upside-down beetle. "They're here for a sumo match that starts in an hour. If you'd been here on time, it would have been empty."

I peer through the swing doors into the arena; there are chairs all the way up to the ceiling, and almost every single one is full. "I can't do it," I say almost inaudibly. "Nick, please don't make me do it."

I look desperately at the floor. If I can just find a crowbar I might be able to pull a few floorboards loose and crawl under them. I can live there forever,

221

like a mouse or a rat. Or a really big and totally pathetic woodlouse.

"Of course you can do it," he says. "They're strangers you'll never see again. Who cares what they think of you?"

I look at the crowd again and the distant stage, and my stomach folds in half. *Nobody* can transform that much in six months. This isn't a few strangers. This is thousands of strangers. Thousands and thousands of strangers. Thousands and thousands and thousands and...

"Me," I decide. "I care."

"They're here to watch sumo, Harriet. Not us. They won't be paying any attention. We get up there, do our thing for half an hour, and then come down again. It'll be..." He twinkles at me. "Coolioko."

I glare at Nick and then sigh in resignation. This is what I signed up for: live catwalks and live television and live octopi and live sumo. Everything in modelling is *live*. There's nowhere to hide.

Plus unless I want to be disembowelled on the spot I don't think I should push Yuka's patience any further.

I nod grimly.

"Excellent," Nick says. "I'll be there, so don't worry, OK?"

That is simultaneously the best and worst sentence I've heard in the last two months. "Uh-huh."

Nick turns to a chair behind him and picks up what looks like a huge white scarf and a very large safety pin. "Here's your costume. See you out there."

And he winks at me then disappears through the doors, into the crowd.

48

I stare at the scarf in horror.

It's a traditional Japanese sumo loincloth, known as a *mawashi*. It's thirty foot long, two feet wide, made of silk and is passed repeatedly around the stomach and between the thighs and secured over the – you know. Front area. And it's worn by *men*.

But I can't afford to make Yuka any angrier, so I take a deep, professional breath as I walk into the changing room, then experimentally wind the scarf up over my penguin pyjamas and secure it with the enormous safety pin. I untie it and wrap it a little higher. Finally, I criss-cross the silk over my entire body and pin it so I'm completely mummified.

That's better.

Now I look like the world's most prudish baby.

I'm on the floor, trying to tug off my pyjamas from underneath it, when the door opens. A young Japanese woman with blue raccoon stripes in her hair

walks into the room, followed by a large group of people wearing black.

People with brushes and lights and boxes and folded-up tables.

People with the serious, focused expressions of highly experienced professionals.

They stare at me, and then the woman with the stripes holds out a beautiful dark blue dress. It's floor-length and silky, with little holes punched in the bottom so that the light shines through it like stars. It has little straps, and a slit up each side. It's beautiful, my size, and exactly the sort of thing Yuka designs.

I am *so* gullible.

"Hello," I say with as much dignity as I can muster. Then I wait patiently for the floor to open up and swallow me whole.

"My name is Shion," the girl says, grinning. "I'm the new stylist." She looks me up and down. "You must be Harriet Manners."

Right.

I am going to kill Nick. That was so *not* funny.

Unfortunately, nobody else agrees with me. I spend the next ten minutes having my hair speedily gelled into a neat bun by a giggling hairdresser, my shoulders sprayed with sparkly sticky stuff by a snorting stylist and my eyes heavily painted in dark blue glitter by a shuddering make-up artist. By the time they've finished with me, I'm so embarrassed by all the giggling and snorting I've actually forgotten to be nervous.

Plus I'm far too busy working out the various forms of punishment I can wreak on my ex-boyfriend. Enormous seagulls I can train to attack him; lime-flavoured sweets I can eat without offering him any. Ominous-looking rain clouds I can get to follow him around.

That kind of thing.

Shion points me down a long corridor in the direction of the stage doors, and I'm so focused on revenge that I'm totally calm. A quick peek through the doors proves that everybody in the crowd really is just minding their own business: chatting, eating, laughing, drinking. Getting ready for the show they've actually paid to see.

Which means I can do this.

Quietly, I slip through the doors into the arena. At the bottom of the stairs leading up to the stage is a pair of amazing, bright pink, glittery high-heeled shoes with six tiny red straps. Attached to them with tape is a little note that says:

It's the shortest possible distance. x

I laugh, bend down and flick the note on to the floor. The shoes are a bit too small, but I manage to wedge my feet into them and get the straps tied.

Then I straighten up, square my shoulders and walk up the stairs on to the stage.

49

The first thing I see is Nick.

He's standing on the other side of the enormous square stage in a pair of dark blue silk trousers and a dark blue shirt buttoned all the way to the top. His head is down and facing away slightly, his skin is glowing, and for the first time I realise – with a painful pang – that even though most of his hair has gone, he still has that tiny curl at the back like a little duck tail.

Then I notice Yuka. She's partially hidden behind an enormous screen next to scowling photographer Haru: hands neatly crossed in front of her, black lace dress on, little black hat perched, face hard and white.

And then I notice the sound of my heart.

Because, as I step towards Nick and he turns and steps towards me, this is all I can hear:

The drum of my heart.

228

My heels against wood.
The quiver of my breath.

The entire crowd is completely silent.

50

In pretty much all of the romantic films I've ever seen, there's always a moment when the hero and heroine meet and the rest of the world becomes a blur. It doesn't matter where they are; the only thing they can see or hear is each other.

All I can say is: romantic films *lie*.

There isn't a convenient fog, misting out the audience. I see thousands and thousands of people: paused, silent and watching me intently.

Quickly, I do my best to wipe the terror from my face and walk like a model into the middle of the ring. I raise my chin and try to get my entirely rigid body to bend into a shape other than that of a stale pretzel.

None of my limbs are working properly. As I jerk awkwardly around the stage, with every movement Yuka's eyes get narrower and angrier, and Haru's hand gestures more demonstrative.

Swallowing hard, I turn away and try another pose. Then I move to the left and try again: curving forward

with my hand on my hip and my right shoulder pushed back.

At which point I realise that Nick is following me.

OK, isn't this hard enough without my ex-boyfriend chasing me around the stage? He's supposed to be a *boy-shaped prop*. In the *background*.

Why is he winding me up *again*?

I flash him a dark look and hobble over to another corner of the stage. He follows, so I move again, but so does he. After a whole minute of being chased in a circle I finally accept defeat. Nick stands close enough for me to feel his breath on my neck, and every single hair on my body immediately stands up.

"What are you doing?" I hiss, bending into another pose. His hand touches my waist and an unwelcome thunderbolt shoots through the right side of my body.

"What are *you* doing?" Nick whispers. "What are you wearing on your feet?"

"Gloves," I snap, changing my pose. "What do people normally wear on their feet?"

"This is a sumo ring. You're not allowed to wear shoes. Especially not heels. The audience is furious."

It's as if the entire stadium suddenly goes dark. My brain shuts down in shock, and when I come back to my senses, I can suddenly feel where the eyes of twenty thousand people are focused: entirely on my shameful, painful, sparkling feet. "B-b-but I d-don't—"

"Take them off," Nick whispers urgently. "Now."

I bend down but my hands are shaking too hard. The red straps are too tiny and there are too many of them. All I can do is paw desperately at the buckles while my eyes fill with water and blood rushes to my head.

Suddenly Nick bends down in front of me. "I'll do it," he says. "Stay still."

He calmly takes my hand to balance me, and removes each shoe like Prince Charming in reverse, bows deeply to the crowd in every direction and dramatically throws the shoes off the stage.

"Now," Nick says with a tiny nod. "Copy me."

51

There's an animal that lives at the bottom of the ocean called a Pacific Ocean Hagfish. When it feels threatened, it oozes a defensive slime from its pores that envelops its predator in a mass of fibrous goo. It then gets trapped in its own goo and dies.

I'm so embarrassed I can't breathe properly. I can't blink. I can't move. I can't pose. I definitely can't model. Like the Hagfish, I am basically starting to suffocate on my own panic.

Rigid with humiliation, I watch Nick go back to his original starting mark on the stage, and then – to my absolute disbelief – turn around and cock his leg high in the air like a dog about to pee on an invisible lamp-post.

Before I can even blush for him – nobody is good-looking enough to get away with that kind of position – Nick looks me straight in the eye, slams his foot on the ground and yells at the top of his voice: "AAAAAARRRRRGH!!"

233

Then he waggles his elbows and blows a tiny raspberry, just like he did in the snow in Russia.

And I can't help laughing, just like I did on my first ever photo shoot, and everything in me suddenly starts to relax.

Trying not to look at Yuka or the photographer, I obediently lift my leg as high in the air as I can, pause and then slam my foot down with an immense "AAAAAAAARGGH!!"

Nick does the same with the other leg and shouts: "AAARRRGH AAAARGH!"

I've never felt less dignified in my entire life and – frankly – that's really saying something.

It's only when Nick hitches up his trouser legs, kicks one leg slowly out to the side and leans into a deep crouch that I suddenly understand.

Sumo. He's doing sumo.

Slowly, I pick up the sides of my dress, compose my face and kick a leg out. I bend into a squat, lift on to my toes and hold it as long as I can.

Then Nick and I stand up straight, take a few slow steps towards each other and do it all over again. And again. And again.

As we get closer and closer – as we stamp and crouch and shout and pace – something amazing starts happening. The crowd really does begin to disappear. They fade and fade until it's just the two of us.

Circling each other.

Stamping at each other.

Staring at each other, as if nothing else exists.

It's only when Nick snarls at me – and I grin and snarl back – that I finally hear a noise from the audience. A gurgling sound that gets louder and louder and louder.

And it's only when I look up that I realise the audience is laughing. When I glance at Haru and he inclines his head slightly, I know I'm going to be OK.

Which means Lion Boy has saved me.

Again.

52

Now, I have many skills.

I can recite the entire Periodic Table and six Shakespearean sonnets by heart. I can tell you every single King and Queen of England since Kenneth the Third in 997, and I can draw an almost perfect circle freehand as long as nobody's watching.

Of my many useless and untransferable skills, however, accurately interpreting subtle facial expressions is not usually one of them. But I don't think that's something I need to worry about today.

Yuka Ito is livid.

"Explain," she says quietly as we climb down the stairs and push through the stage doors. She looks like the White Witch of Narnia just after she finds the first snowdrop. "Now."

Every drop of adrenaline evaporates, and I'm suddenly so scared I feel like I'm flashing colours like a human disco ball: white, then red, pink and green, then some kind of petrified purple colour. "I'm

s-sorry," I stammer quickly. "We were trying to… harness the Japanese culture creatively and—"

"I'm not talking about the poses."

No. Of course she isn't. "I…" I swallow. "It…"

"Where were you this morning?"

"I was… I set my… at least I thought I set my… my alarms didn't…" I'm too scared to complete a sentence.

"You were three hours late." Yuka doesn't need to shout. Every quiet syllable is a pointed jag of ice. "The driver waited outside your building for two hours. He rang your doorbell thirteen times. Where did you stay last night?"

My eyes widen in surprise. *What?*

"I was th… I was th…" *I was there. I was right there.*

"I rang your mobile repeatedly. It went straight to voicemail. You do not turn your phone off while you are working for me."

"I didn't—"

"I explained very clearly that you are not here to party."

My mouth opens in shock. *Party?* Has Yuka ever met me before?

"I wasn't—"

"And when you decide to grace us with your presence, you accessorise my outfit with heels of your own. On a *sumo* stage. A stage reserved for men."

"But—"

Yuka holds her hand up. "No," she says. "I don't want to hear it, Harriet. You have shown rudeness, disobedience and a total lack of respect, and you have done it in front of twenty thousand people."

I've been called a lot of names in my life, but 'rude', 'disobedient' and 'disrespectful' are not three of them. The shock finally knocks the voice back into me. "Yuka, I was at the flat, I set three alarms, I don't party – *ever* – I don't own shoes like that, I wouldn't even know where to buy any—"

"Do not compound errors with lying," Yuka interrupts. "And don't think that completing this shoot exonerates your behaviour. An ability to copy a professional is not what I have flown you halfway around the world for."

There's nothing I can say: she's absolutely right. Without Nick, I would have stood there and quietly drowned in my own panicky mucus.

"I'm so sorry," I say quietly as my eyes start to go blurry.

"If I hadn't already invested so much in you, Harriet,

you would be going home now." Every word sounds like it's been bitten off. "Do not make me regret this decision any more than I do already." And before I can say anything, Yuka turns and walks out of the building.

I stare after her, open mouthed.

"The *mawashi*," Nick says after a few seconds, raking a hand over his head. "It was a joke. I never would have—" but I've stopped listening. I'm already pushing through the doors and running back to the edge of the stage.

If I can just find the note – if I can show it to Yuka – maybe she'll believe me. She'll see that I do respect her, and that I love Japan. That I know I'm lucky to be here, and I'm trying as hard as I can.

That I'm not the person she thinks I am.

But it doesn't matter how hard I look.

The note is gone.

53

I have so many questions, I don't even know where to start.

Actually, that's not true. I totally do.

As soon as I'm back at the flat, I charge straight into the bedroom. Rin's lying on her front on the bottom bunk, reading an English dictionary with her head cocked to one side: pink lace dress on, purple-socked feet crossed behind her. Kylie's sprawled out across the small of her back in exactly the same outfit. Poppy's perched against the wall of the top bunk, carefully painting her nails pink and humming a riff from *The Sound of Music* over and over and over again.

"Why didn't you wake me up?"

They stop what they're doing and look at me.

My cheeks are hot, and my breathing is getting faster and faster. There's a tight feeling around my throat. "You left early this morning, Poppy. Why didn't you wake me up before you went?"

Poppy looks blank. "What for?"

240

"For my photo shoot with Yuka! You knew I had to be—"

Rin knew about the job, but Poppy didn't.

"Oh no," Poppy says, her hand flying to her mouth. "Did you have a shoot this morning? Did you miss it?"

I shake my head. "Rin – you didn't hear the alarms?"

Rin's chin is starting to wobble. "I hear no alarm, Harry-chan. I have whales on."

"What about the doorbell? It was being rung for two hours and none of us heard it?"

Poppy's eyes fly open. "Oh, Harriet, it's been crackling for ages and it finally broke. I left a note about it for you." She points at a small piece of paper duly stuck next to the bed. "And we left another one on the front door asking visitors to ring our phones."

My phone.

I crouch down and start fumbling around under my bed. After three or four seconds, I find it tucked behind a stray pillow. The battery is totally dead.

Oh my God. *What is wrong with me? What kind of person am I?*

Actually, I'd really appreciate it if nobody answers that.

Then something else in my head clicks. I run to the bird alarm, pick it up and sure enough: it's still on *British time*. All my alarms are set to go off three hours from now.

The entire morning has been my fault.

But what about the shoes? I think. Except...

Nobody actually told me to put them on, did they?

Maybe they were a gift. Maybe the note was in the wrong place, at the wrong time. Maybe they weren't even for me.

This is exactly what happens when you just blindly do what notes tell you without asking appropriate questions first. Did Lewis Carroll teach me *nothing*?

Rin and Poppy are staring at me with wide, slightly reproachful eyes, and suddenly I don't want to be here any more. I want to be far, far away, in a universe where I am not such a horrible human being. In a nicer, alternative world where I take responsibility for my own mistakes like a nearly adult, instead of stropping about, ruining things and then blaming everyone else like a spoilt little child.

It's moments like this when my unpopularity is nowhere near as much of a mystery as I'd like it to be.

"I'm so sorry," I say for the billionth time, my face getting steadily hotter. I start backing out of the room.

"I didn't mean to... I don't know what I'm... I'm"
– I blush even deeper – "I'm so, so sorry."

And in a wave of shame, I grab my mobile and the charger, run into the hallway and climb into the cupboard.

54

Before you say it, no.

There is nothing weird about hiding in a cupboard. C. S. Lewis based an entire series of books on the premise that this is what normal people do on a regular basis. Anyway, I don't have any other choice. This is the only piece of furniture in Japan I can fit either into or under.

I shut the door firmly, turn on the light and slump into a large cardboard box full of towels and drying-up cloths. Then I plug my phone in and rummage around until I find one of Poppy's banished chocolate bars. I cram as much of it into my mouth as will physically fit, turn my phone on and hit speed dial.

"Hi. It's Nat. Leave a message or don't. Whatever. I've probably already been eaten by a sheep anyway and this phone is now lying in a big pile of poo, just like my life."

BEEP.

I guess Nat is still pretty angry with her mum. At

least I hope she is, or judging by that message this is going to be the beginning of a really weird and slightly depressing sixth form.

"Hey," I say. "It's me – I just needed to…"

This is not OK. I can't just steal my best friend's modelling dream and then sit in a cupboard, whining about it. A soulmate's job is to make somebody's day better, not worse.

I swiftly adopt my brightest, breeziest, happiest voice and spoil the surprise present I bought for her.

"Umm… Nat, you know you said that looking like a My Little Pony was super cool, right? Well, I found these amazing rainbow hair extensions in Harajuku. What colour would you like? Pink? Purple? Turquoise?" I pause and try to swallow a hard, distinctly unbreezy lump in my throat. "Anyway. Hope things are getting better in France. It's all amazing here and I'm having soooooo much fun." *Rein it back, Harriet.* "I miss you. Bye."

Then I hang up, shove another chocolate bar into my mouth and try a different number.

"*Hello. This is a digital recording of the electromagnetic wave of Toby's voice, which has been encoded on to a binary system of data. Leave your own electromagnetic wave, and I will call you back when*

I've finished playing Plants versus Zombies but that could be a while because frankly it's almost impossible to get through the iron bucket on their head with a few bits of sweetcorn and a cabbag—"

BEEP.

I swallow the chocolate whole. Nat can be quite flaky in the mornings, but Toby always answers his phone. Especially when it's me. It's one of his most redeeming characteristics.

Seriously, what is the point in having a stalker if they're not at your beck and call whenever you need them?

"Toby? It's Harriet. I'm just ringing because…"

Because everything's going wrong and I want him to make me feel better? Because even though I left without saying goodbye, it's his job to be there for me regardless? Because all I'm thinking about is myself?

Again?

"Umm…" I clear my throat. "I thought you should know that if you laid all the Lego bricks sold in one year end to end they would stretch five times round the world. You can put that as a pop-up box in your *Lord of the Rings* video. You know, make it a bit more interactive." My phone makes a tiny pinging noise. I knew those facts about Lego would come in handy one day. "I hope you're having a great summer, Tobes. Speak soon."

Then I hang up miserably and click on the text that's just come through:

HARRIET STOP RING ME ASAP STOP WE NEED TO TALK STOP WILBUR KISS KISS STOP

I stare at it in confusion – my agent seems to be under the impression that his phone sends Morse code – and then close my eyes.

Did Wilbur just call me *Harriet*?

Oh my God: I am in *so* much trouble.

Eyes starting to well up again, I desperately search through my contacts for somebody else to talk to and realise I've run out of options already. Unless I want to confide my problems in one of my local bookshops or the National Trust.

Which means I'm going to have to do what no self-respecting teenager does under any circumstances.

I'll have to ring my parents.

55

It takes a good six minutes for Dad to pick up.

Predominantly because he can't work out where the phone call is coming from. I've rung the home computer from my mobile, and this complicated trick of modern technology creates total havoc. By the time Dad has run round the house, finally worked out what's going on and pressed the right button, all I can hear is him shouting upstairs: "Annabel, there's a video phone in our computer! Was that your idea?"

The webcam finally clears, but all I see is Dad's dressing gown. "Look," he adds as I hear Annabel lumbering heavily down the stairs. "Harriet hasn't died. We've still got a teenage daughter. Cancel the application for a replacement or we'll end up with two."

I scowl. "Nice to see you too, Father."

The dressing gown moves slightly. "Can she see me?" Dad's stomach asks curiously.

"You need to sit down, sweetheart," Annabel says.

248

There's a swift, stripy movement of dressing gown. "Is that better?"

Now all I can see is Dad's left ear. Annabel wheels him across so he's in full screen. Then she pokes her head into the corner of the screen.

"So, what delights of the fashion world have prevented you from ringing us until now?"

I shrug awkwardly. I didn't realise I'd be so happy to see them, but now I feel so homesick I just want to climb through the screen, curl up in the armchair and never ever leave again.

But I can't, can I?

It's just better if she's not here.

"Somebody wants to say hello," Dad says, handing Annabel what looks like an olive covered in peanut butter. "You're so disgusting, Bels," he tells her proudly, scruffing up her hair. The screen suddenly fills with white fluff. "Grrrr-d morning, Harriet. How are woof?"

I smile. "Hey, Hugo."

"I miss you terrier-bly, Harriet," Hugo/Dad says, licking his nose/wiggling his eyebrows. Then the camera points at Annabel's stomach. "Hello, Harriet," a squeaky voice says. "I can't wait to meet you."

"That's ridiculously creepy, Richard," I hear Annabel say. "Our child is not going to sound like a chipmunk."

"It's not my fault if it does," Dad replies. "That'll be your half. It's only fifty per cent Total Legend." He leans towards her belly, pretends to listen and then adds, "What's that? You want to be called Ralph?"

"After the world's biggest rabbit, I presume," Annabel says calmly. Then she looks back at me. "Are you actually OK, Harriet? Are you having fun?"

I swallow, hard. There's no point telling them. They only want to talk about the baby. As per usual.

"I'm great," I lie. My face is starting to hurt with all the pretend emotions. "The campaign's going great, I'm getting on great with my flatmates and Yuka's really, really... great about my incredible modelling skills."

When people lie, they look to the left because that's the part of the brain associated with the imagination. When they're telling the truth, they look to the right because that's the part of the brain linked to memory.

I look to the right as hard as I can.

Annabel frowns. "What's happening to your face, Harriet? Where's your grandmother? Let me speak to her."

Sugar cookies. I keep forgetting that Annabel is possibly related to Gandalf, Merlin and Zeus, all at the same time. "Bunty is..." I have literally no idea. "Umm..."

There's a small knock on the cupboard door next to my head.

"Harriet? Are you in here?"

"If not Harry-chan, we have big problem," I hear Rin giggle. "We have talking cupboard."

"I'm here," I call out, and then turn back to Annabel and Dad. "Oh," I say in my least wooden voice. "That's my flatmates. I should go."

"There's a strange lady at the door, Harriet. She says she wants to see you."

"Cute pink hair and sparkles," Rin adds merrily. "Like Hello Kitty."

I drop my phone.

"What?" I hear Annabel snap into the floor. "What did they just say?"

"Darling?" a familiar voice calls. "Can I stay here tonight? My friend has been hosting a party and it seems to be going on indefinitely. I haven't seen a mattress in days."

"What's going on?" Annabel shouts. "Why don't your flatmates know your grandmother? Where has she been? MOTHER, YOU PROMISED!"

Oh my God. *Do something, Harriet.* Anything.

"Oh dear," I say, picking my phone off the floor and shaking it furiously up and down. "Earthquake." Then I hang up and switch off my phone as quickly as possible.

Slowly, I open the cupboard door.

Bunty's standing there in a blue, floor-length floral dress, with white lace trailing all the way around the bottom and a blue mirrored blouse tied up in a knot at her waist. There are six or seven beaded necklaces of different colours around her neck, bells around her ankles and her pale pink hair has been piled on top of her head and appears to have been secured by a chopstick.

Not a pretty, decorative chopstick.

The kind of chopstick you get in white paper packs at convenience stores that give you mouth splinters.

"What a lovely place to hide!" Bunty says gaily, wrapping me in a hug and patting my head. One of her enormous rings bashes my forehead. "How's your adventure going, darling?"

"A-are you back for good?"

"Absolutely. I thought we could do a bit of girly catch-up. Paint our fingers, pull our eyebrows out and put bits of papaya on our eyes…"

"Nails?" Rin says. "Cucumbers?"

"I think they might be quite dangerous next to the eyes, darling. Let's go for something nice and soft."

Bunty kicks her flip-flops into the corner of the hallway, wanders into the kitchen and pulls the fridge open. "Choccy biccies?" she adds. "For the tummy," she says to Rin. "Not for the eyes. Don't worry, I'm not *insane*. Now, I've got this strange hair that grows out of my cheek and if it gets too long I feel a bit like a cat. What shall we do with it?"

She leans towards Poppy. "Darling, I don't want to be rude but I think you might have one coming too."

"I am a *top model*," Poppy says indignantly. "We don't have *whiskers*."

"How sad," my grandmother says, nodding at Rin and wandering back into the hallway. "They're awfully handy for working out whether you can fit through a small space."

And, just like that, my grandmother is back.

56

Here are a few of the things Bunty makes us do over the rest of the day:

- Mash up various foodstuffs from the fridge and put them on our faces (including soy sauce and rice, salsa and leftover tofu).
- Turn on all the hot taps and have a fully clothed 'DIY sauna'.
- Rub kitchen salt on our legs.
- Brush each other's hair at the same time.
- Moisturise with olive oil and a dash of sesame.

Clearly, my grandmother knows even less about being a girl than I do.

With great aplomb and not a little bit of scariness she powers through: dragging Rin and Poppy back into the bedroom every time they try to escape like the Year Two Class Hamster every time we left the cage door open.

As we crawl into bed, exhausted and marinated

like expensive tuna steaks, I realise I haven't had time to think about everything that's gone wrong. And that maybe I'm kind of glad to have her here, after all.

For the first time since I arrived in Japan, the next morning goes totally smoothly. My grandmother wakes me up with a cup of tea and a bowl of ready-porridge and some kind of de-stressing feather to 'stroke my cares away' (we'll forget that last bit) and I calmly get ready in my neatest, cleanest, most modelly clothes (black trousers, a white vest and some silver ballet flats).

Our taxi takes us into the centre of Tokyo. The buildings get bigger and bigger, the lights get brighter and the crowds get thicker until they look like shiny, dark-suited fish. It's the noisiest part of Tokyo I've been in yet: beeps and chirrups and music are coming from every direction, every building is flashing in different neon colours like lit-up Lego.

The majority of the people on the streets appear to be men. Apart from a pink bunny in a dress, frilly apron and high heels.

That one's probably not.

"Akihabara," Bunty says as she climbs out of the car. "This is the technology centre of Tokyo, darling.

If you want to see something crazy in Japan, you come here."

It's like being in a film set in the future, where there are barely any females and all of them look like they just fell out of an adults-only version of *Alice in Wonderland*.

"The game arcade is a popular Japanese stereotype," a voice says behind me. "Today I shall subvert it."

I spin round to face Yuka. Apparently we're not even doing greetings any more. "Brilliant," I say politely. "Umm… Yuka, this is Bunty, my step-grandmother."

"Nice to see you," Bunty says, taking Yuka's hand and pumping it unceremoniously up and down.

Yuka watches her hand in silence and then manages to extract it. "Yes," she says, and then turns back to me. "I would like to celebrate Japanese culture while also challenging Western perceptions. Every young person can relate to video games."

I'm nodding like a plastic dog in the back of a car, but my stomach is already starting to sink. Contrary to popular belief, not all geeks love *Star Trek* and gaming and fixing other people's printers. Some of us prefer dinosaur documentaries and reciting poetry at strangers while they're waiting for a bus, even after they've been asked not to.

"Fantastic," I lie enthusiastically. "I love arcade games."

"Good," Yuka says as she starts clicking towards a neon orange entrance. "Because you're going to be in one."

57

I love a good metaphor.

What Yuka actually means is that I'm going to be immersed allegorically inside the culture of modern Japanese technology. Or I'm going to be given a gun so I can fight aliens and vampires. Or I'll be scanned into a green screen so that in post-production I come out looking like a computer character. Or...

Or...

Nope. Yet again, I have literally no idea what Yuka's talking about.

Yuka, my grandmother and I walk through the immense building. The arcade is huge and heaving with people, and every square metre of it is beeping and flashing. The first floor is filled with hundreds of computer games: *boinging* and *clicking* and *peeping*. The second floor has things you can shoot and smash and bash and smack. The third floor is lit up by tiles being manically danced on and more photo booths

crammed with squealing girls. The fourth is buried in soft toys. And the fifth appears to be a bowling alley.

At one stage, I see a game featuring live lobsters and a large foam bottom being smacked by a pair of teenagers. A yellow mist hangs in the air, the walls are flashing bright red, and the pale, blank gazes of gamers are everywhere, like zombies.

It's not unlike a sort of twenty-first-century high-tech version of Dante's nine levels of Hell. Except with much better refreshments and clearly marked exit signs.

By the time we make it to the sixth floor, I'm so disturbed by some of the things I've seen that I'm genuinely relieved to be pushed back into a giant cupboard. Except that this one has no chocolate in it and smells quite strongly of cleaning materials.

Bunty follows me in, then sniffs the air, pulls a face and heads straight back out.

"Sweetie pies," she says. "I'm far too old to get into a dark box voluntarily." She turns round and spies a food counter. "Ooh!" she says. "Slush Puppies! I must go dye my insides into a rainbow."

If Annabel isn't a persuasive argument for nurture versus nature, I don't know who is.

Apart from me, obviously.

"Umm, what should I do now?" I politely ask Yuka.

"Exactly what I tell you, Harriet," Yuka says, as in troops her team of stylists and hairdressers. "Do you think you can manage that?"

Here are some interesting facts:

- Manga is the Japanese word for 'whimsical picture'.
- The Manga industry in Japan is worth 420 billion yen every year, which is two and a half billion British pounds.
- It has been a style of Japanese art since the nineteenth century.
- People in Japan consume more paper as Manga than they do as toilet roll.
- Pink lace really itches.

I know this because I've just been turned into a Manga Girl. And also because I asked the stylists and the internet a lot of irritating questions.

My face has been bleached out with bright white foundation, and then given rosy cheeks and dark brown painted freckles. My eyes have been made cartoon-enormous with clever application of eyeliner and fake eyelashes and electric-green contact lenses significantly bigger than the pupil they're stuck to. I'm wearing a pale pink waist-length shiny wig with a shiny fringe that skims my eyebrows, and my dress is pale pink lace covered with hundreds of pink ruffles and bows and diamanté and ribbons and beads and feathers.

There are diamonds and pearls wrapped round my neck and wrists, and on my feet are little lacy white socks with baby blue shoes covered in sparkly silver stars. I even have frilly knickerbockers on, which reach nearly down to my knees and make me look like a Victorian lady at the seaside.

There's no doubt about it: I'm as *kawaii* as a human gets. Rin would be so proud.

Yuka makes a few last-minute tweaks, adjusts my wig and then stalks back out of the makeshift changing room to where Bunty is leaning against a wall with a laser gun in her hands. Bunty's missing every single vampire target, and when I raise my eyebrows she says, "I'm a pacifist, darling. The fact that these poor creatures do not happen to be real is neither here nor there." Then she grins. "Yuka, how lovely and talented you are. It looks like you've been having an immensely good time with a glue gun."

In fairness, I do look like a massive *Blue Peter* project. My outfit is phenomenally heavy. All I've done is walk through the door and I'm exhausted.

I really need to start doing some proper exercise. It's not a good sign when a dress wears your muscles out.

Haru and Naho are waiting in the corner, where six or seven huge lights have been set up. Everything's pointing towards a large glass and metal case, with buttons and a silver metal claw hanging from the ceiling. The whole thing has been painted bright pink, like the world's most girly Tardis. It's what Dr Who would travel in, if Dr Who was also Barbie.

As I get a little closer I realise with a start that the case is full of hundreds and hundreds of tiny dolls. Every single one has pink hair and freckles. Every single one is wearing a pink lacy dress and pale blue shoes. Every single one has massive, staring green eyes.

It's intensely creepy.

"Oh," I laugh nervously, trying not to notice that the eyes of the dolls are following me when I move. "That's me. In the arcade game. I see what you mean."

"Do you?" Yuka says. "Excellent. Now get in."

58

The word 'phobia' is a derivative of the Ancient Greek word *phobos*, which means fear.

Humans can be scared of literally anything. For instance, fear of dust is called *amathophobia*. Fear of peanut butter sticking to the roof of the mouth is called *arachibutyrophobia*. Fear of looking up is *anablephobia* and fear of space is *astrophobia*.

And that's just the As. Go on through the alphabet and there's even *phobophobia*, fear of having a phobia. Which I'd imagine then leads to a fear of irony (I'm not sure what that's called).

I'm not scared of small spaces (*claustrophobic*) or suffocating (*pnigophobic*) or glass (*crystellophobic*). I'm not scared of dolls (*pediophobic*) or things that look like humans but actually aren't (*automatonophobic*). I'm not even scared of sharp, automated metal claws hanging just above your head in a way that could feasibly pierce through your skull and kill you in a matter of seconds.

263

But put them all together in front of an audience? Terrified.

I barely fit into the box. Shion, Naho and Haru have to lift me in, shove me from behind and then lock the glass cabinet so I don't fall back out again. I can still breathe – there are tiny holes punctured into the top – but that's pretty much it. There's barely room to move, and certainly not enough to do more than crouch with my knees by my shoulders.

I feel like Alice when she drinks the potion in the White Rabbit's house. Except that this time there's no chimney or window to stick an arm or leg out of, no cake to eat that will make me smaller, and no lizards running around, yelling at me.

Actually, I'm quite glad about that last point. I don't think shouting lizards tend to help situations like this.

I look anxiously at the expressionless dolls, staring at me. Then at an expressionless Yuka, staring at me. I look at my expressionless grandmother, carefully studying a piece of food stuck to the front of her dress.

I take a deep breath.

Then I take an even deeper breath and remind

myself that I have to do this. Because if I don't, I'm going straight home.

And I give it everything I've got.

59

Something I've learnt over the last six months must have finally stuck.

My body and my brain are actually working together, instead of reluctantly with open hostility, like two work colleagues who secretly hate each other.

I slouch carefully against the glass sides of the box, tucking my knees in and poking my elbows out. Then I move so that one arm is over my head, pressing against the roof of the box. I draw my feet up so that they're stretched in the opposite direction and my head is at a right angle. I use the dress and the edges of the glass: leaning and pressing and bending and unwinding and bending again.

At one point, I'm actually almost upside down: legs in the air, feet on the ceiling, head on the floor, doll clutched in my hand. And – throughout – I try to keep my face as still and as wide-eyed and as expressionless as I possibly can.

Every time I move into a new position, my

grandmother pays less attention to the food on her collar. Shion starts bobbing around like a happy stripy pigeon and Naho high-fives the hairdresser. Even Haru looks mildly jolly.

"*Sugoi, jyan?*" he shouts. "*Kore wa subarashi desu! Iketeru jyan!*"

"Haru says you're doing brilliantly," Naho says straight away. "The photos are incredible."

I flash a quick grin at Naho, and then look at Yuka. With every click of the camera, something is happening to the corners of her mouth: they're starting to move almost imperceptibly upwards.

Yuka Ito is actually *smiling*. In a few clicks, the skin around her eyes might even crinkle.

I've finally done it. I've finally achieved something on my own.

Filled with a bright, hot sense of relief, I'm just shifting my position when something moves.

Something *in the box* moves.

OK. This is precisely the kind of thing that happens when you've watched *Toy Story 1, 2* and *3* too many times, and then written a letter to Pixar asking when the fourth one is due.

I crouch between the dolls with my arms out at the side, and stretch my neck upwards. I'm just reaching out a hand to lean carefully against the other side of the box when the doll nearest it does a little jiggle.

I'm going to say that again. The doll *does a little jiggle.*

I squeak and grab my hand back.

"What's going on?" Yuka snaps.

"The doll," I say before I can stop myself. "It jiggled."

My grandmother looks fascinated. "Did it say anything, sweetie? I make a point of listening to anything inanimate that tries to communicate with me."

Yuka shoots her a look of death and then turns back to me. "Dolls do not move, Harriet." The corners of her mouth are back in their normal position. "Get on with it."

I nod and go back to what I was doing before, except with one small alteration: I'm now numb with fear.

The doll moved. *I saw it.*

Apparently forty per cent of all British people believe in ghosts, and I think I'm now one of them. What if these are the trapped souls of hundreds of children? What if I'm in a haunted arcade game?

Chilled to the core and filled with visions of hundreds of tiny, cold, grasping fingers, I try to keep my face still and make my arms graceful, my legs less rigid, my movement fluid…

Something starts tickling my ankle.

Dolls don't jiggle, I start repeating under my breath as Yuka's eyes narrow until they're almost shut. *Dolls don't jiggle dolls don't jiggle dolls don't jiggle dolls don't jiggle dolls don't jiggle.*

But the tickling gets more and more pronounced, until I can't take it any more.

I look down.

A ginormous cockroach is slowly climbing up my bare leg.

Entomophobia = fear of insects.

Herpetophobia = fear of crawling things.

Fear of enormous black beetles the size of your palm creeping up your leg?

That's just called normal.

I look down, and then up again. "Oh," I say calmly to nobody in particular. "There appears to be a large semi-tropical insect of the order *Blattodea* and the subclass *Pterygota* currently meandering up my *tibialis anterior*."

Or – you know:

GETITOFFMEGETITOFFMEGETITOFFME.

In one graceful, seamless movement, I lurch in blind panic straight into the glass side of the box.

And straight out the other side.

60

There isn't as much blood as you'd think.

That's the good news. The bad news is I don't think there's as much blood as Yuka would probably like.

I've done it again. *Again.*

There's smashed glass and dolls everywhere and, in my lunge for freedom, my dress caught on the metal side of the box and ripped all the way down the skirt. My wig has fallen off, my lipstick is smeared, my beaded necklace has snapped and I've got a metre-long scratch across my arm and tiny bits of glass lodged in my hands. Shion and Naho quickly pick me off the floor, brush me down and stick a plaster over the worst of it, but there's still enough damage to ensure I'm never allowed to get in any glass boxes again.

Not that I'd want to. Like Snow White, I think I've probably had enough of them for a while.

As soon as it's been ascertained that I'm not mortally wounded or going to sue anyone, Yuka's

expression shifts from concern to fury. She thinks I'm making up excuses again.

In fact, *nobody* believes me. Once I'm out of the ruined dress, I clamber around on the floor trying to find evidence, but there's nothing there. I point out that cockroaches can move up to 80 cms per second and *fly*, but it's useless. Unless I can explain how an enormous insect could get into a sealed glass box I'm either:

a) The owner of an exceedingly overactive imagination.
b) Plain old-fashioned bonkers.

Or – worse:

c) Compulsively lying.

Again.

"*Atarashi moderu ni kaeruzo!*" Haru shouts. "*Harriet ga nayamino tane dattandayo.*"

I've studied enough Japanese since Monday to know that *moderu* means *model*, *atarashi* means *new* and *kaeru* means roughly: *change right now*. I'm very glad my translation skills end there.

"Well," Bunty says when the team starts packing

up again. "It's certainly never boring with you around, is it, darling?"

I look to the corner of the room, where Yuka is speaking on her phone. I don't think she's ordering a takeaway pizza.

A few minutes later, mine starts ringing. It's Wilbur. Without a second of hesitation, I swallow hard and cancel the call.

Looks like it's game over.

61

As soon as I get back into the flat, there's a flurry of activity. Rin and Poppy see the plasters and bandages and immediately want to know if I'm OK, have I hurt my head, have I seen the video already circulating the internet?

"Harry-chan," Rin says desperately when I don't respond to a cup of green tea, a rice biscuit or a 'Shouting Vase'. (I'm supposed to shout my frustrations into it to make them go away, but it just makes them go all echoey.) "Maybe you will go walk? Walk makes all person feels better."

"Yes," Poppy says, looking worried. "My boyfriend says that going outside always puts life in perspective. Especially if it's raining."

I flinch and my mood sinks a couple of metres lower.

"Actually," Bunty says wandering around, casually picking things up and putting them down again, "it's a medical fact that exercise just pushes sadness around the bloodstream faster."

That doesn't sound like a medical fact.

"I'll go," I say numbly. Not because I want to walk, but because I don't know what else to do.

"Super!" Rin cries. She jumps up. "*Chotto matteh! I mean – wait!*" She runs into the bedroom and comes back carrying a sound-asleep cat. "Maybe you take Kylie with you? Kylie love walk."

The cat abruptly opens her eyes and gives Rin a look that seriously questions that statement.

I shrug. "Sure."

"I get Kylie ready for you!" Rin stops and then says, "Are you wearing these clothes for a walk, Harry-chan?" I look down. I'm still in the black trousers, white vest and silver ballet flats from this morning. I nod.

Rin claps her hands, then disappears into the bedroom.

When she returns a few minutes later, Kylie is wearing a black jumpsuit with a white collar and little silver booties. Rin grabs a sparkly pink harness, sequined lead and wrestles her indignant cat into it. "Ready!" she says, handing the animal to me. "Enjoy!"

The cat and I look at each other, faces like thunder. For the first time, we're in total agreement.

And I slink out of the front door with the cat flopped unhappily in my arms.

*

There's an old expression: *misery likes company.*

There is *nothing* in the entire world more miserable than a cat being taken for a walk. Kylie's so wretched with despair and disgust at me and the world and everything in it, I feel slightly chirpier simply by comparison.

A walk with my dog tends to go: "Wait, Hugo. Hang on, Hugo. Stop, Hugo. Don't sniff that, Hugo. Stop licking that, Hugo. Leave her bottom alone, Hugo. *Hugo, that is not your ice cream. HUGO! DOWN! NO! HUGO, COME BACK HERE!*"

A walk with a cat goes: "Please get off the floor. *Please.*"

As soon as I put Kylie Minogue down, she defiantly spreads herself flat out on the pavement, and that's it: walk over.

I cajole. I plead. I even try a bit of mild bullying and half-hearted insults. Kylie simply glares at me.

When I tug hard on the harness, she allows herself to be dragged along the floor sideways like a wheely suitcase without wheels.

Eventually – when I've given up all hope – she stands up and walks three paces. I get over-excited, Kylie sniffs a pebble, promptly decides she's done and lies back down again.

It's only when I look up and see an old Japanese lady, dragging a ginger cat along with its eyes narrowed and its legs stiff and its claws outstretched and digging into the pavement that I start to see the funny side.

This is ridiculous. I am ridiculous. *My entire life is increasingly ridiculous.*

I get my phone out of my pocket.

"Hello. This is a digital recording of the electromagnetic wave of Toby's voice, which has been encoded on to a binary system of data. Leave your own electromagnetic wave, and I will call you back when I've finished playing Plants versus Zombies but that could be a while because frankly it's almost impossible to get through the iron bucket on their head with a few bits of sweetcorn and a cabbag—"

BEEP.

"Hi, Toby." I frown. I'm starting to get a little bit concerned. I know it's the middle of the night in England but why isn't he answering? "It's Harriet. Are you OK? I was just ringing to… umm… find out whether we need to purchase our own Bunsen burners for Chemistry A Level. Let me know. Bye."

I hang up, bite my lip and immediately try Nat's number but that goes straight to voicemail too.

"Hi," I say, desperately attempting breeziness. "It's

me. Again. I just wanted to… umm… tell you that I read somewhere that cows can be identified by their nose prints. Can you have a look for me and see if you can tell a difference between them?" I pause and breathe heavily down the phone while I search for another way to say *I need you.* "Hope you're having an OK time. Speak soon. Bye."

I'm trying to ignore the deep ache at the base of my throat. It feels as if I'm trying to swallow a whole apple without biting into it first.

Despite the fact that Kylie and I have got no further than three metres from the flat, I decide that this 'walk' is over.

I tie Kylie to a lamp-post and climb up on to the top of a high wall. Then I ignore the sullen meowing below – obviously *now* she's keen to get going – and close my eyes.

The lump in my throat is getting bigger and bigger, and there's something niggling at me; something at the base of my brain, chewing away like a mouse at a piece of cheese.

I can hear Tokyo in distant beeps and peeps, the indecipherable chatter of my next-door neighbours, an aeroplane lowering itself into Narita airport. It's still hot, but I'm getting used to the smell and the density of the city air: the flowers and the traffic fumes and the incense and the breaded pork and the slightly soapy scent coming from the laundry hanging two floors above my head.

I take a deep breath. That bit reminds me of home. *Home*.

The big lump moves down to the middle of my chest. Suddenly none of this feels exciting any more.

When I was really little, Dad would tuck me into bed and turn off my bedroom light, and everything would suddenly change. Teddy bears and ornaments and books that made me happy and content during the day would abruptly become strange, unfamiliar and scary. The room and everything in it was the same, but the darkness made me different.

That's how it feels now. As if Tokyo is exactly as it was when I got here, but I'm suddenly less capable of knowing what to do with it. Because now it's just me.

I'm in one of the most populated cities in the entire world, and I have never, ever felt more alone in my life.

"My little Owl," a kind voice says. "Look at you, perched up there, just like Humpty Dumpty."

I keep my eyes tightly shut. Yuka was right: my imagination really *does* have a life of its own. Oh my God. Is this the start of madness? Is this the beginning of a downward spiral into seeing vague, shadowy shapes in the wallpaper and having my food mashed up for me before I eat it?

"Are you meditating, Baby-baby Panda?" the voice says. "I've tried to do that ever since I heard Gary Barlow was into it, but I did three sessions and didn't see him. Not even *once*. Such a waste of twenty-five pounds."

I open my eyes. "W-w-what are you doing here?"

"What do you think I'm doing here?" Wilbur says, smiling. "I'm like all the Queen's horses and all the Queen's men, my little Sugar-puff. I've come to put you back together again."

At which point I promptly throw myself off the wall, fling my arms around Wilbur's neck and burst straight into tears.

62

Wilbur takes charge immediately.

"My little Butter-crumpet," he says gently after a few minutes of relieved sobbing (mine, not his). "It's lovely to be appreciated, Mini-chickpea. But you're getting salty water all over my Hermès silk scarf."

"I can't believe you've come all this way for me," I say, ignoring his warning and weeping happily into his shoulder.

"Of course I did, my little Pineapple-chunk." Wilbur pats me on the head, the way you comfort a puppy on firework night. "Fourteen hours squished next to a woman with body odour and wandering feet. Most Fairy Godmothers can just *appear*, so if that's not commitment to a cause I don't know what is. Let me have a look at you."

Wilbur holds me at arm's length.

"Twinkle-monkey, now I *know* something's wrong. What's with the yawn-o-gear? Where has my little Munchkin gone?"

I look down at my outfit, and suddenly I feel like somebody's drained the Harriet Manners out of me.

"I don't know," I admit.

"Then let's get her back, my little Sugar-peanut," Wilbur says. He bends down and unties Kylie, who immediately starts prinking and purring like the contrary little madam she is. Then Wilbur drops a polka-dot holdall on the pavement, climbs on top of the wall and pats the spot next to him.

"I suggest you tell me exactly what the sugar-monkeys has been going on since I last saw you, Teeny-possum."

I take a deep breath and hop up next to him. "I don't even know where to start."

Wilbur nods wisely. "Then begin at the end and work your way through to the front. We can piece the story together from there."

Over the next hour, I tell Wilbur everything. I tell him about the octopus and the dress, my alarms, oversleeping, the pink shoes, the sumo shoot, smashing the arcade game. I tell him how much Haru hates me. I tell him about my new flatmates. I tell him about Bunty. I even tell him about Nick.

For the first time since I've known him, Wilbur listens without a single word.

"OK, Peach-plum-pear," he says when I finally draw to a flushed halt. "Just one question: is there *any* chance you've been abducted by aliens and that the girl in front of me is actually from a world a billion miles away?"

Exactly what kind of magazines has Wilbur started reading?

"No chance," I say reluctantly.

"Because that would make it an *awful* lot easier to get Yuka back on side."

I remember with a sickening thump that it's not just me my behaviour has consequences for.

"I'm so sorry, Wilbur. I just don't think I'm cut out for modelling."

"Baby-baby Giraffe," he says firmly, "not a single thing that's gone wrong has been anything to do with your modelling skills. I thought that you'd have figured that out for yourself by now."

I stare at him. "What do you mean?"

"Tinkle-berry," Wilbur says tying the harness back on to the cat and picking his spotty bag up. He swings it over his shoulder like a slightly podgy Huckleberry Finn. "I mean it's time to find out what the diddle cat is going on."

63

My first instinct on entering the flat is one of panic. Bunty's lying flat on the living-room floor in a shower of flashing lights. It's only when she holds up a crystal necklace that I realise I probably don't need to call an ambulance. She's lying in a small patch of sunshine, waving the necklace so that tiny rainbows bounce around the walls.

Suffice to say, Kylie immediately runs in and tries to violently kill one.

"Bunty-boo," Wilbur says, walking over and prodding my grandmother with a stripy sneaker. "May I join you?"

"Of course, darling. Take a pew."

Wilbur lies down next to her, and they both watch the rainbows in silence. Finally he says, "Any ideas?"

"Quite a few, as it happens."

"About—"

"Exactly."

"And the—"

"I thought so too. Nothing yet but it's getting there."

"What's going on?"

"Nothing to worry about, my little Paper-flip-chart," Wilbur says with a smile.

"Harriet, darling, why don't you go into the bedroom and have a little look round? See if there's anything *missing*?"

The mouse in my brain suddenly wakes up and takes another nibble. I shift uncomfortably.

"Harry-chan?" a small voice says from the doorway. "Do we have visit? Is it Ted? Do we need more presents?"

"Is it Nick?" Poppy says from behind her. "I've been calling and calling him and…"

They spot Wilbur, and there's suddenly silence. A strangely long and uncomfortable silence. The kind of silence you could drink, if you were interested in drinking silences.

"Poppy," my agent says. "Cherry-winkle, I haven't seen you since you jumped shipski to that other agency without cancelling our contract first. How's tricks, Pumpkin?" There's a slight edge to Wilbur's voice that I haven't heard before.

"Umm – hi, Wilbur," Poppy says awkwardly, tucking

her golden hair behind her ear and standing on a different foot. "Nice to see you again. How are you?"

"Fandabby, naturally, Darling-cake." Then he looks straight at Rin. "And how's my little Rin-chops?"

Wilbur knows *Rin*? How does Wilbur *know Rin*?

Then I see that Rin has gone bright red, and has immediately grabbed Kylie and buried her face in Kylie's fur. "Wilbur-San," she says, dropping into a low, formal bow. "Iamfinethankyouandyou?"

"Marvelly," Wilbur says, sitting up. "And tell me, Sheep-pudding: have you found much work since Yuka dropped you from the Baylee campaign and replaced you with Harriet?"

Rin abruptly steps backwards until she's pressed against the wall with Kylie held protectively in front of her.

What the sugar cookies is going on?

"Not so much," she says in a small voice.

"Not at all, I've heard," Wilbur says, flashing a glance my way.

I suddenly realise that although Rin said she was a model, she hasn't actually mentioned a single modelling job since I got here.

"I am OK. I enjoy the chill time." Rin's cheeks are now scarlet.

"Of course you do," Wilbur says. "Who doesn't just *adore* penniless, anonymous unemployment, Rabbit-nose?"

My head is starting to make an incomprehensible buzzing sound. *Rin* used to be the Baylee model? I replaced her? I ruined her modelling career and I didn't even *know*? I've Googled *everything in the world that has ever happened ever,* and it never occurred to me to look up the model I replaced last year?

"B-but I don't understand," I say, looking at both of my flatmates. "What are you saying—" and suddenly the mouse in my brain stops chewing.

Annabel changed the time on my alarm clocks.

While I was getting ready to leave the house for the airport, she changed my watch, my phone and all three alarm clocks. Dad had to help her screw on the back of the little bird because it was too tight.

A fraction of a second later, the mouse sighs and clonks me gently round the head.

I charged my phone the night before the sumo shoot. I *know* I did, because I had to get my six-piece adapter kit with snap-on plug out of my suitcase. And plug it in next to the doorway. *Not* under my bed.

There was no note about the doorbell next to my bed when I went to sleep.

The shoes at the sumo ring were *pink*, *glittery* and *too small*.

My brain continues making a few more whirring sounds, and – finally – the mouse stands up, rolls its eyes and punches me straight in the face.

No. No.

NO.

Feeling sick, I turn round and run to the bedroom; hoping I'm wrong, hoping I've made a mistake, hoping I've jumped to irrational conclusions. But I haven't.

The corner of the room is empty.

The cockroach trap is gone.

64

Six months ago, I had a list.

It was a list of all the people I thought hated me, and I carried it around with me everywhere. I added to it, and I studied it, and it grew and grew and grew. Eventually, I realised I was wrong and I crossed the names off and threw the list away.

Maybe I shouldn't have been so quick to do that.

I've travelled halfway around the world and fooled myself into thinking that there's a place for me here. That I fit in. That people actually want me to.

But now I'm back exactly where I started.

It looks like somebody still hates Harriet Manners after all.

65

Bunty and Wilbur don't leave my side for the next twenty-four hours. It's no longer my New and Infinitely Less Glorious Plan 3 (NAILGP3).

It's theirs too.

They take me for slightly rubbery sushi from a conveyor belt. They take me to see a Hollywood blockbuster at the Waseda Shochiku Cinema. They follow me to the Meguro Parasitological Museum, and then promptly go outside to vomit (it has the longest ever tapeworm found in a human: it's nearly nine metres long).

By the time I meet Wilbur at Tōkyō train station the next morning, I'm pretty sure that one of them is standing outside the bathroom every time I go to the toilet, just to make sure nobody's followed me in.

"Cooo-eeeee!" he screeches across the enormous, incredibly busy concourse, pushing his way to meet me. "Over here, my little Chicken McNugget!" He's wearing a bright pink suit with sparkly wings drawn

on the back, and a leopard-print cap. "Back to genius attire, I'm incandescent to see." He looks me up and down. "What's the inspiration this time, Buttercup?"

I smile. "My father made it for me."

Wilbur looks carefully at my denim dungaree dress, stripy leggings, neon-green trainers and the white T-shirt with the huge word **MODEL** written on it in red marker pen.

Let's just say: Dad finally noticed my satchel.

"My Father Made It For Me," he sighs happily. "You light up my life, Sugar-lump. You really do."

Bunty nods from behind me. "Your turn," she says, pushing me gently towards him.

"Got her," he says, grabbing my arm as if we're playing Harriet Relay. "Go home and guard those two backstabbers."

"On it. Poppy's having a bath, and I may or may not have propped a chair outside the door. Rin's trying to train her cat to roll over, so that should keep her occupied for the rest of the day."

"Just don't let them leave the house," Wilbur says, and then blows my grandmother a kiss and starts leading me through the train station with his arm tucked through mine as if we're two teenage girls, not one and a slightly portly fashionista.

I assume we're going on the metro, and am already weak with relief that it's not rush hour so we won't be physically crammed into a carriage by a little man wearing little white gloves and a hat, like a really aggressive Fat Controller from *Thomas the Tank Engine*. But Wilbur steps on to the up escalator.

"The shoot isn't on the underground?"

Wilbur tinkles with laughter. "You think we'd risk making you stand up on a moving vehicle?"

OK, I asked for that. "So where are we going?"

"Think about Yuka's subverted thingummy-jiggery. You're a smart cookie, Coffee-bean, why don't you tell me?"

The butterflies in my stomach go completely bonkers.

"Mount Fuji?" I squeak, gripping his arm. "We're going to *Mount Fuji*?"

At that precise moment, we get to the top of the escalator and Wilbur points at the instantly recognisable, long, shiny white train pulling into the station.

A pointy-nosed train with a blue stripe running down the side of it.

The most famous train in the entire world. Apart from Thomas, obviously.

"We certainly are," he says, patting my head. "And we are getting there on *that*."

*

The first time Dad brought Annabel home, she brought me a book about mountains. *Everest. K2. Kanchenjunga.* But Fuji was always my favourite because – unlike the others, hanging out in the Himalayas – it didn't have any friends.

I guess I felt a certain empathy with it.

In a flash, I suddenly understand what it is Yuka's doing. She's using fashion to challenge cultural stereotypes: living fish in a dead fish market. Women on a sumo stage. People trapped inside a computer game instead of by it.

The more I know Yuka, the more I admire her.

It's just a shame the feeling is almost definitely not mutual.

Wilbur and I wait by the smooth white electronic barriers that stop people climbing on to the track. Then we clamber up the stairs on to the Shinkansen and take our seats. I'm so excited, if the windows opened I'd be like Hugo on long car journeys: head out, tongue halfway down my chin, drool hitting the unlucky person behind me.

"By 2008 these Bullet Trains had made enough trips to circle the earth 30,000 times," I tell Wilbur breathlessly.

"At top speed it takes a train three minutes and 45 seconds to stop," I inform him as the train starts gently accelerating.

"In 47 years there have been 7.1 billion trips made on the train, and never a fatal accident," I say as a beautifully dressed woman in a hat and gloves starts walking down the aisles with refreshments, like an air hostess from the 1950s.

"Ooh, peanuts," I add happily.

As we slide out of Tokyo, everything slowly changes. The buildings get smaller and smaller, and the gaps between them get bigger and bigger. Suddenly – with an almost audible pop – there are big green stretching fields and tractors and little squat houses with peacock-blue tiles on the roof and dogs barking. The ground gets very flat, the sky gets close and bright, and there are people: bent over, wearing big flat hats and picking rice. We're going so fast that I'm literally pinned to my seat: my entire body is heavy and I have to *pull* myself down the aisle to the toilet like a little tree-swinging monkey.

There's a sudden peace, and for the first time in days I feel like I can breathe.

The only thing I can't really wrap my head around is how everyone else on the train can be so *nonchalant*.

In fact, the majority of the people on here are actually fast asleep: eyes rolled back and heads lolling against the people sitting next to them.

"People can get used to anything, Possum-breath," Wilbur says quietly. "You don't go into raptures every time you see the London Eye, do you?" Then he raises an eyebrow. "Actually, my little Kidney-bean, *you* probably do."

I look at my lap. Well, it *is* the world's largest cantilevered observation wheel.

Fifty minutes and six hundred breathless observations later, the train stops and an electronic voice says in a cut-glass American accent: *"Now arriving at Shin-Fuji station."*

"Is this it?" I burst out, standing up too quickly and smacking my head hard on the overhead compartments. Ouch. "Are we here? Are we at Mount Fuji? Can I see it? Can you show it to me?"

As if it's a shy kitten, and not a volcano 3,776 metres high.

"This is us, my little Butternut-squash," Wilbur says, then he points out of the window. "And who's that?"

I turn, but even as I'm turning I know, because Wilbur's got that twinkle.

That Well-What-Do-You-Know twinkle.

That What-A-Coincidence twinkle.

That Fairy-Godmother-Before-The-Ball twinkle.

That One-Day-I'm-Going-To-Get-Shot-By-Harriet-Manners-And-It'll-Be-All-My-Own-Fault twinkle.

My eyes meet Nick's and every single one of the one hundred trillion cells in my body leaps into the air. With difficulty, I lift my hand. "Hey," I finally mouth through the glass.

"Hey," he mouths straight back.

66

One day, I'm going to be the kind of ex-girlfriend who moves in a bubble of composure and indifference, leaving former suitors sobbing in her wake.

Today is clearly not it.

Not only did Nick see me smack my head on the overhead luggage compartments, he also sees me miss my first step off the train and fall straight on to the platform floor. He immediately reaches out a hand to pick me up, but I shake it off, put my hands on my hips and thrust myself off the ground. "Exercise," I tell him imperiously, bending a couple of times to demonstrate. "It's important to practise lunges wherever possible."

"Obviously." Nick nods. "It's rule 452 in the Fashion Modelling Handbook."

What? Why has nobody given me this book yet?

He smiles. "And rule 593 is Break Everything in a Twenty-Metre Radius, so you're clearly a natural."

Oh.

I blush and pretend to look for my train ticket in my satchel, even though I know it's in my pocket.

"Come and give me a kiss, Prince C," Wilbur announces as I search fruitlessly for a suitable comeback. "I haven't seen you for yonks and diddly yonks. How's that big brute of a country treating you?"

"Fine. Freezing cold, though."

"Australia's a contrary mare, and no mistake," Wilbur agrees, shaking his head. "Sunny at Christmas, cold in summer. What does Santa wear there, I wonder?"

"Red board-shorts," Nick says as he starts leading us out of the tiny station. "He's big into surfing."

"*Well*," Wilbur exclaims triumphantly, "no *wonder* he's got such red cheeks and nose by the time he gets round to us."

"Did you know," I blurt out, "that if Santa Claus was real, in order to deliver presents to 378 million Christian children all over the world, his sleigh would have to move at 3,000 times the speed of sound with 214,200 reindeer and the air resistance and the centrifugal forces involved would cause both the reindeer and Santa to explode?" I pause. "Not that I think Santa's real," I add. "I'm just saying if he *was* real."

Oh, for the love of *sugar cookies*. Nice way to not look like a *silly* child, Harriet.

"Aaaand she's back," Wilbur says, patting me on the head as if I'm a slightly dim-witted Labrador.

"Did you bring any Polaroid with you?" Nick asks as we start walking towards a large white van with blacked-out windows. "Haru's run out."

"I'm a professional, darling. Of course I have Polaroid film." Wilbur opens a flowery bag with a rabbit printed on it. "Now, is Yuka ready for this cherub?"

"That's not exactly how she's referring to Harriet at the moment, but – yes."

"And how about the… you know?"

"Ready. It pains me to say it, but my aunt is a genius."

"That good?"

"Uh-huh."

It's like they're talking in code. To be honest, I'm not even sure I want to know what they're on about.

So far my modelling career has consisted of: jumping around in snow with bare feet; being covered in gold paint; getting attacked by an octopus; feeling humiliated in front of 20,000 people and being put in a glass box.

Judging by past experiences, I would imagine they're now planning to wrap me in clingfilm and drop me off the top of a mountain attached to an elastic band. It's for the best all round if I just don't ask.

"And any sign of…" I say to Wilbur, lifting my eyebrows. I can totally do code too. *Ha.*

"What?"

"You know."

"No, what?"

For God's sake. How come when *I* try to be all mysterious, nobody understands what I'm talking about?

I blush. "Poppy or Rin," I whisper under my breath. "Any sign of them?"

"None," Wilbur whispers back. "Your grandmother's still guarding the flat like a gloriously sparkly Pyrenean Mountain Dog. She texted me to say she's got them baking wasabi cookies. It's going to be fine this time, my little Human-firework. We've made absolutely sure of it."

My shoulders relax, but only slightly.

Over the last ten years, Alexa and her minions have shown me so many shades of hatred I could draw you an Unpopularity Rainbow.

I know the shade of hatred you get when you tell people they've used the wrong word in a sentence;

the shade when you've just had a six-page spread in *Harper's Bazaar*; the shade when you've accidentally tripped in the school canteen and thrown baked beans and chicken Kiev all over the back of the person in front of you.

I even know the shade of hatred that comes from telling people about shades of hatred, and offering to draw them an Unpopularity Rainbow.

But I'm not sure anyone has ever hated me enough before to change my alarms, wear out my phone battery, plant a pair of culturally offensive shoes on me and manhandle a cockroach, all to try and get me fired when I'm 6,000 miles from home.

Not even Alexa.

67

I've had a picture of Japan in my head for more than a decade. Skyscrapers, flashing lights, crowds, technology, sushi, girls in cute outfits and dogs in clothes and a random mountain floating in the air somewhere behind it.

In other words: Tokyo.

As we drive away from Shin-Fuji train station, I suddenly realise there's an entire country that I had ignored completely.

Huge green fields full of tiny purple flowers, dense thickets of gnarly woods with tiny roads winding through them. Huge bright blue skies, silence and rustling and birds; little restaurants with wooden chairs and paper lanterns hanging from the ceilings; regal red temples built into rocks. In between the trees and the flowers are enormous shining lakes: sometimes seasoned with tiny boats and fishermen, sometimes with windsurfers, sometimes completely empty.

And – looming behind it all, reflected perfectly – Mount Fuji.

Proud and completely alone.

The only thing that could possibly make the journey more amazing would be *not* being squidged against the van door, curled into a stiff, semi-fetal position. I'm squashed next to Nick in the front, and every time we go round a corner, his left knee brushes against my right knee, or his left elbow brushes against my right elbow, and I spring a little further into the door as if I've just been electrocuted.

And there appear to be a *lot* of corners.

Wilbur's not helping. In fact, he seems to be going out of his way to make it worse. "Nick, Sugar-pot, tell Harriet where we are now."

"This is Fuji Five Lakes."

Three minutes later: "Nick, Monkey-bum, tell Harriet where the name Fuji comes from."

"I think it translates to *without equal.*"

One minute: "Nick, Orange-pip, tell Harriet what those flowers are called."

Cue laughter. "How would I know, Wil? Purple ones?"

I'm not a naturally violent person, but after three-quarters of an hour of this I am *seconds* away from smacking Wilbur's head against the seat in front to get him to shut up. Just so that I can stop blushing scarlet and avoiding eye contact and trying to hide my sweaty palms by cramming them between my legs. Just so I can stop saying 'ah' and trying to sound all mature and indifferent.

Just so I can stop pretending I can't feel Nick's shoulder knocking sporadically against mine or his foot three centimetres from mine or that it's slightly killing me.

Finally, we pull into an enormous, muddy car park. I'm out before the engine's switched off. Next time, I am *so* sitting in the back.

I hop straight into a puddle.

Nick laughs and carefully climbs over it. "That was pretty selfless of you, Manners, protecting my jeans like that. You're like some kind of girl knight."

I blush and shake the muddy water from my leggings.

"Owl-cakes," Wilbur says, clambering out and stretching like an enormous pink sparkly cat. "Can I leave you to entertain yourselves? I'm just going to go pull the brief out of Yuka."

I glance nervously at Nick and then away again.

I'm not entirely sure that *entertain* is the right word. When a frog vomits, it ejects its entire stomach and uses its forearms to empty out the contents.

There's a small chance I may be about to do the same thing.

"Sure," I say.

"Absolutely," Nick says, and – to my distress – his nonchalance sounds totally genuine. "Take your time."

"My darlings," Wilbur sighs. "If time belonged to me I totally would."

And he skips towards a familiar big black car waiting on the other side of the car park.

68

Studies have shown it takes exactly four seconds for a silence to become awkward.

I think somebody needs to tell Nick this.

He's still standing in the car park with his hands slung nonchalantly in his pockets. There isn't a flutter of discomfort or embarrassment on his handsome face.

Five seconds: nothing. Six seconds: nope. Seven seconds: nada. Eight sec—

"Come with me," he says abruptly, looking up. I'm forced to quickly pretend I've been studying an imaginary pigeon in a tree just behind his head.

"Pardon me?"

He awkwardly scratches his head. "Please? Unless you want to spend the next ten minutes standing in a car park?"

Pretend, Harriet. Pretend as hard as you can.

"Actually," I say in a desperate attempt to sound

like I'm not bothered either way, "white vans are quite interesting. Did you know that you would need 772 of them to move one billion Cheesy Wotsits?"

Yeah. That'll work.

He'll either think I'm totally over him or inordinately obsessed with private transport. And cheese-flavoured snacks.

"Of course," Nick says, nodding seriously. "Everybody knows that. Let's go."

He turns and starts striding towards the other side of the trees. I start objecting that Wilbur won't be able to find us again, that we'll get into trouble, that we'll get lost, and then I realise that with every hesitation he's getting further away. So I set my shoulders into their most cool, unbothered position and saunter casually after him. Then – because he's so fast – I saunter a little more quickly.

Then I break into a cool, unbothered kind of jog.

I'm just about running – cool and unbothered, and breathing quite heavily through my mouth – when the trees suddenly clear.

In front of us is an enormous, sparkling lake. A few flossy white clouds are hovering in the sky, which is now starting to deepen to a faint lilac colour with a slightly pink horizon. The lake is surrounded by a grey pebble beach and tiny flowers, and directly behind it is Mount Fuji.

We are totally alone.

I suddenly feel uncomfortable. As if I'm doing something very, very wrong.

I turn around and start walking quickly back towards the car park. "Harriet?" Nick says, and I pause then turn to face him. "Are you OK?"

I half nod without saying anything.

"Here." Nick reaches into his pocket. He walks forward and hands something to me.

"What's this?" I look at the money he's just forced into my hand. "What are you *paying* me for?"

"Hold it up."

There's a picture of a man on it with big bouffant hair and a bushy moustache. "Hideyo Noguchi, the famous Japanese bacteriologist?"

Nick frowns then shouts with laughter. "Not that side. Turn it over."

On the other side of the note is a little circle: a blue picture of a mountain topped with snow, reflected in the lake below it. I must have used 1,000-yen notes at some stage in the past week but I've never noticed it. I look back at the view in front of us. "Is this—"

"Where we are now? Yes. This is the exact spot where that picture was drawn. I wanted you to see it."

There's a silence while I try to process this.

"*Why?*"

"I don't know," Nick says. "I suppose I wanted to give *you* something this time."

We both look at the floor while I fiddle with the corner of the note. Then I say quietly, "Poppy's very beautiful, isn't she?"

I sort of feel as if I need to put her name out there, like a line in the sand.

Even though it's not actually sand: it's pebbles.

But you know what I mean.

Nick glances at me sharply, and a deep line appears between his eyebrows. He pauses, then says, "Yes, she is. But I prefer you."

The awkwardness in my stomach is getting tighter and tighter, and the urge to run away is unbearable.

What the sugar cookies is Nick *doing*?

I suddenly don't want him to say anything else. I feel as if I'm about to lose the boy I knew for good. And not to someone else this time: to a different version of himself. One who is a cheat.

Which is so, so much worse.

"I think we should stop talking to each other now," I say in a brittle voice. "Frankly, I think you're being awful."

Nick flinches. "Harriet—"

"There you are, Chuckle-monkeys!" a voice cries behind us, and a hand in a twinkly pink suit lands on my arm. Wilbur beams over my shoulder. "The light's running out, Pizza-bottom. We need you to get ready now."

I glance briefly at Nick, but he's staring at the lake: profile outlined against the sky, face totally unreadable.

Whatever he was going to say has gone.

It feels like it's not the only thing.

Swallowing hard, I follow Wilbur quietly back across the car park. But not before I've folded the note in half.

And dropped it on the floor behind me.

69

I am *so* ready to be transformed.

I want the full works. I want to be primped and prodded and coloured in and brushed. I want to be preened and polished and glossed and gleamed and sprayed and beautified and augmented until I look like a proper, real model. Like somebody completely different.

Which is why it's a bit disconcerting when Shion pulls a curtain around me, ties me into a long, floaty white dress with two pockets and a bit of white ribbon round the middle, and then starts walking me back through the car park.

There's no hairdresser here. No make-up artist. No assistants. Just Shion and me.

"Umm," I say politely as she gently winds a couple of purple flowers into my hair. She nods in satisfaction then hands me a pair of rubber flip-flops. "Where's my usual… garnish?"

As if I'm some kind of fashion hamburger.

Shion smiles. "No garnish today. Yuka wants you

311

completely natural. I'm on strict orders not to touch you with a single product." She grimaces slightly and leans closer to my face. "Although I am *so* tempted to quickly just touch up those two zits with a bit of concealer but" – she sighs – "we'll just have to leave them for Photoshop."

What? They're sending me out *like this*? Exactly as I am?

This wasn't part of the deal.

I don't even let Nat take photos of me like this.

I'm desperately trying to pinch some colour into my cheeks and lips the way Scarlett O'Hara does in *Gone with the Wind* when a cold voice behind me says, "Can you swim?"

Yuka's standing a metre behind me. I have literally no idea how long she's been there. It's like having a shower and only seeing the massive black spider in the corner right at the end. "Sorry?"

"Can you swim?"

Fifty-four per cent of the world's population can't, but Dad ensured I was in the minority during a particularly traumatic trip to Cornwall. "Yes."

"Good." Yuka nods. "This is the most important shoot. It is absolutely pivotal that everything goes to plan. Is that perfectly clear?"

I swallow. "Yes."

"Now, I am going to do something I have never done before in my entire career."

I look at the lake nervously. "Umm… what?"

"This."

And in one smooth motion, Yuka turns and walks back to her car, then climbs in and it drives away.

70

The relief is immediate.

It's as if the Narnian winter has abruptly thawed, and everyone in a twenty-metre radius can suddenly take off their metaphorical big furry coats. Within seconds, Shion's humming under her breath; Naho taps out a tune on her notepad; Wilbur takes his sunglasses off and wipes them on his shoulder pads. Even Haru perches on a log and rubs his forehead.

Yuka has obviously realised that the best thing she can do for her own campaign is be nowhere near it.

I follow Shion towards the water and then realise that Naho, Haru and a couple of the assistants are pulling on thermals, huge, waterproof onesies, hats and thigh-high wellies.

I'm going in, aren't I. I'm actually going into the freezing cold lake. In nothing but a summer dress. And flip-flops.

Of course I am.

*

I don't want to point out the obvious, but I'm recently heartbroken. I'm wearing a long white nightie and flowers in my hair. And now I'm being sent into a large body of open water.

Has nobody read *Hamlet*?

One of the assistants shyly holds out an extra waterproof costume to Wilbur and is promptly greeted with hysterical laughter. "My little Peanut-butter-spoon," he finally wheezes at the startled girl. "I'm not wearing that: I'd vomit in my own mouth. Plus, I can't go in water, Pea-pod. I'm like sugar: I'd dissolve on the spot. I think I'll just stay here and keep a lookout for danger like a cute little meerkat."

Then Wilbur puts his mirrored sunglasses back on and gives me a knowing, wry nod.

He really *is* like a guardian angel.

Albeit one with wings stitched into the back of his suit rather than a functional part of his outfit.

I'm just trying to work out how to get into the water without ruining yet another dress when a hand lands on my elbow. "Do you need help?" Nick's now dressed entirely in yellow waterproofs, like the world's most beautiful Paddington Bear. "Because unless you're Jesus, Manners, you're going to have to get a bit wet."

Every cell in my body is now numb, apart from the area directly under Nick's hand. That's on fire.

"Actually," I say, trying to extricate myself, "that's not true. If I was a water strider with hydrophobic feet, such as a *Gigantometra gigas*, I would be able to walk on water by shedding vortex filaments into the water and simply propelling myself forward."

"What's a *Gigantrometra gigas*?"

"It's sort of like a big stick insect."

"And are you sort of like a big stick insect?"

I look at my non-hydrophobic feet. "No."

"Then you're going to get wet." Nick holds out his arm like a man in a black and white film. "Hold on to this."

No. Yes. No no no no no *no*.

"Thank you," I say with great dignity, taking a step forwards, "but I am perfectly capable of—"

The world suddenly tilts as I plunge down.

Nick grabs me before I hit the water and straightens me back up again. "Please, Harriet. That's why I'm here. I've been paid to make sure you don't knock yourself out and drown. Will you *please* let me do my job without fighting me the entire way?"

I open my mouth and then shut it again and nod.

It's only as we get deeper that I start to notice just

how beautiful this dress is. Out of water it's deceptively simple, but there are actually dozens of layers, cut at slightly different angles so that they swirl out in huge billows as the water pulls them in different directions. Despite being white, there's so much material it's not transparent at all. It's slightly mermaidy, slightly Lady of Shalott (yet another heartbroken lady who didn't fare very well in lots of water).

I slip on another rock as we reach the team, and Nick swiftly moves so that his arm is around my shoulder.

"*Yoku yatta, Harriet. Kimiwa migotoda,*" Haru says in an almost unrecognisable, low, calm voice. "*Demo, sono kakkou ha samuku naika?*"

Naho smiles at me. "Haru says you're doing brilliantly, Harriet. He also wants to know if you're too cold?"

I shake my head. All I can feel is Nick. The rest of me may as well have vanished completely.

"*Mizu no nakani suwatte moraukedo, daijyoubu kana?*"

"Is it all right if you sit down in the water?"

I try not to notice Nick's arm move and his hand rest gently on my waist. The world is starting to tilt again, even though this time I'm not actually slipping anywhere.

"*Jyaa, sorosoro hajimeyouka?*"

"Ready to start?"

Nick's hand moves and seems to slip slightly under the cloth tied around my middle. It fumbles a bit just at the small of my back and I can feel myself blushing from the roots of my hair all the way down to my toes. Apparently the sun's core is so hot that a piece of it the size of a pinhead would give off enough heat to kill a person 160 kilometres away.

The way I'm burning right now, I reckon I could obliterate everyone from here to South Korea.

But he's not mine.

There's a line between being supportive and being gropey, and he has just totally crossed it. "Nick," I snap, "what on earth do you think you're playing at? Get the hell off me."

"I'm trying to find the button," he says. "Sorry. I thought it would be easier than this."

I stare at him. That is so unbelievably rude.

"*What?!* Is that some kind of horrible metaphor for—"

But I don't finish, because Nick suddenly beams at me. My stomach promptly stands on its tiptoes then

318

flips over backwards and everything inside me falls apart. "Got it," he says, leaning forwards.

Before I can stop him, Nick kisses me gently on the cheek.

And my entire body is covered in light.

71

For a fraction of a second, I actually think that the light is coming from me. That my emotions are so strong, I've rendered them a literal, physical, visible fact. I'm a scientific phenomenon.

Then I think, Wilbur was uncannily prescient and I've just burst into flames.

It's only when Nick pulls away and I look down that I realise the light's coming from the dress. Every single fibre of the material is a hair-thin LED, woven tightly together, and the whole dress is now shining neon white with tiny clustered knots of light around the neckline like stars.

I am glowing and glittering all over, and the light is spreading through the water and swirling around me.

Never mind metaphors. Never mind lightning bugs.

Nick has *literally* just lit me up.

Above me, the sky is starting to change colour into a dark, gold-ish pink, brightening to red at the horizon,

and tiny dots of stars are forming in the blackness. In front of me, lights from the car park are bouncing off the water and an assistant is holding a soft golden light over my head. And below me, my dress is reflecting and shining through the water.

There is light everywhere. I'm surrounded by it, and covered in it, and full of it.

At some point I'm going to have to come back down to earth again. But for a few minutes, I'm going to stay exactly where I am.

Suspended somewhere a few metres above it.

"*Jyunbi ha iikai?*"

"Ready, Harriet?"

I nod blankly and silently lower myself into the freezing-cold water. Now that Nick's no longer touching me, it's incredibly, ridiculously cold.

And I don't care in the slightest.

"*Kirei dane?*" Haru says, gesturing around as the camera starts clicking and I stare into space somewhere over his left shoulder.

"Yes. Beautiful." Nick nods and looks at the mountain carved against the horizon behind me. "Without equal."

And then he looks directly at me.

72

Whatever Wilbur has done to protect me, it works.

The shoot goes perfectly. I sit quietly in the cold water for ten minutes, then bend into it, then lean forwards on my elbows. Finally I lie down completely so that Haru is shooting directly over me and my wet hair and glowing skirts are swirling around my head like I'm a water nymph trapped in some kind of magical, ghostly seaweed. I even manage not to inhale water into my lungs or drown.

Everyone is utterly delighted.

"*Shashin kara kannjyou ga afurete kuruyo, Harriet. Kimino kokoroga mieruyouda.*"

"There's so much *emotion* in these pictures, Harriet," Naho translates happily. "Haru says it's like he can see right into the middle of you."

Sugar cookies.

I quickly blink and try very hard to be a little less transparent.

*

322

Finally, Haru gives a satisfied nod, Naho wraps a towel around my freezing shoulders and we all splash and slip back out of the lake again, where Yuka is waiting for us.

I'm not even vaguely surprised. I'm going to guess she got less than three metres down the road before spying with her night-vision binoculars.

"*Umaku ittakashira*?" she asks Haru stiffly.

"*Sugoiyo*," Haru says with a nod, and I beam. That means 'excellent'. "*Honntouni sugoi noga toretayo*."

And then it happens again – Yuka's smiling. No, Yuka Ito is *grinning*.

Even Nick looks startled.

"Excellent," Yuka says, smoothing down her dress and carefully composing her face. She looks me up and down and then clicks her fingers. "What are we standing around for? I'm not paying anyone to catch pneumonia. Get my model dry."

Wilbur is going bonkers on the beach behind us. He's shouting and spinning in little circles with his pink jacket pulled over his head. "BOOM! I told you, Peaches! I told you my little Frankie-chops would knock it right out of the park!" He bends down and starts attempting Russian dancing on the pebbles.

Yuka frowns. "If you're going to be working directly

for me, William, I strongly suggest you stop that immediately."

Wilbur pauses in his crouch-jumping. "For the bajillionth time," he says indignantly: "It is Wilbur, with a bur and not an iam, and I would thank you to—" Then he stops and stands up straight. "Working for you?"

Yuka gives an almost imperceptible nod as she climbs back into her waiting car.

Wilbur's face goes all red and shaky, and then he physically explodes. "OH, MY MINI-HUMMINGBIRDS, THIS IS THE BEST DAY THAT HAS EVER BEEN BORN IF DAYS WERE BORN WHICH THEY'RE PROBABLY NOT BUT WHO CARES I MADE IT! I'M IN! I'M FINALLY IN PROPER FASSSHHHIIIOOON."

And he grabs my arm and starts swinging me round in manic giant circles. The way Nat and I used to spin years ago before I slipped and smashed into a park bench and had to be taken to hospital to get eight stitches in the back of my head.

I blush and spin, giddy and pink-cheeked.

I can't believe it: everything's going to be OK. The campaign's a success and nobody's angry with me. Wilbur's got his big job, and I've kept mine.

And Nick?

Nick *kissed* me.

Which I can't even think about until I've stopped being spun in nauseating circles. There's only so much discombobulation a brain can handle.

Wilbur finally lets go of me and I dizzily stagger a few metres into the nearly empty car park.

Nick is on the phone, facing the other way. He's talking quietly but I can still hear him.

And I really wish I couldn't.

"Poppy?" His voice sounds tight. "What are you talking about?"

There's a silence while my inner ear rebalances and the world slowly stops dipping and diving and gyrating around me. I think I'm going to be sick.

He's on the phone to her *already*?

"Of *course* I care," Nick continues impatiently. "You know I do. Don't be ridiculous."

Suddenly, all at once I'm aware of the water dripping from my hair down my nose and on to my top lip, and the icy droplets running down my arms and legs on to the floor, and the sogginess and dampness of my towel.

Apparently 300 million cells in our body die every single minute, and for the first time in my life I can actually feel them: shrinking and shrivelling all over me.

"I'm coming back now," Nick says. "Stay there."

And without even looking over his shoulder, Nick puts his phone back in his pocket, climbs on to a scooter and drives away.

Leaving me, unseen and speechless, behind him.

73

Here are a few new equations for you:

LOVE = 1 first kiss + 400 plus subsequent smaller kisses + 182 days + 278 daydreams + 186 phone calls + 2,087 texts + 1 last kiss.

LOVE = 4 nights spent crying − 2 months waiting for him to come back − 8 weeks of not being able to open a magazine or watch television in case he's in it − 63 days of getting sad every time you see a seagull or a lion or a raindrop − 11 days of pretending you're over him − a lifetime of never being able to eat lime-flavoured sweets, ever again.

LOVE = nearly ruining your GCSEs because all you're thinking about is him.

LOVE = turning into a total idiot.

I have wasted six *whole months* on Nick Hidaka.

In the space of six months, Mercury has gone round the sun *twice*. In six months, I could have walked all

327

the way across the width of Russia, or cycled over America, or sailed to Brazil. It took Jack Kerouac three weeks to write *On the Road*, and Charles Dickens six weeks to write *A Christmas Carol*. I could have written *five classic novels* in the time I spent thinking about a boy. I could have spent 444 days on Jupiter, and 391 days on Saturn and 1.4 really luxurious days on Venus.

Instead, I filled my head with big black curls and lips that curve up at the corner; with green smell; with shouted laughter; with a boy who disappears whenever he feels like it and says whatever he wants and only ever thinks about himself.

You know what?

I am never liking a boy again, ever. When I get back to school, I'm going to invest all the extra time and brain space into learning Apalachee or Tsetsaut or Susquehannock, or some other language that has been totally dead for more than a hundred years.

And it will *still* be more productive.

"Done, my little Twinkle-bottom?" Wilbur says, tapping me on the shoulder. I take one last look at the space Nick has disappeared into the way he always does, like the proverbial genie.

Am I done? Is that it? Am I finally ready to let go?

"Yep," I say, turning to Wilbur and taking a deep breath. "This time I think I am."

I spend the rest of the journey back to Tokyo quietly staring out of the Shinkansen window at little lights scattered at random through the fields, while Wilbur lightly snores beside me.

By the time we pull back into Tokyo station, all I want is to have a hot shower, pull my penguin pyjamas back on and climb into bed with a crossword puzzle.

But it doesn't look like that's an option.

"Poppet-cakes," Wilbur says in a daze as the train pulls to a stop. He rubs his eyes. "I know I have a *super* vivid imagination, but is that who I think it is?"

I look out of the window at a small huddle of people in black. Shion, Naho, Haru and a few assistants. And – almost entirely hidden in the middle – Yuka. Like some kind of tiny, fiercely protected, Faerie Queen.

"Perhaps they're here to give us presents?"

Maybe that's how modelling works. Maybe when you do a really good job at a shoot they all rush back to greet you at the station with a surprise basket of cupcakes or kittens and maybe a few celebratory personalised banners.

Then I see Wilbur's face. It's gone very white and

very wobbly, as if all the bones have just been whipped out through his nose.

"My little Bumble-bee," he says. "Maybe I'm not such a good meerkat after all."

74

We get off the train in silence.

Wilbur and I stand as close to each other on the platform as we possibly can.

"Come here," Yuka says. "Now, please. Both of you."

I've been to the headmaster's office at school plenty of times before. In Year Seven, I was called in to receive the Biology Award and the History Essay Award and the Debate Team Award. Then I went in again in Year Eight to accept the Physics Award and another History Essay Award. In Year Nine I got the English Award, and then in Year Ten I had to go back so that he could give me quite a large book voucher and inform me tensely that I wouldn't be winning any more awards because it was upsetting the other students.

But I have never, ever been called in because I'm in trouble.

I imagine it would feel exactly like this.

331

Wilbur and I look at each other, and then start creeping down the platform, like two little children playing *What's The Time, Mister Wolf?* I'm so hysterical with fear and nerves, I'm quite surprised when Yuka opens her mouth and the first line out of it isn't 'Dinner Time'.

"Who gave you your first break in modelling, Harriet."

Her voice is terrifyingly gentle: in exactly the way a cat gets very slinky just before it pounces on a mouse.

I clear my throat. Technically Nick 'discovered' me, but the tiny part of me that knows how to stay alive steps in just in time to stop me saying that. "You."

"And who has given you work ever since."

"You."

"And is *this*" – Yuka gestures serenely around her – "what normally happens. Are fifteen-year-old girls normally picked out of school trips and handed highly paid international jobs for a world-class designer with no castings, no competition, and no experience?"

I can't help but feel that this is a slightly leading question. "No?" I guess weakly.

"Correct. Most models go on hundreds of castings and are rejected hundreds of times. They struggle for years against themselves and each other. Very few make any real money. Those that do have a few years, at best, before they are thrown aside. Fashion is hard work, fickle and unforgiving. It eats girls like you for breakfast."

I suddenly feel as if I'm in a Roald Dahl novel. Hasn't Wilbur said something like this before?

"I understand."

"No, Harriet. You don't understand, because I made sure of it. I gave you an exclusive contract from the beginning to ensure you would not be part of that world. And I have done everything I can since to keep you away from it."

My eyes widen. Has my entire modelling career been a sort of glamorous babysitting?

"But… why?"

"I saw qualities in you I wanted to keep. And I was worried that the industry would take them away from you."

I have literally no idea what qualities she's talking about.

"Th-thank you?" I stutter, face flaming.

"And in return," Yuka continues, "you have shown me disrespect, arrogance and disobedience. You have lied, you have been late, and you have failed to follow a single one of the basic rules I gave you."

I shut my mouth abruptly and look at Wilbur in a panic. His entire face is now a shade of mossy green.

"N-n-no, Yuka," I say, but there's so little saliva in my mouth that my tongue's starting to make a sticky, clacking sound. "I didn't... I haven't... you don't understand—"

"Yes, Harriet," Yuka says quietly, "I think I do." She reaches into her bag, pulls out a newspaper in English and hands it to me. There's a full-page spread: a large photo of a much, much younger Yuka in black lace, and the caption:

INDUSTRY ICON STEALS DESIGNS

Fashion icon Yuka Ito has broken her contract with fashion powerhouse Baylee in order to set up her own label. A source close to the fashion icon says: "A small group of us models have been flown all over Asia for the launch of her new label and it's all super top secret. I was so excited to get my shoot in Tokyo."

A spokesperson for Baylee said: "Yuka Ito is currently signed exclusively to our label. While she did design these clothes herself, until her contract

expires, they technically belong to us. We are seeking legal advice."

Yuka Ito has so far been unavailable for comment.

"I-I-It wasn't me," I say urgently, looking back at the article. *'Us models'?* That's not even grammatically correct. "Although I know it *sounds* a bit like me I didn't tell anyone about—"

But I did, didn't I?

I knew precisely how important it was to keep my mouth shut – I promised Yuka and Wilbur that I would – and I still let the secret out. Trying to make two girls like me was more important than keeping my word.

"I should have explained earlier," Wilbur says, stepping forwards while a hot, burning wave of shame knocks the wind out of me. "It's not really my little Monkey-bum's fault, there's been some unprofessional activity going on—"

"Enough," Yuka says. "I'm not interested in hearing any more stories." She turns to me and says flatly: "Do you think it was a coincidence that you were positioned in Tokyo, Harriet."

I blink. "Umm..."

"Japan is my home. You were to be the face of

the whole campaign. But that was clearly the worst decision of all. So you're fired. I trust this is one instruction you won't have a problem following."

"Now just a second—" Wilbur starts, and Yuka turns to him.

"And you're fired too, William. Please take Harriet back to the flat, collect her things and go to the airport. Your tickets will be waiting for you there."

Wilbur looks as if somebody has snatched the battery out of him. He gets visibly smaller. "It's Wilbur," he says. "With a 'bur' and not an 'iam'."

"I don't think it really matters," Yuka says. "We will not be working together again."

75

Neither of us says another word for the rest of the journey home: we're both locked in our own private miseries.

I've been waiting to come back down to earth with a bump for a while now. Wilbur, on the other hand, has almost definitely never been near it before in his life.

Finally, the taxi stops and I gently tell Wilbur to wait in the car while I get my things. He stares at me blankly, and then looks at the leather seats. "I suppose," he says, "if I'm going to cry and snot uncontrollably it may as well be somewhere wipe-clean, right?"

"Umm, yes," I say with a tentatively supportive little pat. "That's the spirit?" Then I climb out of the car and make my way over to the flat.

Nobody else appears to be at home, so I tiptoe into the bedroom as quickly and as quietly as I can.

I need to get out of here before either Rin or Poppy returns.

337

I'm like a feather. I'm like a mouse. I'm like a ninja of invisibility and poise and—

"Are you going?"

Sugar cookies.

I turn around, and there is Princess Poppy: leaning against the doorframe with her perfect golden hair spilling over her shoulders and her perfect shoulders tensed and her perfect arms crossed and her perfect mouth set in a totally straight and expressionless line.

I start throwing items haphazardly into my suitcase. "Uh-huh."

"That's such a shame."

I flinch and start lobbing everything faster: trousers, shoes, shirts.

"I mean, what with you sneaking around with other people's boyfriends and stuff, it's a real pain that you can't stick around."

My stomach plummets. Poppy's cheeks are pink, her blue eyes are gleaming, and I've never, ever seen anyone look more angry or more perfect. "God, no, Poppy: I didn't—"

"I know *everything* so don't lie as well."

I shut my eyes briefly. Thanks, Nick. Thanks for blaming me. "Poppy, I didn't see it coming, I wasn't prepared. I would have pushed him away, I-I didn't mean to hurt you..."

"Why can't you just LEAVE. HIM. ALONE?"

I feel sick. Is this all my fault too?

Did I want Nick back so hard that I somehow turned it into a real, physical thing? Maybe I should start focusing my magical powers on curing cancer or winning a Nobel Prize, instead of hurting people.

"I should go," I say quietly. "I'm so sorry, Poppy. If I had known all the trouble I'd cause, I wouldn't have come."

I zip my suitcase up, even though some of my belongings are still scattered around the room, and start wheeling it into the hallway. My sleeve gets caught on the door handle, and I'm now so utterly desperate to get away I strongly consider leaving my arm here and just going home without it.

"I'm glad Rin did what she did," Poppy says as I finally yank myself free and stumble into the hallway. She puts her hand on the door and my stomach goes cold. "I think maybe it's best for everyone if you're not here."

And she slams the door behind me.

76

My New and Infinitely Inglorious Plan (NIIP) is now as follows:

- *Apologise to Wilbur.*
- *Fly home.*
- *Apologise to my parents (and the bump).*
- *Apologise to Nat and Toby.*
- *Make up some kind of T-shirt that says SORRY IN ADVANCE as a cunning pre-emptive tactic*
- *Go to bed for the rest of the summer.*

But when I come out of the flat I see Wilbur, leaning against a lamp-post, talking on his mobile phone. His voice is quiet and his shoulders are slumped. It's as if all the bright colours have been drained out of him.

And suddenly I can't face him.

I can't face anyone at all.

I'm not proud of what I'm about to do next, but I do it anyway.

I pick up my suitcase so that the wheels don't make giveaway squeaks. I tiptoe awkwardly behind Wilbur. I turn the corner of the street. I put my suitcase down.

And I run away.

All right: technically I *wheel* away.

I have no idea where I'm going. I'm just pulling my suitcase in the opposite direction to the flat.

I keep my eyes on the floor, and I walk. I walk and walk and walk in the hope that if I walk fast enough, far enough, I'll discover exactly what it is I can do to make everything slightly less terrible.

By the time I've calmed down enough to take in my surroundings, I've managed to meltdown all the way into the heart of Tokyo. There are brightly coloured lights everywhere: flashing on the streets, climbing up the enormous buildings, soaring into the sky. Ten-metre televisions are yelling from the corners, hundreds of people are swarming everywhere and every three seconds or so there's a high-pitched bird peep, followed by an answering peep from hundreds of metres away.

*

I am totally and utterly lost.

With a different type of panic setting in, I desperately try to find my bearings. There's a Starbucks, some kind of enormous train station and the biggest zebra crossing I have ever seen running across five different roads. It's so big that everyone has to wait on the pavement, and – when the peeps start – simultaneously scramble across the road in a vicious star shape: criss-crossing and bumping and shoving.

It's like a huge computer game testing coordination and timing, and I know from harsh experience that I have precisely neither of those things.

I wait six entire crossing cycles before I can find the courage to step out and then take my deepest breath and start pulling my suitcase across. There isn't much time: when the beeps start speeding up, you have ten seconds to reach the other side before the cars start again. And they *will* start. I've already witnessed at least two people put their hands out and physically *push* against car bonnets to stop themselves getting run over.

Getting hotter and hotter, I desperately try to manoeuvre my way across but my suitcase keeps getting stuck, people keep pushing me, blocking me, physically holding my arm so that they can go in front.

By the time the beeps start speeding up, I'm only halfway there. And I can't turn back because that would take longer and then I'll just have to do it all over again. Somebody shouts something in Japanese at me, and I realise – to my horror – that I've stopped, frozen on the road like a terrified rabbit.

My heart is hammering, my eyes are starting to fill up.

I've managed to take a bad situation and make it a hundred times worse, all on my own.

Well, me and the Tokyo road planners.

I've just begun to start running to catch up with the people ahead of me when I hear a *whoosh*.

The world spins around.

And the road jumps up to meet me.

77

Thankfully I don't die.

The bicycle just clips me, and the only real damage is a bloody knee and elbow and quite a large hole in my leggings, pride and mental stability. A tiny lady swoops down to pick me up and guides me gently across the road. By the time I've stopped shaking enough to thank her, she's gone.

Rocking my suitcase on its side, I ignore the dubious glances from the crowds and sit heavily on the floor next to it.

I want to go home.

I want to go home more than I have ever wanted anything before in my entire life.

I want to be in my tiny stupid bedroom, putting fossils on overcrowded shelves and trying to stop my dog from eating talcum powder. I want to be studying Shakespeare and Milton and star constellations; I want to be worrying about chemistry formulas and physics

equations instead of dresses and poses and octopuses and kisses. I want to see my dad dancing around the living room and I want to see Annabel laughing at him and Hugo getting all over-excited. I want to see Nat roll her eyes at me and Toby wipe his nose on his jumper. I even want to see Alexa. Nice, predictable Alexa. Who hates me with the least amount of effort and national newspaper coverage possible.

I just want everything to be exactly how it was.

Maybe this is what happens to the butterfly and the frog. Maybe they go to so much effort to grow wings and legs and run away, and when they see a little bit of the world they just feel sad and lonely and end up hopping straight back home again. Where they belong.

I pick my phone up and ring Dad. There's no answer.

I try Annabel: her phone is off.

Then I try Bunty: engaged.

I call Nat and get her voicemail again, then try Toby. It rings a few times before suddenly switching off.

Did Toby just *hang up* on me? Am I now so pathetic that my own stalker just cancelled my call?

That does it.

I pull my jumper tightly over my head. And I start crying.

78

I don't know how long I cry for.

In fairness, people don't normally time themselves. All I know is that I cry long enough for my face to get all swollen and weird-shaped, and not quite long enough to forget what it is I'm crying about.

Not one person stops to ask if I'm OK. Not a single stranger asks if they can help. Not a human soul interrupts to offer poignant words of wisdom and kindness and—

"Are you OK?"

I sniffle and wipe my nose on my jumper. All right. Maybe I should have been a bit more patient before I attacked the entire human race. I nod.

"Are you sure?"

The voice is muffled and indistinct. "Yes. Thank you."

"Because," it continues, "for somebody who thinks they're OK, you spend a hell of a lot of time rolling around on pavements."

Slowly I remove the jumper and wipe my eyes.

347

"Hey," Lion Boy says with a small smile. "There's my girl."

I look at Nick, with his beautiful face and his beautiful hair and his beautiful cheekbones. I look at the way he's slouched, and the way his lips curve as if the world is permanently, irresistibly funny.

To summarise, I look at how incredibly beautiful and perfect he is.

"Go to hell," I say, pulling my jumper back over my head.

I hear Nick sit down next to me. I immediately whip my head out again like the furious tortoise I am. "I'm not sure your geographical knowledge of the afterlife is very strong," I say through my teeth. "Do I need to draw you a map?"

"I didn't realise this was your pavement."

"*Actually*," I snap, and then stop. Stupid Japanese laws about public pavements. "Leave me alone, Nick. I mean it. *Now*."

He opens his mouth to respond, and then sees the blood on my hands and knee. "God, Harriet. What happened? Are you hurt?"

I jerk away from his hand. "No," I snap, struggling to stand up. "I am not hurt."

I'm suddenly so angry it feels like the contents of my chest are about to rush out of my ears like the magma inside Mount Tambora in 1815 (the biggest ever recorded volcanic eruption). "Get lost, please. Go away. Go on, *shoo*."

Nick's lips twitch and his nostrils flare. "Did you just *shoo* me, Harriet Manners?"

And my head bursts.

"*WHO THE SUGAR COOKIES DO YOU THINK YOU ARE, NICK?* You may be a supermodel and you may be beautiful and charming and cute and funny but you're also just a *boy*! You're just a boy, and I am a girl, and every time I breathe in there is a molecule that used to be part of a dinosaur in it which I assimilate into my body which means that I AM PART DINOSAUR, POSSIBLY T-REX, AND YOU DO NOT GET TO TREAT ME LIKE THIS."

I'm so swept up in a torrent of blind fury that I am making little claws at random passers-by. Nick blinks and then grabs one of my T-Rex hands. "Hang on a second, Harriet—"

"And OK," I continue fiercely, shaking him off, "you're probably part dinosaur too, but you're probably a Dilophosaurus with a rubbish frilly neck or a Linhenykus which only had a little pointed finger where an arm should be like this." I hold my forefingers out by my armpits and wave them around uselessly.

Nick snorts and I take a cross little hoppy step towards him.

"Oh, *that's* it. Am I not *mature* enough for you? Not *interesting* enough for you? Too *silly* for your epic adultness? Well *you're* the problem, Nick. Not me. Don't you *ever* try and make me want to be someone else again. I am just *fine* the way I am." I grab the handle of my suitcase. "And this time *you* can sit and watch while *I* disappear."

I turn to sweep elegantly away, but Nick holds on to my suitcase. I cannot *believe* that on top of everything he has now totally ruined my dramatic exit.

"Can I say something now?" he says, lifting an eyebrow. "Or do you have more second-rate dinosaurs you'd like to compare me to?"

I scowl and stick my nose in the air. "Whatever."

"Great. First of all, it turns out somebody has been sabotaging the campaign. I only found out at the lake. I had no idea before. We thought you were just being clumsy as usual."

OH MY GOD HOW DARE HE—

Oh, OK. I suppose that's a reasonable assumption to make. "I already figured *that* out yesterday, genius," I say, rolling my eyes. "Poppy and Rin."

"No," Nick says, frowning. "Not Rin. She actually helped us sort everything out."

I abruptly sit down on top of my suitcase. "Oh."

"Harriet, Rin hasn't got a bad bone in her body – plus she adores you. She's getting a T-shirt made with both your faces on it. She wanted to make your friendship 'official'."

I'm so relieved I feel like crying. Of all the girls I've ever thought might be my friend – other than Nat – Rin's my absolute favourite. I'm suddenly filled with so much happiness I have to desperately claw back a few remaining strands of anger to finish what I need to say. "So it was Poppy. *Big* surprise."

"It was to me."

"I bet," I say in my most sarcastic voice. "Don't you know your own *girlfriend* very well?"

"Usually," Nick says, raising his eyebrows. "But Poppy's not my girlfriend. She never has been."

79

There's always this excellent moment in really good action films where everybody's kicking and fighting and there are legs and arms and bodies everywhere, and suddenly somebody leaps into the air and it all goes very slow, and very quiet, and you just *know* that the end is somehow coming.

As if we're all hanging in the air, waiting for somebody to pull the move that changes everything.

"*Uh?*" I say.

"I have never dated Poppy," Nick repeats, and there it is: the metaphorical boot in my face. "*Ever.* She's just a model I worked with on that D&G shoot in Paris. I had absolutely no idea she'd told you we were together until Rin called me at the lake."

I suddenly hear that overheard phone call again. '*Poppy?*'

He wasn't talking *to* her: he was talking *about* her.

"But—" I try to swallow but it's not really working. "You came to the flat... she said—"

352

"Exactly. *She* said. I didn't. We were doing another shoot that evening, but the reason I'd raced over was to see you. I was waiting for you at the airport, but you looked so happy and excited to be in Tokyo... I guess I didn't want to confuse things. So I decided to turn up at your flat instead and do it properly."

My mind makes a little whirring rewind motion.

He *did* turn up a few minutes after I did.

And at no stage did Poppy *ever* refer to Nick as My Boyfriend in front of Nick. She kissed his *cheek*.

"B-but what about the sumo match?"

"I waited for you." The corner of Nick's top lip twitches. "For *three hours,* Manners. But then you made it brutally clear you were over me."

I suddenly remember his white, punctured face on the steps.

He wasn't confused, he was *hurt*.

I feel abruptly guilty, and also a tiny bit pleased with myself. *Ha!* I am an excellent, excellent actor. Nat is going to be *delighted* when I tell her.

"So at the lake..."

"I had to give it one last shot. But you gunned me down again, so the kiss" – he shrugs and looks pained – "I guess I was kind of saying goodbye."

It's a good thing I'm sitting down, because if I wasn't

standing would be a bit of a problem. You know how my bedroom always looked strange and unfamiliar once the lights went off? Now it's the other way round. The lights have gone back on, and everything looks completely different. Unexpected. Brilliant.

"But..." I pause and blush.

The sumo. The lake.

Nick's been totally innocent the entire time.

Oh my God, I have been *so horrible* to him. I said he was part Linhenykus. Nobody deserves that. Except maybe for—

I blink. "Why would Poppy pretend like this? And how did she even know about me?"

He shrugs. "Poppy's the kind of girl who gets exactly what she wants. I think she kind of lost control when it didn't work this time. I suppose she thought if she believed in it enough, and if she got rid of you, I'd end up with her. Which I wouldn't, because she's a nightmare and also" – he twists his finger up to his head in a way that politely suggests *bat-poop crazy* – "and... and I talked about you in Paris. *A lot*. She basically had an entire character-assassination arsenal at her disposal. Sorry about that."

I look at Nick's beautiful face, all screwed up and flushed and anxious, and suddenly know *exactly* why

Poppy put in so much effort. "But... Nick, you *dumped* me, remember?"

"No, Harriet," Nick sighs. "I told you *really* clearly that I was gonna leave you alone for a couple of months while you did your exams. I should've realised you'd zone out and stop listening – you *always* do that when you panic. I should've sent a supporting document or an email afterwards or recorded a message or something."

And the last piece of the puzzle slots into place with a click, like an enormous, romantic Rubik's Cube.

All I actually remember from that conversation over two and a half months ago is 'we shouldn't see or speak to each other any more' before I went into internal meltdown mode.

And, though I'll obviously never admit it to the Nobel Prize committee judges, there *was* quite a lot of time spent with Nick when I should've been revising.

Like, almost all of it.

Who wants to revise biology when you're going out with a supermodel? Even *I'm* not that much of a geek.

Oh my God. I am *such an idiot.*

Nick smiles awkwardly. "I said I'd be back when

your exams finished. But you made me think I'd left it too late."

The text. It arrived the day after the end of my exams.

"So… you still like me then?"

"Don't you get it yet, Harriet?" Nick says in total exasperation. "I *like* that you know about the stars in rain and the shape of clouds and the heartbeat rate of a hummingbird. I like that you know that giraffes don't have vocal cords and sharks can't stop moving. I like the way you stick your little nose in the air and stomp your feet and frown just before you laugh. I like how your ears go red when you're embarrassed and your freckles get darker when you're angry. I like that little crumpled paper ball your chin makes before you cry. I like that when you're shouting at me you physically pretend you're a T-Rex. I like *you*, Harriet. Why is that the only thing in the universe you find so hard to wrap your big fat brain around?"

I suddenly feel like I'm at the lake again: as if I'm covered from head to toe in lights. I have absolutely no idea what to say to any of that.

"My brain isn't big and fat. It has a totally normal fat quantity, which is roughly half of its dry mass."

Oh. Apparently I do.

Nick grins. "My point exactly."

It feels like two strings have been attached to the corners of my mouth and somebody is pulling them upwards. "And is this all because of you?" I gesture around me. "Am I in Tokyo because you made it happen?"

"Nope." Nick shakes his head. "This time I'm here because of you. I actually begged Yuka for this job. I had to organise *dresses* and stuff. It nearly killed me."

Nick pulls a face, but underneath the usual calmness is something I haven't seen before: uncertainty. And I suddenly realise with a pang that all of this has been for me.

Nick found me, seven months ago. For me, he left. For me, he came back again. He made me laugh when I needed to; he annoyed me when it helped me; he saved me when I couldn't save myself.

For me, he tries to keep it simple.

There are 7,123,024,873 people in the world, and Nick keeps choosing me.

I look at him – sitting on the pavement, pulling at the holes in his jeans – and he suddenly looks so earnest, and so worried, and so nervous, and so totally *un-Nick*, that there are only two possible things I can do.

So I do both of them at the same time.

I leap up from my suitcase and I lob myself at him so quickly he falls over slightly and has to steady himself on his elbow. "Thank you," I say into his ear. "Thank you for liking me."

And I kiss him as hard as I can.

80

Reasons to Think About Nick

1. *He always thinks about me.*

I don't know how long we kiss for.

Let's just say it's long enough to make the entire world and everybody in it melt and turn to vapour, and not quite long enough to get us arrested.

Which is good. My urge to see the inside of a Japanese prison is only a very small and transient one.

"OK, I just have one more question," I say when I finally pull away, flushed and beaming with my lips all tingly and my heart all swoopy and my hair all sticky-outy, like a small dog who's just been harassed with a hairdryer.

"Of course you do." I'm pleased to note that Nick looks exactly the same as me, if not a bit beamier and more rumpled.

359

"How did you find this all out? Poppy didn't confess all, did she?"

"Obviously not. FYI she's currently on her way back to England. Yuka is absolutely furious and she's made sure Poppy's agent knows it. I think Poppy's next modelling job will be staring vacantly out from a kitchenware catalogue with her hands on her hips," Nick says. "Rin, Bunty and Wilbur helped, but most of it came from somebody else."

"Who?"

Nick points into the distance. "Him."

I follow his finger and stare at the huge crowd of people walking across the zebra crossing, dodging the bicycles. Then I stare a little bit harder. Because walking through the middle of them – wearing a T-shirt with a guitar drawn on it and a bright purple velvet jacket – is Toby.

Right, I give up.

I clearly know nothing about people at all.

Slowly, I stand up and wait for Toby to reach me. He starts playing *Three Blind Mice* on his T-shirt. After a few wrong notes he shrugs. "It's so very important to make an entrance, isn't it, Harriet? Although in hindsight, I wish I'd worn the drum-kit

T-shirt. It's a bit easier to play under pressure."

I stare at him, too startled to speak.

"Hey, Nick," he adds chirpily, waving with his spare hand. "I liked the wellies you were wearing earlier. Do you think they'd go with this outfit, or would it get a bit sweaty around the knee area?"

"*Toby*," I finally manage. "What are you *doing* here?"

"I'm your stalker, Harriet. I've been here the whole time. What kind of terrible stalker would I be if I wasn't?"

"But—"

"I'm getting really good at it, right? I don't think you knew I was here *at all.*"

"But *how* are you here? You're not even sixteen yet."

"Oh, I'm here with my parents. They said we could go on holiday anywhere I liked to celebrate the end of my exams, but I just couldn't decide where to go. That is until some information came to my attention last week." And he actually winks at me. "They think I've been *really* busy with a school project."

Toby looks extremely chuffed with himself. "I mean, you're at my school, right? And this was a *fascinating* project. I found all sorts of incriminating evidence."

He pulls out photos and crumpled bits of paper and audio recordings and maps and drawings.

All this time I thought I was alone. But really I was surrounded constantly by people who cared about me: Toby, Nick, Wilbur, Bunty, Rin. I just couldn't see them.

I don't know whether to be incredibly touched or slightly creeped out.

"Toby – why on earth would you follow somebody *6,000 miles*?"

"5,937 miles, to be precise." He points behind me. "Do you know what that is, Harriet?"

Oh dear. I patiently follow the direction of Toby's finger. "It's a statue of a dog."

"Not just any dog, Harriet. That's a dog called Hachiko. He was a brown Akita dog and he was adopted in 1924 by a Tokyo professor called Hidesaburo Ueno."

"Ah." I nod politely. After everything he's done, the least I can do is listen to one of his random facts. I make people do this for me all the time.

"Every day for a year Hachiko would come and greet Hidesaburo after work here, at this exact spot at Shibuya station. In 1925 the professor suffered a stroke at work and died, but Hachiko returned to the same spot every single day for nine years waiting for him to come back."

Tears suddenly spring to my eyes.

"The dog waited for the rest of his life, and when he eventually died the people of Tokyo built a statue in the place he used to wait to commemorate his loyalty, and the fact that he never, ever gave up."

I bite my lip. That's one of the most beautiful stories I've ever heard.

It's also exactly why I love dogs. Kylie Minogue would have waited about thirty seconds before going home with the next person who had food in their handbag.

"But it still doesn't explain what you're doing here."

"Yes, it does, Harriet. I'm your Hachiko."

And before I realise what's about to happen, Toby darts forward and kisses me.

81

OK:

- Two kisses with two different boys in five minutes is not something I want to encourage.
- Ever.
- All kisses are not the same.
- *Ewwwwwww.*

Toby really goes for it.

I mean: he really, *really* goes for it. He twists his head from left to right as if he's trying to unscrew a light bulb from my mouth, and then attempts to lick my top lip, and then sort of opens and shuts his mouth like a baby bird trying desperately to get fed.

He tangles my hair in his fingers so I can't get away without physically pushing him with both of my hands and losing quite a few strands in the process.

Which I do, obviously.

"*Toby,*" I snap, wiping my mouth on my hand.

364

"*Seriously*. You have to wait for a *signal* before you kiss a girl. I did not give you any kind of signal *at all*."

Toby looks completely undisturbed. "Did you not? I thought I saw one."

"*What* signal did I give you?"

"You were looking very pretty, Harriet. And kind of boggle-eyed, like a little owl."

I sigh. "That's very nice of you, Toby, but a) that's just my face and b) *prettiness* is not and never will be a kissing signal. It's important that you realise that as soon as possible."

I glance anxiously at Nick who looks – if anything – slightly amused. Isn't he supposed to be fighting for my precious honour round about now? Isn't he supposed to be throwing Toby against a wall and telling him not to touch His Woman again?

What kind of rubbish love triangle *is* this?

"That was my very first ever kiss," Toby tells Nick. "How do you think it looked from there, buddy?"

Nick grins as I blink at both of them. "I think maybe you went in a bit too fast," he says. "She looks a bit shocked."

"Right." Toby gets a little notepad out of his velvet jacket which – I've just realised – was his Charlie and the Chocolate Factory costume from two Halloweens ago. He scribbles something and then frowns. "Perhaps a simple customer announcement would be best? *I am about to launch a kiss*. That kind of thing?"

Nick shouts with laughter.

For God's sake. Bella never had to put up with this kind of friendly, bonding nonsense in *Twilight*.

"You realise I'm still here, right?"

"Kissing is important stuff, Harriet," Toby says solemnly. "We boys need to discuss it just as much as girls do, you know. And we can't just read *Cosmopolitan*." He pauses. "Actually, we *can* but when our mums find it under our beds we have to have really long and confusing conversations about it."

"Tobes, I really think maybe we should look into getting you a hobby other than me."

"Actually I don't want to be rude, Harriet," he says thoughtfully, "but you're not quite as good at this whole kissing thing as I had hoped. You just kind of stood there, smacking me quite briskly with your hands. It was a bit of a disappointment, if I'm being perfectly honest."

My eyes widen, and Nick quickly stands up and puts his arm around me. He kisses my forehead. "I'll volunteer for now," he laughs.

Then he holds up his other arm. A taxi stops

immediately and Nick pokes his head through the window. "*Sumimasen*," he says flawlessly. "*Tokyo-eki made dekirudake hayaku onegai shimasu.*"

I keep forgetting Nick's half Japanese. I may have to ask him to speak in other languages all the time. I had never realised bilinguality could be so attractive. "Where are we going?"

"Back to the beginning," Nick says with a grin, opening the car door for Toby and me.

I'm just not sure which one.

82

Here is my absolute favourite fact of all time:

99.99999999999999999 per cent of every atom consists of empty space.

It sounds simple, but do you know what that means? It means that every single thing in front of you *right now* – the chair you're sitting on, the shoes on your feet, the glasses on your nose, the chocolate in your mouth – is mostly not there.

And *that includes you*.

I know: mind-blowing, right? It doesn't matter how many times I'm told this fact, it's almost entirely impossible to process. And when it finally sinks in, it's hard not to find it a bit overwhelming.

As I open the door to the flat I'm hit by a waft of sequins and lace and beetroot and perfume as Bunty, Rin and Wilbur all launch themselves at me. Within

seconds a glitter-covered Rin is wrapped around my neck. There appear to be pink feathers in her hair. And some in Wilbur's too.

I *knew* I shouldn't have left them alone with my grandmother.

"Oh, Harry-chan!" Rin says into my T-shirt collar. "We are so very mistakable about Poppy! Kylie found cockroach box in her handbag! She is a naughty, naughty pretty girl!"

I notice the distinctly missing affectionate 'chan' from Poppy's name. I think that's as harsh as Rin is going to get. "I'm sorry," I say, patting her on the back. Then I say what I haven't said for ten years: "Umm – would you like to be friends?"

"Ooooh!" Rin says, clapping her hands in delight. "Yes please! I will come to seeing you in London! I will see Big Ben and Wheel and wear Top Hat and we shall be spoiling for choice and shall have BIG BLAST!" I laugh and Rin suddenly spots Toby. "It is nice to finally meet you," she says, bowing slightly. "I am Rin. You must be Ted."

"I'm not Ted, I'm Toby. Did you know that teddy bears have killed more people than real bears have?"

Rin's eyes widen and she turns to me. "*Harry-chan!* He is just like you!"

I nod and grin at him fondly. "Yup."

Toby's eyebrows raise. "Are you going to try and kiss me again, Harriet? Because I strongly suggest you check your emails first in case I blow your mind and reading is rendered physically impossible. I think there might be something important."

I frown at him and immediately turn and head straight to the bedroom to get my laptop. Seriously. Do I have to change all my passwords *again*?

Through the thin paper walls I can hear Wilbur's high-pitched voice in the bathroom. With every second it's sounding more and more like the agent I know and love.

"Really?" (Pause.) "For diddling?" (Pause.) "For *shiddling, diddling*?" (Pause.) "For *shiddling diddling middling piddling*?" (Pause.) "*NEW YORK?* OH MY DONKEY-CAKES! Are you McKidding me? I am the *King* of interested!"

There's another pause and then Wilbur's head pops round the bedroom door. He puts his hand over the receiver. "Yuka's not the only designer in the world, my little Caramel-macchiato," he whispers with a wink. "Let's not forget that." And his head disappears again.

I blink at the door, and then back at my computer.

For the attention of Harriet Manners
From the office of Yuka Ito

It would seem that new information has come to light. As a result, I would like to apologise and am withdrawing my offer of redundancy, effective immediately.
   Yuka Ito

And, just like that, my adventure has come full circle. Things are back exactly as they were at the beginning. As if I'm still the geek hiding under a table at The Clothes Show Live, just about to be thrown haphazardly into the world of fashion. As if I'm still a girl who doesn't know who she is or who she's supposed to be.

   As if nothing has changed at all.

   Except it has.

   I take the deepest breath I can find, and then type:

Dear Yuka,

   I would like you to release me from my exclusive contract with you. I will not be accepting my job back.

   I really appreciate everything you have done for me, but whatever those qualities you see in

me are, they're not going anywhere. This is me, and I'm stronger than I look.

I want you to give me the freedom to grow up, even if it's scary. I want that adventure.

Thank you for everything you have taught me. Goodbye.

Harriet

I'm just about to press SEND when Bunty wafts into the room.

"Did you get an apology, sweetie? I'll give that to Yuka, at least. She always knows when she's backed into a corner."

I blink at my grandmother for a few seconds, and then my brain clicks. *Nice to see you.* When she saw Yuka outside the Arcade Hall, she said *nice to see you.* Not *nice to meet you.*

"Do you *know* Yuka?"

"Of course I do, sweetie. We've run in the same circles for years. I've been trying to tell her what's been going on this whole time, but she just refused to listen. Typical Yuka. All talent, no ears."

I stare at Bunty in amazement.

I don't want to sound ungrateful, but can people *please* start telling me stuff?

"AND BOOOOOOM!" I hear Wilbur shout at the top of his voice. "LONDON CAN KISS MY GUCCI BOOTIES. AMERICA, HERE I COME."

"Now, darling," my grandmother says as I send the email and shut my laptop. Without warning she slams me into her embroidered breasts again. "It's been lovely spending some proper, quality time with you, but it's time to get going."

I blink in disappointment. I was really starting to like her. I was kind of hoping we could spend a few weeks getting to know each other properly, and that it might be the start of a proper granddaughter-grandmother relationship of the non-Little Red Riding Hood/Wolf variety. "*Now?*" I ask her boob sadly.

"I'm afraid so, darling. We have a plane to catch."

"*We?*"

"Yes, sweetheart."

Bunty pulls back and I suddenly notice the bright expression on her face. She looks exactly as I felt earlier at the lake.

"Annabel has just gone into labour."

83

Oᴋ.

I don't want to point out the obvious, but Annabel has gone into labour an entire *month* early. My new sibling is clearly a maverick with no respect at all for plans, schedules, appointments, or other people's itineraries.

Just like my father.

Fifteen hours later, Bunty and I emerge at Heathrow only to be hit by a whirlwind of shiny hair and handbag and scarf and perfume, like a kind of girl-bomb.

"You're *home*!" Nat shouts, almost knocking me over. "*Finally!*"

I look over her shoulder at the trolley she just hurdled. I have never seen her run that fast for anything, ever. Maybe she shouldn't have given up PE for A Level after all.

"What are you doing here?" I laugh as she covers

374

my cheek in little hard bird-pecks. "I thought you'd still be in France."

Nat flushes and manages to look cheeky and delighted all at the same time. "Erm, well..."

I narrow my eyes at her. My best friend looks totally incandescent. She's also wearing a lot less make-up than normal and her hair hasn't been straightened. Her natural scraggy curls are back and her fringe is slightly sticking out on the left-hand side. It's *very* un-Nat-like. "Nat, what's going on?"

"Hmm?" My Best Friend picks a bit of fluff off my hoody. "So – how was it? Did you see any dogs in dresses? Did people talk Japanese at you?"

"Excuse me," Bunty says, smiling and handing me a little carton of coconut water. "Stay hydrated, darling. Air conditioner is a killer. I'm just going to go and find us a taxi outside."

And she scoots off, her flip-flops making a *clack clack clack* sound on the floor. I turn back to Nat. "Right," I say. "What's happened?"

"Well, umm..." She clears her throat, looks at the ceiling and then looks at the floor. "Ooh – I like your shoes. Are they new?"

"Of course my shoes aren't new, Nat. My shoes

are never new. Stop changing the subject."

Two red spots appear on her cheeks. "I *may* have…" she starts. "I mean, it's *possible* that… I *could* have…"

"No offence, Nat, but this is like trying to talk to a dolphin. Try to get a whole sentence out."

"I met a boy."

The coconut water I'm sipping gets spat all over her.

"The guy with the *green lycra*?" I shout. "The guy with the *olive oil*? The guy with the *meaningful salt*?"

"It's not like that," Nat says indignantly. "He's… lovely. And sweet. And *super hot*." She goes a bit dreamy. "And he has this way of cracking his knuckles when he's nervous that's *so cute*. And he can *totally* kill it at Guitar Hero. And he has this amazing lilting accent like his voice is… on a boat or something."

Like his voice is on a boat?

"Oh my God, Nat. You've got it really bad."

She blushes even deeper. "I know. That's kind of why I'm here. Mum found out and dragged me home again. She said falling in love was enough punishment for anyone so we were quits."

I laugh. "Is that why you disappeared?"

"Not really. Oh, Harriet, I feel so embarrassed. I

gave you such a hard time about Nick. I don't think I quite realised until I met François that it's not really like that. You can't protect yourself from it. Nothing exists but them."

"François?" I laugh. "He's French and his name is François?"

"Some French people are called François, Harriet," Nat says crossly. "It's a thing. It happens."

I smile and we start heading outside the airport. "You were wrong about Nick, by the way. I'll tell you all about it in the taxi."

"You know what?" Nat sighs. "Maybe I don't know anywhere near as much about boys as I thought I did. They're quite complicated, aren't they? I think this might be the start of a lifetime of confusion."

She links her arm in mine. "So, did you have a good time? Did it live up to the epic Flow Chart? You know we've still got loads of time left to do that stuff together."

I think back to the bright lights, and the booming televisions, and the beautiful shrines, and the madness of Harajuku. I think about Mount Fuji, and the Shinkansen, and Tsukiji and the video arcade and the sumo hall; about my lit-up dress and Charlie and Kylie Minogue and the cockroach. I think about Yuka and

Bunty and Toby and Haru and Naho and Shion; about Rin, who waved us off at the airport wearing a pink tutu and gave me the friendship bracelet I'm wearing now.

I think about Nick, who kissed me again before I got on the plane and had to literally push me into check-in because I decided last minute I wasn't going anywhere.

Then I think about how different I feel to the way I did when I went there. As if I'm still me, but stronger. As if I've found my wings, and I finally know what to do with them.

"Yes," I say with a grin as Bunty opens a taxi door and we climb in. "As far as adventures go, I'd say Tokyo was pretty coolioko."

84

I don't like hospitals.

Let's be honest: nobody actually does. Ostensibly they're about making people better, but they're not. They're about reminding us that at some stage we all get sick, and we all hurt, and we all get lonely, and sometimes there's nothing anybody can do about any of it.

The only thing on my mind as we walk through the big metal doors into the waiting room is that the last time I was in this exact hospital, I had a mum. And when I left three days later, I didn't.

I suddenly feel horribly sick – right through to the middle – and it hits me just how much my feelings towards this baby are about the fact that it might take Annabel away from me. Because that's what babies do, isn't it? Babies change everything.

As we walk across the big green floors, I try to focus on the rhythm of my breathing and the beating of

379

my heart and the tap of my trainers. Then I feel Nat gently grab my hand. "It's going to be OK, Harriet. Look."

I glance up and there's Dad doing some kind of Riverdance in the hospital corridors. Every time a nurse or doctor walks past, he grabs them and spins them in a little triumphant circle.

This must happen more often than you'd think, because they just wait patiently until he lets them go and then continue with a slight smile down the corridor.

Nat kisses my cheek. "I'll go and get a cup of tea. See you in a few minutes?"

"Offspring Number One!" Dad shouts across the hospital as my non-kissing soulmate disappears through the doors. He immediately wrestles me into a bear hug and tries to whirl me in another circle. "You're back! That's your name henceforth, by the way. Or maybe 'Good' and I shall call your sibling 'Bad' and we'll have an entire set of Manners."

He lets go and I steady myself. "Is..." I swallow. "Does that mean Annabel's OK?"

Dad looks at my face and then wraps me up even tighter. "Of course she's OK, sweetheart. She was always going to be OK."

I can feel my chin starting to do the crumpled-up paper-ball wobble. Dad kisses the top of my head and pulls away. I finally notice his T-shirt. In big letters in red marker pen it says **MY DAUGHTER'S A SUPERMODEL**, and underneath, in little letters, it says: **THE OTHER'S JUST SUPER**.

"It's a girl? I have a baby sister?"

"You certainly do," Dad says with a grin that almost cracks his face in half. He ruffles my hair, and for the first time in my entire life I don't scowl and try to smooth it back again. "I think it's time you met her."

85

The room is totally quiet.

Sunshine is streaming through a window, and there's a small, comforting beeping sound. Annabel's sitting calmly in bed in a clean white nightgown. Her blonde hair is smoothed into its normal impeccable bun, her face is peaceful and her cheeks are rosy. If it wasn't for the fact that she isn't wearing a suit and there's a small, snuffling bundle of material in her arms, you wouldn't know anything had changed at all.

Except it has.

I lurk nervously in the doorway while Dad bounds straight into the room like an excited Labrador. "WIFE-FACE!" he says loudly, and then claps his hand over his mouth. "Sorry," he says in a fake whisper. "I meant wife-face, lower caps." He leans over the bed and peers at the lump in Annabel's arms. "When do her eyes open?"

"I didn't give birth to a kitten, Richard. Her eyes have already opened. She's asleep."

"Don't be so sure, Annabel," Dad says firmly. "They're smarter than they look. Harriet used to have this trick of pretending to be asleep when actually she was listening and storing it all up and getting ready to spout it all back out again just when you least expect it. We need to be prepared. This one looks wily too."

"Good," Annabel says, affectionately rearranging a few of the blankets. "The wilier the better." Then she looks up to the doorway. "Mum? Can I have a word?"

Bunty nods and jingles into the hospital room. She's surprisingly quiet.

"I'm sorry, Mum," Annabel continues. "I've been far too harsh. You've done an amazing job taking care of Harriet. We couldn't have done it without you."

There's a pause and I see Annabel searching for the right words, which is something I have literally never seen before.

"I've changed my mind about your kind offer. We'd love to have you stay with us for the first month or two." There's a pause. "*I* would love you to stay."

Bunty kisses Annabel on the forehead.

"Thank you, darling. I know I haven't been around in the past as much as I should, but I'd really like to change that."

She can be such hard work sometimes, you know.

I don't think I can handle any more.

It's my first baby, and you know I love her to pieces but...

I just think it's best for everyone if she's not here.

They weren't talking about me.

They were talking about Bunty.

A tiny squeak escapes from my throat, and Annabel looks up. She stares at me for a split second and then twists towards Dad.

"Take Tabitha, please," she says, gently thrusting the bundle at him.

"*Tabitha?*" Dad says. It's only when he takes the baby and fits her swiftly into the crook of his arm that I remember he's actually done this before. "Tabitha Manners? As in Tabitha from *Bewitched*?"

Annabel laughs. "It's also Aramaic for *gazelle* and the cat in Beatrix Potter so it should keep us all happy. I'm sure if we do enough research we can find a few record-breaking owls and koalas too." Then she turns back to me. "Come here, Harriet."

I walk towards her and sit gently on the bed. With a slight wince, Annabel bends down and gets a piece of paper out of her handbag. She hands it to me.

On it, written in perfectly neat handwriting, double underlined, it says:

THE MANNERS FAMILY

- HARRIET
- TABITHA
- RICHARD
- ANNABEL
- BUNTY

"You see that?" she says quietly, pointing to it. "You're still at the top of my list, Harriet."

She nudges me with her shoulder, and my world suddenly falls straight back together as if it never exploded in the first place.

"Oh, *what*?" Dad moans, leaning over us. "Are you *kidding* me? I'm *third*? It's my surname in the first place: I gave it to you little name-stealers." He looks at the bundle and gently prods it with a finger. "I've got your card marked, Missy, and I know where you live."

"Can I see her?" I ask nervously. "My sister?"

Dad grins and carefully hands me the bundle, and I stare down at Tabitha.

I don't believe it. I actually do not believe it.

Not only is my new sister a maverick with no respect at all for timetables and plans, apparently she has no interest in statistics either. Less than two per cent of the world has red hair and it's a recessive gene.

She's even more ginger than I am.

"Another top model in the making," Dad says proudly, looking at both of us. "Annabel, you are so incredibly lucky I'm genetically such a hotty."

At that precise moment, Tabitha opens huge blue eyes and looks at Dad with a calm, unimpressed expression that says: *Seriously? Billions of fathers in the world and I got landed with this plonker?*

And I am suddenly absolutely certain that I'm going to love her more than I've ever loved anything, ever. Even maths. Even English. Even history.

Even more than *physics*.

My phone beeps. I quickly give my tiny, adorable sister a gentle kiss on the head and then hand her back to Dad.

Coming back to England tomorrow. ;)
Nick. xxxx

I grin happily and then look over at Bunty, who's vaguely sniffing some flowers next to the bed. Then at Tabitha, yawning and wrinkling her little red nose. Then at Dad, humming under his breath and trying to get Tabitha to high-five him with her tiny palm. Then I look at Annabel, still gazing calmly at me.

She wrinkles her nose and I wrinkle mine back, and I suddenly realise that it doesn't matter how far I go, or how lost I am, or how lonely I feel. I fit in here. I always will.

That's how I know I'm home.

Acknowledgements

Thanks to my wonderful editor, Lizzie Clifford, for helping me discover 'the statue in the stone', and to my agent Kate Shaw, whose patience and kindness gave me the time to find it. Thanks to the whole team at HarperCollins, who have supported both Harriet and myself with passion and tireless creativity from the start, and to Pippa Le Quesne, whose guidance is always illuminating.

Thanks to my family: to my amazing Mum and Dad, always proud of me whether I deserve it or not, and my grandparents, for the world's best cuddles, advice and jam tarts. Thanks to Flossy, for trying so hard to kill my keyboard, and to my little sister, Tara: my best friend, and the only person I'd give up my giant teddy-bear with the blue bow for.

Enormous thanks to Julian and Naho for their incredible generosity, and for re-translating my terrible Japanese without mocking me too heartily. Thanks also to Kristin, Laura and Sarah, for years of support and friendship. You have made many dramas so much smaller.

Finally, to everyone who has read and loved Harriet: you have brought her alive, and I couldn't have done it without you.

Thank you. x